The New Year's Resolution of Greta Baker

HELEN TREPELKOV

Black Rose Writing | Texas

ISBN: 978-1-68513-040-4
PUBLISHED BY BLACK ROSE WRITING
www.blackrosewriting.com

Printed in the United States of America
Suggested Retail Price (SRP) $20.95

The New Year's Resolution of Greta Baker is printed in Garamond Premier Pro

*As a planet-friendly publisher, Black Rose Writing does its best to eliminate unnecessary waste to reduce paper usage and energy costs, while never compromising the reading experience. As a result, the final word count vs. page count may not meet common expectations.

ACKNOWLEDGEMENTS

First and foremost, I want to thank Black Rose Writing, Reagan Rothe, and his talented and dedicated team for their support and belief in me.

I am also extremely grateful to my editor, Lisa Petrocelli, who did a fantastic job editing my manuscript.

Many thanks to my husband and our two daughters for their love, support, and many insightful suggestions.

A very special thank you to my mother, who is still my greatest motivational force and who suggested I should write in the first place, and to my late father, who told me that I had the strength to do it.

Last but not least, I am thankful to my grandchildren, whose light and laughter fill my life with happiness and purpose.

The New Year's Resolution of
Greta Baker

CHAPTER ONE

The crystal ball had just completed its 75-foot, one-minute-long descent. The number "2020" lit up. The new year was here. Greta loved the tradition of replaying the New Year's celebration of a century ago. It was so much more fun then. Lots of people, laughing, and cheering. So much better than the nowadays holographic projections into the sky.

Greta nibbled absentmindedly on her grapes. At $29.99 a pound, they were worth every penny. She got them because of the Spanish superstition she had read about many years ago. Spaniards have a tradition of eating twelve grapes at midnight on New Year's Eve for good luck, one for each stroke of the clock. It was an important year for Greta. She and her husband, Gregory (he preferred to be called Greg), were finally ready to have a child. So why leave anything to chance? Every little bit helps.

Greta felt happy. She had spent a great New Year's Eve with Greg, her best friend Susan, and Susan's husband, Mike. Shortly after lunch at Susan's, they decided to go bowling. They went to a real bowling alley, instead of just renting some hot virtual reality app. Greta did not like the VR games. She rarely played them, usually when she wanted to take her mind off work and relax a little, but was too busy to leave her desk for a long time. Sometimes, no matter how long she kept staring into her computer, the article she was working on refused to budge. The cursor would just blink sadly, at the same spot, the right words stuck hopelessly somewhere in the midst of rambling thoughts produced by her industrious brain.

They were at the only bowling alley in town that had survived the VR revolution. There were fewer people bowling now than during their last outing, and they got two adjoining lanes without any problem. The huge alley, abuzz with life just ten years ago, and requiring reservations well in advance not only to get two lanes next to each other, but just to get in, was now practically empty, with only two more couples at the far end of the hall. It was immediately evident that the place was struggling to stay afloat. It was not spic-and-span even during their last visit, but now the wall paint and the floors were dirtier, lanes were fewer, snack portions smaller. The dull, bored faces of the few remaining human personnel lit up the moment their party arrived, displaying eager agitation and readiness to accommodate any wish, however frivolous—anything to save them from their involuntary idleness and allow them to kill time until the end of their shift, and maybe postpone the impending layoffs. They reckoned, quite correctly, that each customer put them a little further from the doomsday of closing for good.

The depressing atmosphere spoiled Greta's mood, but soon she was immersed in the game. She was winning, having scored two consecutive strikes, which did not happen often. She could not make herself take the game seriously. In fact, she would stop caring about winning and shy away from it the moment emotions got heated. It was too intense, too visceral for her. At such moments, she felt as if she were running neck and neck in a herd of hungry animals on a scent, smelling other animals' sweat, touching their wet bodies. She did not like that feeling. Greta stirred uneasily in her armchair at the mere thought. Susan seemed to enjoy it, however.

Greta feared her friend at such moments. Not only did Susan take the game seriously, she lived and breathed it. Susan's congenial gaze became harsh, fixed, it seemed, on something inside her, and her rotund body morphed into a heavy projectile, capable of destroying anything that stood between her and her goal. Greta preferred not to be in her friend's way at those moments.

Having tried, unsuccessfully, to regain the lead, Susan suddenly disappeared. A few minutes later, she emerged triumphant, carrying a huge tray with a round of beer and a mound of chips for the party. Men cheered, welcoming a nice cooling break. After an almost imperceptible hesitation and a resigned sigh, Greta took a gulp of her beer. It was common knowledge that she was ridiculously incapable of handling alcohol. It turned her into mush. Oh well, Greta did not want to look like a prig.

Now that both couples were firmly settled on having children in the near future, Greta and Greg had started to pay more attention to their health. Susan was making fun of Greta for thinking about giving up alcohol altogether on the New Year celebration. She called her an overzealous perfectionist and jokingly questioned the ultimate success of their toils. After an indignant outburst from Greta, who hated this crude side of her friend, Susan relented, but still insisted that being a little tipsy would only make the process more enjoyable. Didn't Greta agree? Susan was hopeless. Useless to argue with her. She could easily chug four or five beers a day and was one of the last ones standing as far as smoking was concerned. Only when the insurance companies began to charge smokers obscenely high fines did she finally resign herself to a healthier way of life. Susan's idea of watching her health, and her weight for that matter, meant substituting a Bud Light for a regular one with especially fat-laden foods. She loved beer and refused to entertain the thought of having food without it. She conceded that she was considering switching to Bud Light for good after knowing for sure that she was pregnant.

Greta did not win. Susan did. Greta was soon safely curled in a warm blanket in her seat, sipping her only beer, and enjoying the spectacle of the game.

No need to get aggravated over trifles, Greta calmed herself. It was just one beer and a sip of champagne to honor tradition. She fixed her cashmere throw that was constantly sliding to the floor, and popped another grape into her mouth. After the game, they all had dinner at their place—just takeout from their favorite local joint. Susan and Mike planned to stay overnight and ring in the New Year, but they all got so tired, they had to give up the idea and settled on a much more modest plan of lunch the next day, just Greta and Susan. The men hated such outings. Both preferred to have their meals while sprawled comfortably on their couches.

Greg went to bed shortly after midnight, but Greta lingered. She was too excited and happy, and not quite ready to smolder her feelings by sleep. Thoughts and emotions were fizzing in her brain like her unfinished champagne. Pride and joy mostly, but also fear... Soon, hopefully, she was going to be a mother. The timing was perfect. At 32, she still had a couple of years to allow for unforeseen delays. Women were encouraged nowadays to give birth at a young age. Insurance companies imposed much higher copayments for older mothers. The out-of-pocket expenses skyrocketed after 35. Greta smiled, lost in pleasant memories.

CHAPTER TWO

It was cherry blossom time. That year, they were able to make it to DC. Greta felt the anticipation and excitement that did not diminish as time went by. It had been quite a few years since they made it to the National Cherry Blossom Festival. At the turn of the last century, the new four-day weekend was finally legalized and all companies were mandated to adopt the new workweek. Greta suggested adding one day to the weekend, but Greg made it very clear that to take any additional days off was out of the question. The breakthrough seemed very close, and that made Greg impatient and unable to concentrate on anything else. Greta knew how difficult he was to deal with during those final stages and tried to leave him alone. He was serving the whole of humanity, and this noble cause made him uncompromising and quite ferocious at times.

This time, however, everything seemed to effortlessly fall into place. Greta managed to secure a room in their favorite hotel that was sold out a few hours after she made the reservation. She also snatched a table in one of the trendiest new restaurants for one of their evenings. On top of that, the peak of the festival fell on the weekend when Greg did not have to show up at his lab, which allowed Greta to see him in one of his rare moments of relaxation and accounted for his more positive outlook on the upcoming trip. Greg was not exactly a fan of cherry blossoms. In his eyes, all this ephemeral and delicate frothiness did not justify the fuss.

Early in the morning they hopped into the underground. The underground, deeper than the subway of long ago and with dozens of new lines, replaced all other modes of public transportation. Greg and Greta had to stand during the length of the trip, elbowing the neighbors at every abrupt turn. They endured the unavoidable crowds at the exit and finally joined the throngs of people marching in dense rows toward the Tidal Basin.

"Is it even worth it?" grunted Greg every time somebody's elbow nudged him or some child's shrieking sounds of disappointment or delight made him jump. He was already dreaming of the forthcoming good meal and glass of wine in one of the capital's historic bars. Greta did not seem to notice the crowds. Her eyes were fixed on the pink-and-white cloud in the distance. "Watch where you're going, Greta! This is why you always trip. We are still a good ten minutes away from the blossoms."

Greta was very much aware of her habit. She would dart forward, her eyes glued to the object of her present esthetic obsession, only to be cut short in her race by a mundane stone or parking block. This time she lucked out. They reached the flowering trees without incident. Once under the canopy of flowers, Greta stopped noticing people altogether, her eyes editing them out before her photo app did. All she saw or cared about at that moment were the blossoms. Against the cloudless blue intensity of the sky, with the branches all but invisible behind the blossoming clusters, the flowers seemed to float, weightless, around hordes of humans, gently touching their cheeks, kissing their foreheads. The delicate petals seemed to flirt with their hands raised high to the sky, as if determined to use this brief moment of beauty to secure a small piece of eternity. A wild, indomitable fire was running through Greta's veins, filling her with rapturous joy at witnessing the beauty and triumph of life. Famished and tired, but reluctant to miss a single moment of the transient splendor, she finally dared to call it a day only after the sun had set.

Having made the full circle around the Basin, as usual, they went for dinner at one of Washington's institutions. They sat in a booth across from a massive mahogany bar. There were not many customers yet, and the quiet dignified atmosphere of the restaurant was in stark contrast with the vibrant experience of the day, pleasantly intensifying both, but at the same time having a sobering effect on Greta. Greg considered it a well-deserved prize for his patience and a display of great agility, albeit lost on Greta. He maneuvered among people, trying not to lose her from his sight when she darted from one place to the next without ever looking back.

A large family arrived and was seated two booths down. Greg was facing the boisterous clan, while Greta was sitting with her back to them. It looked like parents took their children, their spouses, and grandchildren to an early dinner. The grandfather, a man close to 70, with short white hair, was wearing immaculately ironed shirt and trousers with a razor-sharp crease—quite an anachronism even for a man his age, considering most fabrics were replaced by wrinkle-free materials years ago. A woman of about the same age with fine features, wearing a navy, sleeveless dress revealing beautiful shoulders and well-toned arms, was sitting at his side. A strand of pearls that perfectly matched the whiteness and evenness of her teeth adorned her neck and made her look livelier and younger. Around them was a whirl of five or six children, with cropped hair for boys and long locks and bright-colored ribbons for girls. Two pleasant pairs were orchestrating the process.

"What's wrong, Greg? It looks like you haven't heard a word I said." Greta turned her head to see what was happening behind her back that apparently was affecting Greg. Before she could repeat her question, Greg put down his glass, took both Greta's hands into his, and said simply, "Let's have a child, Greta."

·　·　·　·　·

Greta and Greg met at a huge charity event. A new state-of-the-art laboratory, dedicated entirely to the research of the universal antivirus vaccine that would safeguard not only against the known strains of the viruses, but also against many future ones, was being built with a grant from one of the Big Tech magnates. Susan worked for the sponsoring foundation and was one of the organizers of the gala. She helped Greta get exclusive coverage of the event. Greta worked for one of the largest food companies in the country. Consumer-good giants tried to maintain an active social stance with as many journalists on their staff as they could afford to showcase their donations to various popular causes. This was an effort to recruit new adherents and increase sales by enticing consumers into purchasing their products by compelling social policies. Greg was there in his professional capacity as a scientist.

Hundreds of people gathered in the huge lobby with three-story-high ceilings, marble floors, and floor-to-ceiling windows. It was a highly anticipated event, the importance of which it was hard to overestimate. The opening of the lab was impatiently awaited by hundreds of scientists eager to tackle the daring project with the newest equipment.

Viral pandemics had been regularly plaguing humanity through the twenty-first century and as it was all too obvious, were not likely to disappear in the twenty-second. The research in the field had been conducted for almost two centuries now. There were some promising leads, but as soon as it looked like the universal vaccine was finally in the offing, the perfidious shape-shifting viruses mutated so drastically that it made many of the findings obsolete.

The crowd was huge and growing. Serving bots were noiselessly maneuvering among people with their trays of hors d'oeuvres and champagne. One of the guests, explaining something vehemently and gesticulating with both hands to help him drive his point across, stepped back in the heat of the moment. His hand swept through a tray of hors d'oeuvres. Some guests chuckled. The serving bot, the empty tray on the helplessly extended hand, was just standing there, his front panel blinking red, signaling for the help of a human supervisor. A man in a dark suit, not a tuxedo like all the other men present, was already making his way through the crowd.

"Why do you have to move so silently, you creepy creatures! You scared me to death!" the man yelled. Then, his face dark-red and swollen, slightly bulging eyes heavy with anger, he turned around and hit the bot across the front panel, again and again.

Greg was one of the man's opponents, and they went back a long way. His name was John Drake. They had attended the same university and had been working in the same field since then. Their paths never crossed until recently, however, when they both zeroed in on the universal vaccine, albeit having different approaches to the issue made them rivals rather than colleagues. John was a very promising virologist known among his peers as an exceptionally short-fused and arrogant man, impossible to work with. Greg was about to interfere when he looked up and saw Greta making her way toward the commotion. The words of reproach froze on his lips as he followed the graceful, seemingly effortless moves of the girl through the crowd. Her face with big blue-green eyes in the aureole of golden hair was floating against the blurred motley background, suddenly remote and unimportant.

At first, her face reflected professional eagerness to get closer to the epicenter of the incident. But as soon as she realized what was going on, Greg saw red blotches appear on her pale cheeks and her clear blue-green eyes narrow and become prickly and gray, as the ocean in a thunderstorm.

"What do you think you're doing? How dare you hit him!" Everybody remained silent, stunned by the violence of her outburst and curious to hear the man's response.

"Him? Come on, it's just a piece of equipment, like a computer," sneered the man.

"It is a *feeling being*, not a computer! I don't think you should hit a computer either, for that matter, out of respect for the human thought and labor that went into producing it."

"To hear you talk, I'm not allowed to hit anything, not even a toaster."

"Precisely," replied Greta coldly. "I don't believe you are. But we are not dealing with a toaster here; this is a very complex issue."

At this point, Greg finally regained the gift of speech and interfered. "Oh, John, don't be such a scaramouch! I think you should apologize to the lady, my good man, and also to the bot. The AI phenomenon is not understood by us in all its complexity, but it is very likely that robots do, indeed, have feelings. Better safe than sorry, wouldn't you agree?" He turned to the crowd for support. Everyone acquiesced.

"You surely are joking! Not on my life," hissed the man. "And don't you hope I will forget it." He darted out of the hall before anybody had time to make up their mind as to whose side to pick.

Greg asked Greta out the next day. In a few months, they were married.

CHAPTER THREE

Greta was sitting in the armchair facing the window in their living room. The city lived and breathed around her. The familiar skyline with its skyscrapers and obligatory windmills on every roof reminded her of cute hedgehogs from a children's book she liked to read when she was a little girl. Today, however, it looked different somehow, more groomed and solemn. It seemed to have acquired a new dimension, became brighter and deeper, like an apartment after a thorough spring cleaning, when the sun casts its rays through the spotless windows.

The red-and-green eyes of the holographic streetlights were duly changing color on the now mostly empty flyways. They were introduced only a few dozen years ago, when it became obvious that the street level could no longer accommodate both commercial and private traffic. Planocars and flybots, their smaller versions, became affordable and soon after, ubiquitous; extra strata of traffic were created. First, just two, at 150 and 300 feet. When they proved widely successful, two more were added, at 450 and 600 feet. Holographic images were a natural choice for streetlights. The holiday-like light display, jarring at first, soon became a familiar sight.

Holiday Greetings! and *Happy New Year!* signs, indispensable for this time of year, were hovering over the East River. Holographic reindeers with Santa Claus in his sleigh in tow were zipping through the night sky. Christmas trees aglow with ornaments and menorahs with flickering lights were at every intersection.

Greg and Greta's jobs allowed them to pay the luxury real estate tax, affording them an apartment on the 130th floor with a practically unobstructed view of the city. They also enjoyed a less crowded altitude lane for their planocar, now parked neatly in its spot on the terrace—another asset not to be scoffed at. With cities so heavily overpopulated, living space was rigorously monitored. They decided against a bigger place and settled on a spacious one-bedroom. The progressive tax on urban square footage on top of a one-bedroom apartment, deemed by the State to be big enough for young couples without children, was rather steep.

Greta looked around with pride and satisfaction, her eyes lovingly caressing every item—the sofa she got with her first bonus on the new job, the slick floor lamps, the bright frasadas from Peru. The kitchen upset her a little. As with all electronics nowadays, her kitchen appliances were on a six-month lease. The speed of the technological progress made it unreasonable to buy equipment that became obsolete in a matter of months, and the constant turnover made it harder to preserve the character. The space had a tendency to look like an operating room, sterile and impersonal, but one could not have it all. Kitchen towels livened up the space and at $49.99 apiece were a bargain. Greta smiled remembering how frustrated Susan was that her friend would spend money on something so futile. Whatever. With the new restrictions on consumer items, she considered her choices a success.

Greta had always loved to add small flourishes to practicality. Susan, on the other hand, liked to stretch her dollar to the very limit. She was a prisoner of love for a good deal and her overall pecuniary efficiency. She was very good at managing money and avoiding emotional spending. Good old Susan.

Susan, her best friend. They went back a long way. They cut classes together in high school to go on double dates, they roomed together at college. They had no secrets from each other. They had each other's back. She trusted Susan. She was seeing her for lunch today and couldn't wait to tell her all the latest. Greta leaned back, smiled, and closed her eyes.

CHAPTER FOUR

Greta and Greg had applied for the Big Child Lottery, to win the right to raise their child themselves. At first, Greg was very much against the idea. The State was so much better equipped to raise children. What did Greta know about this process? He was certainly clueless. Wasn't it better to leave it to the professionals? And what about her career? It took her almost a year to make him change his mind. The Lottery was quite expensive, and the odds of winning very slim; practically nil, in fact. Still, Greta and Greg could afford it, so why not? Winning the Lottery would be a surefire way to secure this right. If they didn't win, they would have to go through the rigorous selection procedure.

The moment a woman became pregnant, the process of stripping the new life of any shred of mystery began. The covers were removed one by one until the future Homo sapiens stood there in all his naked glory. Comprehensive DNA tests were carried out, graphs and diagrams were created, possible developmental scenarios charted until no dark corner remained. The percentile risk of every known disease, as well as the child's natural proclivities, were meticulously calculated and evaluated at the very onset of new life.

Then, dozens of specialists were put to work and powerful quantum computers engaged to create the unborn human's perfect life. All the thinking was done well in advance and all possible doubts and torments were wisely removed to avoid costly mistakes. You knew what to eat and how much, what sport to practice, what education to get, and what job to hold to live the longest, healthiest, and most successful life. Your life's course was sequenced, closely monitored, and updated as time went on—a fine here, a higher premium there—nudging you back on track should you stray.

Humanity did possess the technology to alter the human genome so as to create a perfect human being. However, what constituted a "perfect human being" was widely a gray area and specialists unanimously agreed that more research was necessary before bioengineers could be given the green light to proceed. In the meantime, meddling in human blueprints was strictly prohibited and punished by life in prison without parole. The only exception to this rule was the elimination of life-threatening and quality-of-life altering birth defects. There was a comprehensive list revised every year. "No Life Lost" was the motto.

Upon the child's birth, parents left the baby at the hospital, where he or she would undergo more extensive testing, and the optimal course of upbringing and education, as well as a perfect diet and exercise regimen, were fine-tuned.

The standard procedure was quite straightforward. It was immediately dubbed a stroke of genius and the Nobel Prize in Economics was bestowed upon its creators, along with numerous accolades. It allowed the ideal placement of each individual, which streamlined the economy and made for fulfilled, satisfied adults.

Fishing out the nuggets of natural predisposition from birth and nurturing them into solid skills allowed society to develop happy individuals without wasting time. All the dull, repetitive, strenuous manual tasks, as well as the noncreative sector of intellectual ones, were performed mostly by the robots. Thus, every child was given the best opportunity for a successful and happy life, using his or her potential to the fullest. The economy, in the meantime, enjoyed the best labor it could expect, considering the ban on bioengineering methods, incorporating every ounce of the human's physical, intellectual, and spiritual potential. In order to raise such individuals the educational process had to be scientifically based and strictly monitored. A special branch was created that prepared specialists to take care of children from birth. Parents could no longer be trusted with raising their children. Not every adult was born to be a good parent, certainly not in view of modern economic demands. Child-raising became a centralized industry, only the State being well equipped to perform this most important and delicate task.

The child was to live in a State-sponsored nursery, and later in a boarding school. Parents could visit or take the child home for a daily two-hour period, as long as it did not interfere with or distract the child from her or his rigorous routine. There was very little leeway since nothing was left to chance in order to assure the child's successful education. Yearly assessments and less invasive monthly corrections were in place to ensure that the chosen course was on target. As the child grew older, a series of thorough tests served the same goal.

The possibility of creating an ideal society where everyone could realize their destiny without cutthroat competition or lengthy searches for the right path, became a reality. The path was revealed to individuals from the start—bright and shiny. For the first time in the history of humanity, a man could see his future as envisioned by Mother Nature. From time immemorial, there were some who fought it and tried to change their destiny. The defiant hordes flocked to the Moon colony. They were given a fair chance to try out their own ideas. Those who tried to change things on Earth were sent to Mars, with no right to come back, to create their own vision of human paradise.

The difficulties began when the parents expressed the desire to raise and educate their children at home. An alternative way was put into place. Each metropolitan district allowed a small share of prospective parents to raise children independently. No more than 0.01% of all expectant couples were given that right per calendar year.

Greta was thinking for the umpteenth time how lucky she was. Should she have decided to become pregnant just three years ago, she would have had to delegate raising her child to the State. Thank God the neo-feminists managed to win back the right of parents to raise children, though with huge restrictions. First, future moms and dads had to register with authorities and undergo a series of tests, ranging from simple general health screenings to more sophisticated ones, aimed at determining whether the couple was psychologically fit to be full-time parents. Upon successful completion of the tests, a rigorous examination preceded the signing of the parenting contract.

There was one major caveat. The contract stipulated that should the parents-to-be meet all requirements, pass the tests, and be granted the permission to raise their child at home, they had to remain together until the child's 18th birthday. A divorce did not just mean the immediate placement of the child into State custody, but a very substantial fine, prorated based on the number of years left until termination of the contract—in other words, the child's age. The parents' separation was fraught with unpredictable complications, and the trauma could be so severe as to compromise the child's successful development. Needless to say, the financial burden of achieving the seamless transition, although varied from child to child, was usually considerable. It was imperative for parents to stay together for another reason, as well. One of the parents had to quit his or her job and take care of the child full-time. The remuneration of that parent was understandably substantial, almost on par with registered State educators. Should parents split, the State would replace this parent into the initial field of work, which usually also entailed a sizable expense.

CHAPTER FIVE

Susan was sitting on the terrace in her favorite spot overlooking the Hudson River. She enjoyed the gorgeous view of the New Jersey skyline, while soaking in the rays of the sun, unusually warm for this time of year. She chose an apartment on the second floor because it was much cheaper than the apartments on higher floors. She did not enjoy dishing out so much money in luxury taxes for the pleasure of feeling suspended in the air over other buildings' rooftops. Susan smirked. She had no doubt in her mind that she had outsmarted everyone, big time. She felt like she was on a cruise boat gliding noiselessly down the river, the majestic skyscrapers on both banks just a stone's throw away.

She was idly following the monotonous moves of their house robot from the corner of her eye. The robot was vacuuming the carpet. Every time the brush came into contact with a piece of furniture, the robot would start a funny little dance until it picked up every speck of dust and resumed the unobstructed path. The same exact scene replayed itself over and over, time after time, day after day. The shtick could take up to a minute. Susan went through the pain of measuring exactly how long the meticulously performed senseless procedure could take on previous occasions. "What a dummy," whispered Susan, unable to hold in her frustration when the robot seemed to be stuck in one place, attacking the leg of her favorite chair (amazing find on a local antique site when she and

Mike were on their spontaneous summer escape to Pennsylvania). The blatant awkwardness and inefficiency of the whole process frustrated Susan, graceful and nimble despite her voluptuous form. Susan was one of the lucky few, hence, ferociously envied by other women. Her body did not lose sex appeal and agility despite a few extra pounds, which had an uncanny ability of settling in just the right places. It was especially fortuitous for Susan, who had an extreme aversion for any form of self-restriction, exercise in particular. The consequences of this character flaw were amply compensated, however, by her ability to impose self-serving restrictions on those around her. Instead of twisting her body into unnatural poses or forcing it to do boring and painful movements, Susan would much rather contort other people's minds by gently manipulating them into accepting her point of view. She perceived it to be a much more sensible and easy way to approach any situation, including her looks.

• • • • •

It was time for Susan to get moving. Greta sounded strangely excited yesterday, when they were making the arrangements. She wondered what the reason could be. Well, she would find out soon enough.

They were having lunch at Nostalgia, which was Greta's idea. It was her turn to choose the venue, so Susan did not make a fuss. It was a rule they had established a long time ago—taking turns at picking the venue—and they stuck to it. Susan was not excited to fork over twice the amount she would normally spend, but this was a very cool, new, "old-fashioned" place, according to Greta, and they absolutely had to try it. Cultured meat and plant-based food had supplanted traditional animal meat many years ago, and since then had taken on new shapes, far removed from the conventional ones, dictated by animal anatomy. Susan did not mind some old-fashioned foods once in a while- she was especially partial to chicken wings – but she did not see what all the hype was about. They were so overrated. Besides, all those natural shapes looked so crude, come to think of it. Susan preferred the no-nonsense meals of the traditional molecular gastronomy diners.

Greta had no doubt read some review of the place and was now under its spell. Funny duck. Public art installations, exhibitions, theater, ballet, concerts, new books, any cultural event of note, for that matter, did not go unnoticed. New food venues were subjected to her scrutiny as well. Greta exulted in new tastes. Every week, she would comb through all reputable publications on the subject, gleaning the events she found especially noteworthy. She seemed convinced that life could not be full unless one attended all cultural events in town. When Susan once tried to find out why she would go to such lengths over trifles, Greta vehemently stated that it allowed her to keep her focus on the main things in life. Susan had never heard anything so absurd and naive. How could seeing Leonardo da Vinci's works or listening to Bach, let alone trying some absurd new dish, help with your career or personal matters? Why, then, was Greta, wised up by such illustrious mentors, still not a team manager by age 32? Not to mention her personal life was rocky at best, her relationship with Greg, the longest so far, not all smooth sailing. At times, Greta was impossible, making similar pronouncements with no rhyme or reason. Susan did try and joined Greta on her outings a few times. It did nothing for her. Susan resisted the temptation of making cutting remarks, however, although wicked barbs trembled at the tip of her tongue. Who needed the aggravation? Besides, the cultured shrimp salad on the menu looked good.

The consumption of products of animal origin was strictly prohibited. Animal-rights activists could finally rejoice, having unequivocally won an important battle. The satisfaction of people who found abominable the seemingly innate tendency of humans toward subjugating the weaker ones was, however, short-lived. The abuses of robots were on the rise, and although the idea that robots could have feelings was still unproven and extremely controversial, the number of their advocates was growing rapidly. Not that Susan cared one way or the other. Not so Greta. What a loopy girl. Just the other day, Susan's robot stopped behind her in its usual noiseless fashion, and Susan almost tripped over its lower limb as a result. Even worse, she broke the heel of her new shoe. Oh, Susan really lost it that day. She was kicking her household helper with the ruined shoe until her hand hurt. Greta almost burst into tears, but not because she felt sorry for her friend. She pitied the robot, convinced by propaganda of the Robot Rights Movement. Sometimes Greta could be really annoying.

Susan was not completely devoid of hedonistic inclinations, but convenience and price prevailed. The molecular gastronomy had all but cornered out the old methods of food preparation. Why bother with eating, let alone cooking messy, reconstituted pieces of food of different shapes and sizes? The new technology, once mastered, was much easier, cleaner, and faster. Susan didn't bother with that, either. Every building had a food delivery unit in the basement with a vast rotating menu. Susan liked the rectangular and square packages you just emptied on the plate, *et voilà!*, dinner was served. You could easily consume them on the go, if need be. She could also order a fly-in from the many food delivery businesses should she fancy something more exotic. Of course, she would have to pay extra for delivery because extra drones created additional traffic and were usually at the root of most traffic jams. For that reason, Susan rarely resorted to this option.

Susan was not alone in thinking this way. The concept was so deeply entrenched that many households eliminated kitchens altogether, transforming them into walk-in closets. Susan did not go that far. Greta, on the other hand, would have been appalled at the very idea of not being able to concoct something special in her kitchen when she happened to be in the creative culinary mood, which was not often, despite the staggering amount of kitchen equipment and gadgets Greta had amassed. Susan liked to point this out every time Greta and Greg had Susan and Mike over for dinner and served food from one of the delivery joints in their neighborhood.

The preferred methods of fueling bodies seemed to have come full circle. The proud humans of the twenty-second century were often shocked to learn that many centuries ago a great number of ordinary Romans, as the excavations of Pompeii had revealed a long time ago, had small basic kitchens and were very likely to have appreciated the convenience and regularly eaten takeout for dinner.

Modern science allowed a myriad of new exciting creations, using the products' nutritional value to the fullest and combining them in the best way. Chefs were carried away with new perspectives of cooking and presenting dishes previously unknown. And yet, although there was no shortage of possibilities, new dishes, and new artful, creative presentation, the food aficionados demanded something drastically different, something bolder, even less perfect. Bored by perfectly balanced flavors and wine pairings, they wanted to be surprised, to tingle their taste buds in new unexpected ways. Some hotheads among the brainiacs even started to float the idea of the imminent end of the restaurant industry, as the achievement of perfection meant the end of the road. The phoenix myth was revised. Every living thing or activity, having exhausted its potential, having reached its own supreme, that is, perfect state, had nowhere to go, and when movement stops, life stops. It had to die and resurrect in order to travel the road of life again. Susan and Greta were too engrossed in their own lives to pay attention to such gibberish.

For this very reason—what goes around comes around—or due to the unquenchable entrepreneurial zest feeding on human boredom (probably both), the almost forgotten idea of old cooking methods started to take hold once again. Old-fashioned restaurants that would have seemed like an outlandish experiment just a dozen years ago, took root and became wildly popular, all the messiness of the old-fashioned eating process notwithstanding. These restaurants started to pop up like mushrooms after rain, but by consensus amongst the Gothamites, the standard bearer was Nostalgia, where guests could experience the frills of eating out from years past.

The tables had flowers at the center, tablecloths with matching napkins (not the usual paper, biodegradable kind), and waiters instead of the conveyor. These extra touches were hailed as a great success by customers. The flowers were fake and the waiters were robots, but the place was still quaint enough to position itself as a throwback to the twenty-first century, and it undeniably had a warm, friendly vibe.

Greta loved the ambiance of those new places, although they were not for the faint of heart. The food was supposed to look like you were eating real animal flesh. Susan's imagination was not as vivid as Greta's, and this particular aspect of the new presentation did not bother her. It took Greta a few days to warm up to the idea, even though the shrimp on the menu had never been one of the namesake crustaceans swimming happily in the ocean. The regular food chain aggravations seemed benign compared to legends of generations past—that they were victims of slaughter by their big brothers—the humans. Greta had to concede that her fears were highly exaggerated. The prototype from the zoology book looked nothing like the neat pink specimen on her plate.

CHAPTER SIX

Susan clearly was ill at ease. For some time, she had been pulling absentmindedly at the fringe border of her napkin and seemed to have taken a sudden interest in the posse of colorful pansies on their table. Her eyes were stubbornly fixated on the small orange flower with a purple middle. Susan had not interrupted Greta once, which in itself was a first. The exuberant, ever-so-slightly condescending manner gave way to tense listening, by far the longest stretch of Greta's uninterrupted talking in the history of their friendship.

Greta was too excited to relate her news to notice the unusual behavior of her friend. She babbled on and on for quite some time. When she finally stopped and looked at Susan inquisitively, Susan exclaimed, "I can't believe it. You, too!" Greta gasped, but before she had time to say anything, Susan went on, "I was just about to tell you when you called me. I just didn't want to steal your thunder and was waiting for you to tell me *your* news first. Now it turns out we both are about to have babies and want to raise them ourselves. I have just entered the Lottery, too. How funny is that?"

The word "funny" grated on Greta's ears, but she was too much in shock to dwell on Susan's choice of words. For some reason, she thought Susan was not even interested in children yet, and was saying it for Mike's sake. Greta could not picture Susan as a mother. The news threw her off. She did not know her friend that well, after all. Greta was a little disappointed, too. She was not looking to monopolize the right to raise children, but she was hoping to have her moment. All this time, she had been painting a different picture in her head. She saw Susan being surprised, even incredulous, and maybe just a little jealous, asking questions about how the Lottery business worked. It was a fleeting feeling, however. In a moment, she was already happily chirping about how much fun it would be to become pregnant at the same time and go through the experience together.

Susan breathed in relief. That was a close call. She observed Greta from the corner of her eye. She could not help admiring her. Her face was not beautiful in the traditional sense, but it had an enigma about it, just as her whole personality did. The secret was in her eyes, an intense shade of blue-green, that trapped one's gaze and held it in sweet captivity, innocent and wise at the same time. You couldn't help feeling preemptively forgiven for all your sins, past and future, the absolution being absolute. Susan hated to admit it, but she needed Greta. With her, through her, Susan felt complete. She was the yin to her yang. She was her best buddy.

Greta seemed genuinely happy and not suspecting foul play. *The gullibility of this girl is appalling, to say the least*, thought Susan, completely assured of her victory, with the usual feeling of superiority and disdain. Susan had to keep one jump ahead. She was competitive, with both feet firmly on the ground, which translated to her strong belief that she had to have the best, the soonest, and in bigger quantities than any of her acquaintances and friends. Especially her friends.

The electronic waiter wheeled noiselessly to their table and put the plates in front of them. Greta hastily grabbed one from the tray and was about to go on with her narrative when she was suddenly stopped in her tracks by Susan's sharp voice. "Way to always grab the best piece, Greta! No, really! How selfish can one be?" Greta stopped in mid-sentence, taken aback by the unusual outbreak, so uncharacteristic of her friend.

"What are you talking about?" she asked in dismay.

"You took the freshest salad with the plumpest shrimp and left me this half-wilted sad one here."

"I just took the closest one, Susan," Greta said soothingly. "I think you're talking nonsense, but here, do you want to exchange plates? I just put my fork in the salad and haven't started eating yet."

Susan calmed down as fast as she snapped. "Oh, it's alright. I guess you will need more vitamins sooner than me," she said cheerfully. "What happened to our idea of doing it together?"

"But we are doing it together! You make no sense, no sense at all," started Greta, but Susan interrupted her.

"I meant to discuss the whole thing with you today, to find out whether you would be onboard. You, on the other hand, seem to have your mind all set. What if I were not ready yet, you didn't even bother to consult me! It's true, you can drop your career at any point. Oh, sorry, I forgot, you don't even have a career! You are a pushover, Greta. You let people take advantage of you. If it weren't for me, you would be stuck with the crappiest assignments. You probably enjoy sitting for hours at your computer, trying to find the best word to describe the shape of today's clouds, for all I know."

"Please, Susan. You're not making any sense. We were both ready to have children months ago; nothing has changed. Greg and I want to raise our child, but we just decided it last week, and I am sharing the news with you right away."

Suddenly, Greta began to fuss, almost as uneasy as she was excited just a few hours ago. Hurriedly standing up, she inadvertently bumped into the leg of the table. Susan's water glass, still half full, fell, and in a matter of seconds, the water started to trickle down Susan's skirt.

"Oh, Susan, I'm so sorry," mumbled Greta in distress. Her Vital Signs Device beeped. Damn it! Orange warning.

Vital Signs Devices, VS devices for short, were a relatively new contraption, introduced when the population of people 65 and over reached thirty percent. It had aroused a great controversy. The device was implanted in an individual's underarm and was constantly transmitting their vital signs to the central station where they were stored. There were three levels of alerts according to the danger—yellow, orange, and red. Only doctors and insurance companies had access to the data. That way, doctors had complete databases of their patients' pulse, blood pressure, sugar levels, and other important health information at their fingertips. Most importantly, the device was set to signal should any of the signs change drastically or reach critical red levels. The person in question was immediately contacted and help was on the way should the case warrant it. The old, the sick, and the lonely swore by it. Others (mostly the young and reckless crowd) found it an intrusive and annoying gimmick introduced to help health insurance companies squeeze yet more money from their prey. Blood alcohol level was one of the vital signs, and fines for reaching the red level were hefty.

"Oh, it's not a big deal, don't worry," countered Susan quickly, trying not to lose countenance again. *Klutz, klutz, klutz,* she was thinking in the meantime. *Just like my darn robot! The girl is incorrigible! She can't even walk and talk at the same time, quite possibly not walk and think, for that matter. What a multitasking disaster! Oh well, whatever,* Susan thought in a more benevolent manner, feeling sorry for her pitiful-looking friend, still in complete consternation, offering to dry-clean her skirt. *At least no damage is done, the skirt will dry nicely, it's just water.*

"Oh, don't even think about it. It's such a special day today! I'll take care of it myself," she said out loud, a carefree smile on her face, and hugged her friend as they parted ways.

•　　•　　•　　•　　•

Susan is really fantastic, always has been, thought Greta, suddenly full of gratitude, the stupid incident immediately forgotten.

CHAPTER SEVEN

It was their senior high school year. Greta was impatiently waiting for the Homecoming Dance. She liked this guy, Jim, and she was sure he liked her, but was too shy to approach her directly. They just looked at each other during classes. She had great hopes that this dance would finally help them establish some sort of contact.

Greta had her outfit planned out. She put on white cigarette-leg jeans with high-heeled sandals and a pale green tank top that went very well with her eyes. Her matte, perfectly smooth skin was glowing from within, both from a two-month long indolence of hot summer days and the anticipation of a romance. She checked herself in the mirror and felt satisfied with the result. Skinny by nature, her body looked especially trim and toned after months of swimming and hiking. Her hair seemed to have soaked in the mixture of sun and salt that one could smell with a small effort of imagination.

Greta opened the door of the dance hall. Powerful rhythms shook the room, punching Greta in her chest, stabbing her ears; the hissing colorful flashes blinded her. The dance floor resembled a wounded multiheaded hydra, the shapeless mass of students twisting and twirling in the feverishly pulsating light. She knew she could never reach this level of ecstasy, complete abandon, and immediately felt intimidated and out of place. She stood there, not knowing what to do or where to go. She was so beautiful, her outfit stood out so well against the dark background of the room, appearing and disappearing in the fluorescent flashes, as if teasing, luring her catch.

Once her eyes became accustomed to the maddening cadence, she spotted Jim. He was at the other side of the hall, looking even more lost than Greta was. She started to slowly make her way toward him through the throngs of distorted odd shapes, the interlacing, unrecognizable bodies.

Her siren-like looks attracted attention. She got noticed. A few boys asked her to dance. She was too shy to say no right away, so it took her about twenty minutes to finally get close to Jim. She stopped for a moment to catch her breath and looked around. At that moment she noticed her friend Susan making signs to her with one hand while holding a glass of red punch in the other. She was maneuvering in her direction with extraordinary agility and smiling widely. Greta's heart sank. Yet she stopped her journey and waved back. Susan, excited, had reached her at last. Someone from behind must have given her a push, or so it seemed. It all happened so fast. Susan lost her balance and the contents of her glass landed on Greta's white jeans. Aghast, she watched as the ugly dark stain got bigger.

"Oh, no, oh, Greta. I'm so sorry, I'll leave with you and drive you home."

Greta searched the room to see what Jim was doing. She saw a girl approaching him, two drinks in her hands. She looked back again as she was leaving the hall. The girl was dragging Jim, laughing happily, to the center of the dance floor.

Susan was really fantastic. She dry-cleaned Greta's pants and took her to lunch the next day.

CHAPTER EIGHT

Susan was enraged. She did not see it coming. How could this dreamy, almost fey-looking girl pull her act together? Appearances could be deceiving; Susan needed no better proof than that. She kept an eagle eye on all of Greta's moves and never allowed her to take the lead in any endeavor. In her head, however, she had labeled Greta as useless a long time ago. That was probably what cemented this friendship even more, on Susan's part, for she could not have allowed anyone around to outperform her.

They went back as far as high school. Susan, Greta, and a group of their classmates went to Fort Myers for one week after freshman year. The grandparents of one of the kids had a house there and graciously—and courageously—invited the whole gang to stay with them. The fact that the grandfather was a former Marine must have played a big role in their decision-making process. The idea did not sit well with any of the kids' parents, but finally, after more than a week of deliberations, the lucky few who managed to secure the parental blessing boarded the six-a.m. flight and by eight a.m. were already basking in the sun on the beautiful and conveniently secluded beach. For the first few days vegging on the beach remained their activity of choice, their long, lazy tanning sessions punctuated only by short dips in the wonderfully refreshing water. They needed to cool down their slowly roasting bodies and get rid of the light buzz from the beer supplied by the older cousin of one of the local boys.

When the sun finally set, enveloped in its blazing red-and-orange cape, they had chips with more beer and binged on all kinds of TV shows, happy from the thought that they were done with studying, for the time being at least.

Grandparents did not interfere with their lives as long as they were home by ten p.m. and remained reasonably quiet for the rest of the night. Paradise, however counterintuitive that idea might seem to those who did not luck out, is known to bore people into all sorts of adventures. After a few days of perfect life, the restless teenagers started to look for alternate venues to enjoy themselves.

The same enterprising boy who monopolized the beer supply came up with the idea of nearshore fishing. His friend had a boat with all the necessary equipment and was ready to take them out to sea for a symbolic price. The trip turned out to be a fun experience, although they did not catch any fish. So, they went out the following day as well. The sea was a bit rougher that day, and although they did catch a few small fish, the fun started to wane. On the third day only Greta and Susan showed up. The grateful guy, in an effort to spice things up a bit, suggested the girls try fly-fishing for barracudas. He had two cuda tubes. After three uneventful hours, Greta, who was fishing alone while Susan was flirting with the boy, hit it big. She managed to bring in a forty-inch barracuda. Their efforts remained fruitless for the rest of the day, although Susan, who had immediately joined Greta, insisted on staying past sunset.

When they were leaving the boat, Susan asked their captain to take a picture of them with their catch. Greta, repulsed by the huge monster with fang-like teeth, was not in a hurry to pose holding the fish. Susan was. For many years, Susan, masterfully avoiding mutual acquaintances and potential exposure, showed the picture as testimony of her own prowess. After the trip, Susan and Greta became best friends.

Susan could always relax with Greta. They were not on the same track. Not even on one plane, for that matter. So how could she best her in such an important issue? How could Susan lose her guard to such an extent? She missed all the telltale signs, so obvious now in hindsight—languid looks at babies, staying a little longer than usual in front of baby stuff. The little Greta was probably not so naive, after all. No use dwelling on it any longer.

First things first. Damage control. She googled "Big Child Lottery." It was to be held June 1. It was open for entries until May 1, but Susan did not want to take any chances. Feverishly, she spoke in all the necessary information. Now, at least, she and Greta were even.

What a superb idea, to get out of her stupid job in such a glorious way. Susan felt a bout of insurmountable jealousy. She had been contemplating quitting her job for some time now. It did not make her happy anymore and she was bored. Mike had told her so many times that he would support her. Susan was convinced that behind his magnanimity lay his fear of losing her. He was just too afraid that she would find another man and tried to limit her contacts with other people, but the offer was still on the table. Susan, however, needed to exit with style. Now that the ubiquitous use of household robots made the term "housewife" devoid of meaning and hopelessly archaic, not that she found the endeavor glorious, God forbid, the perspective of becoming just a "significant other" made her cringe. And Greta had figured it all out before Susan, who would look like a sorry copycat if she followed in her footsteps. Yet the idea was too good to pass up. She had to beat Greta at her own game.

Registering for the Lottery was a breeze. She reached for her Personal Assistance Tablet, PAT for short, and dictated "independent parenthood" with resolve. She quickly glanced over the cautionary introductory pages and clicked on "Registration." The initial process was easy. She quickly completed the straightforward questionnaire. Her finger hovered for a split second over the "submit" button. Then, uttering "Damn you, Greta!" under her breath, she hit it with such force her finger slipped over the key and almost missed its mark.

CHAPTER NINE

Susan could not believe her eyes. The next available spot for an interview was not until late October. Her first reaction was disappointment. An almost ten-month wait. She heard it was complicated, but she did not realize how many couples were interested, until now. Grabbing a beer and calming down, she concluded that on second thought, it was for the best. There was so much to think through, and it was not her habit to leave things to the last moment. She gave herself a pat on the back for not postponing the registration. All of a sudden, a thought hit her. Her eyes narrowed and her lips slowly extended in a smile. If Greta waited a few more days, there was a good chance she would miss this year's quota altogether. Wouldn't that be ironic? Just like Greta.

A phone buzz interrupted her daydreaming. Annoyed, Susan glanced at her PAT. It was Greta. Her face on the screen looked worried. She was impatiently fidgeting with her hoodie's drawstrings. "There is no time to waste, you have to register immediately, Susan," she almost screamed. "I decided to do it, just in case I don't win the Lottery, which, let's face it, is the most likely outcome. At first, I didn't want to do it ahead of time, everything in its time, you know me, but they register for early November now. You have to do it ASAP. I didn't even finish the registration, I wanted to let you know. Talk to you later!" She hung up. Susan did not say a word.

Greta called again a half hour later. She sounded very excited. She was so lucky, she told Susan. She got the interview for mid-November. If she had waited another day or two, she would probably have missed this year's quota.

Greta inquired whether Susan had registered successfully. Susan replied that she had. She sounded contrived. The whole situation left a bad taste in her mouth and she wanted to leave it behind as soon as possible. Why did Greta have to drone on and on? With an imperceptible sigh, Susan assumed her usual cheerful, carefree manner, assured Greta she was fine, thanked her for her help, and wrapped up the conversation under the pretense that something urgent had come up at work. She was not sure yet how she would explain the situation to Greta. Maybe there would be no need to explain. Worst case scenario, she would tell her it was a glitch that her registration went through before Greta's.

She took another beer from the fridge. She badly wanted a cigarette. Smoking at home was prohibited and exorbitant fines were imposed on those who dared to disobey. Rules were strict and enforced rigorously.

Susan was not affluent enough to smoke at her leisure and pay the hefty tab for self-destructive habits and antisocial behavior. It was absurd to think she could dupe the extra-sensitive air-pollution detectors that would immediately alert the special task squad. It was even more useless to hope she'd go unnoticed by the omnipresent, ever-watching, deceptively vacant eyes of the CCTV cameras, especially considering that the ratio of these cameras was one per every three citizens. The hopelessness of such attempts was proven on many occasions by the few desperate souls who tried to smoke in the forested park areas or hide under the awnings late at night.

The rules took effect more than five years ago, but she still missed her cigarette breaks on the terrace with a cup of coffee or a drink. Now, if she wanted to smoke, she had to go to the lounge in the cellar. The lounge was set up to discourage the habit. Its decor was in dire contrast with the sleek opulence of the lobby. It was windowless, with a few pictures of tobacco plantations in basic frames on otherwise bare concrete walls, and brown armchairs of rudimentary ergonomic value, circa 2000. Bright red ashtrays on small side tables and powerful air-purifiers in the corners completed the look. For a while, Susan bravely ignored the ignominy of smoking in those surroundings until last summer, when the insurance companies jacked up the premiums for smokers for the second time in one year, bringing it up to prohibitive heights for the majority of the middle-class population. Susan had to quit. She left one pack, however. Just in case. It looked like it was time to break into her pack.

Angrily, she took out a cigarette from her stash and went to the terrace. She was about to light up, but then her hand stopped in midair. After a short but intense internal fight, reason triumphed. She started to slowly walk back. Then, suddenly, lifting her head high and tossing her hair in silent defiance to the unavoidable damage from the impending fine, she lit her cigarette. Her VS device buzzed, letting her know she had to tone down her stress level.

To curb the spike of sudden neuroses due to quitting creative activities, such as knitting or painting in small social groups and team and individual sports, were pushed heavily and even encouraged with monetary bonuses. Susan redirected her attention to desserts.

It was so easy to watch weight now. It practically watched itself with the crop of new monitoring applications. It was now enough to just scan the information on the meal package to keep track of your calorific intake and the percentages of essential nutrients. The more sophisticated ones allowed you to key in your food preferences and the app would come up with menus tailored to satisfy your personal tastes, while in keeping with the optimal nutritional values based on your individual chart. The apps kept track of your food consumption, allowed substitutions, and if you deviated from their suggestions, made the necessary adjustments. You could not deviate on the last day of the week, however, unless you did not mind the extra cost for medical insurance, which was based on the weight deemed healthy for you, among other things.

With so much help one was hard-pressed to gain weight unless one ignored the app's warnings. Susan had one weak spot - sweets. Hence her constant battles with extra pounds that always sent her doctor into a tizzy. She usually had to pay extra for her medical insurance, but these fines were much smaller than the ones for smoking; she considered it money well spent.

Susan remembered an op-ed discussed by her coworkers in the wake of the last hike. The author went to great lengths to calculate exactly how much money it cost per year in premiums to smoke, to drink, and to eat what one wanted. One thing was clear—chosen few could afford the pleasure of their own poison, or any poison, for that matter.

Susan was still pacing the room like a trapped animal when she imagined herself with needles knitting a winter scarf or some such item for Mike, and her irritation gave way to laughter. She sat there, thinking, for a few minutes. Then, putting away her beer, calm and focused on the task at hand, she said Greta's name into her PAT's mic. "I' m so sorry, Greta, I really couldn't talk to you normally. I'm so glad you managed to register. I myself registered soon after I came home and was about to call and tell you that they were running into late October already, but Dan called. You remember Dan, my coworker? He is impossible. He went on and on and on, and I had a hard time wrapping up the conversation. But I couldn't not pick up, I blew him off twice already when we were having our lunch. It was really an urgent matter."

•　•　•　•　•

"You got October?" Greta's face fell. She did not remember any Dan, but what did it matter? "Oh, lucky you. How stupid of me to wait all this time! Oh well, it's okay, I guess." It was not quite okay. Greta had a very unpleasant feeling of having been duped, but she could not put her finger on exactly when and how. Now Susan, who jumped on the bandwagon at the last minute, was 2,452nd in line, while Greta was 49 women behind, being 2,501st; not that it mattered. Still, it was annoying. *Oh well*, Greta tried to shake the nagging feeling. *It's my own fault. I should not have waited until the last moment.*

They chatted for a few more minutes. Greta was visibly upset, so after telling her that this way, Greta would be in the loop by the time of her interview, having learned all there was to know from Susan's experience, Susan cut the conversation short.

. . . . . .

Susan tried to watch a VR movie. She usually preferred the older, passive kind. The newest, interactive VR was too much of a strain. She had to do enough thinking in real life to need any artificial stimuli. She had stubbornly fumbled through her extensive library for almost an hour, but that night even mindless non-engagement sitcoms, her favorite genre, failed to cure her foul mood. She gave up at last and, unhappy and angry at herself, went to bed. She tossed and turned for a few hours unable to fall asleep. Mike came home around midnight and was surprised to find her in bed at such an early hour. He made an attempt to find out whether she was sick, but Susan pretended to be fast asleep.

Susan planned to bring up the Lottery with Mike that evening, but had a change of heart. It could wait until tomorrow. She did not foresee any difficulty in convincing him. He actually tried to broach the subject a few times himself, but she nipped it in the bud. So, hopefully, Mike would rise to the bait without much ado.

Mike was a staunch presence in Susan's life. Everything about his husky figure screamed dependability. He was, alas, too predictable, too transparent, not intriguing or challenging enough, and, thus, boring. But not in a million years would Susan let go of him. Ambitious as she was, she did yearn for someone flashier, but as a shrewd level-headed woman she realized it would inevitably mean more trouble. She also knew she was no arm candy herself. So, she just kept Mike to herself and did not go out in public with him, especially to work events, unless it couldn't be helped.

Susan, her thirtieth birthday behind her, had yet to discover what love was. It was her darkest secret. When her friends were debating the "to love or be loved" issue, she would remain remarkably quiet, her personal experiences invariably one-sided. Her friends were usually too caught up in the discussion to pick up on her silence or too well-mannered to show they did, let alone comment on it.

In her early twenties she laughed it off as nonsense. She dismissed all the stupid behavior, like spending half the rent money on clothes, losing sleep, failing exams, with an unshakable feeling of superiority. She prided herself on never losing her head. But as she was nearing her thirtieth birthday, she started to wonder. Maybe she was missing out on something. An unsettling, disquieting feeling would creep in, usually late at night, when Mike was already fast asleep, harder to get rid of as time went by. She felt a sting of jealousy when some friend or acquaintance of hers would talk about being in love.

She was fond of Mike. He was low maintenance, straightforward. She did not have to think about him when she was not with him. He left no unresolved questions or innuendos. He was like a good old cooking pot you had inherited from your grandmother that could be used to cook anything from oatmeal to chicken soup to risotto with equally great results, and that did not require any special treatment besides basic cleaning. Once you were done, you just stashed it in its usual spot on the shelf and forgot about it until the next time you had to cook, perfectly sure that you would find it in the same condition you had left it.

Susan met Mike at a friend's birthday party. He was the birthday girl's new boyfriend. He was sitting quietly in a corner and did not engage in any of the usual activities, such as drinking, flirting, or most pathetic, gossiping. Susan came alone. She was in-between boyfriends at the time, which suited her just fine. She was not contemplating settling down anytime soon. Her career was finally taking off. She had landed the coveted managerial position with a well-established charitable institution and enjoyed life to the fullest. This quiet guy impressed her. He had presence and commanded attention. He seemed to be exactly the timid yet dependable sort she had been looking for; she had enough moxie for both of them.

She asked Mary, the birthday girl, about him. His name was Mike. Mary's eyes shone and she became red to the tips of her ears whenever his name came up. She was obviously head-over-heels in love with him. Susan had no difficulty in finding out everything there was to know about him. Mike was a computer whiz (Susan was not surprised) with a big tech company, who had just recently relocated to New York from the West Coast. He knew no one in town and felt lonely. He was very much into modern music and art. Susan's mind, not unlike a computer, recorded all the pertaining data and minutes later churned out a course of action.

Grabbing two glasses of champagne, she accosted Mike with a shy but charming smile and soon they were chatting as if they had known each other for ages. Susan deftly played her Southern origin card and implied she felt slightly intimidated by the city. She was careful not to stress the point, for every one of her friends knew fairly well that Susan was not intimidated by anyone or anything. All the information supplied by Greta on art exhibitions had finally proven helpful. Susan had always had an excellent memory. She had no use for all this information about artists, their lives and their work, but it did not go in one ear and out the other. Mike and Susan exchanged phone numbers and agreed to see the retrospective of a famous French artist together the next Friday. Two weeks later, Mike stopped responding to Mary's calls. In a few months, Susan and Mike were married. Mary was invited. She sent the couple a nice gift, but declined the invitation.

•   •   •   •   •

The results of the Lottery were duly published on June 1ˢᵗ. Both Greta and Susan could hardly sleep the night before the big event, although they realized that the chances were close to zero. Indeed, there were no surprises. Neither of the young women won.

CHAPTER TEN

Mike, his hands shaking with excitement, triumphantly put his PAT in front of Susan, who was enjoying her usual after-dinner beer while watching some light show. "Here, Susie, we've got the interview reminder! It's October 25th," said Mike.

Susan looked at him gloomily; her ease and contentedness evaporated in a matter of seconds. The news brought her back to the looming issue. She did not happen to share her husband's jubilation. She was not in the habit of leaving anything to chance if she could help it. The baby issue was new territory to both of them. She still had no answer to the most important questions. *What are they looking for and what do they want to find out? What kind of questions will they ask?*

Susan felt like smacking Mike right in his radiant face. *What is he so happy about? Empty-headed idiot!* They were definitely not on the same wavelength at the moment. Only too aware that it would not be a good time to make a scene, Susan darted outside under the quickly concocted pretext of a sudden headache. That could have fooled no one but Mike, who just stood there in consternation.

Stupid Greta with her constant superstitions and surprises! Couldn't tell Susan her plans about children earlier. Now Susan had so many things to think about.

Susan had never given much thought to the idea of motherhood. She may have never warmed up to the idea without Greta's help.

Now that she and Mike were considering unassisted parenthood, the idea of so many required tests seemed preposterous, even revolting. If she had to suffer these deprivations for nine months and go through all this trouble, shouldn't she have the right to decide whether to raise her child or allow the State to do it, not vice versa?

At least they already had a spare room they could convert into a nursery. Susan gave herself a tap on the back for mentioning to the authorities during their last move, quite prematurely, that they were planning to start a family. Even if prospective parents were not considering independent parenthood, they were still allowed to have one separate room per child, tax free. At present, Mike liked to use this small but cozy room as his personal sanctuary. Susan liked to watch movies late into the evening, so whenever he did not feel like joining her but was not ready to go to bed, he would use the room to decompress. Susan did not understand Mike's need for privacy. She did not mind other people around her, as long as she could do what she wanted. Usually, she could.

When Susan's voluptuous body entered any space, it seemed to seduce every creek of the room into living by the beat of her heart, the decisions of her mind, the laws of her body. It was not a spearheaded attack, but a soft invasion by her seemingly protean mass, like mercury or slime, confining the victim to a minimum of livable space. She mesmerized him or her into complete surrender, all with a disarming smile, the poor soul feeling too ashamed to inconvenience such a nice person or worse, look boorish or aggressive.

Most of the time, it was Susan who controlled the remote, and she chose what they would have for dinner or where their next vacation would be. Susan always presented a compelling case, and Mike would usually agree with her. In the beginning of their relationship, Mike would sometimes put up a fight, but Susan's infallible logic would soon quench his dissent. She was convinced she knew what the right thing was for them, and had convinced Mike. Mike was so used to this state of affairs that he gave her the reins in practically all of their dealings and would acquiesce to Susan's ideas without even thinking of his own.

Of course, Susan could let Greta have her interview and inspection first, and get the feel of the land from her. Greta was too naïve and romantic to talk to her about such issues directly, but with carefully crafted questions Susan was sure she could get a lot of precious information out of her. But that meant giving her a small advantage. Considering how tough the competition was and how small the quota, it did not seem wise. Susan did not believe in giving ground. She had to find another way.

Those were Susan's thoughts while she meandered around the Independent Parenthood building. Still deep in her thoughts, she mindlessly fell into step with two young women who had just left the building. She was idly listening to their wearisome chitchat when suddenly she heard something that made her almost cry out in excitement.

"Don't forget that the Flynns rescheduled the inspection for this coming Wednesday, Agnes," one said before they split up.

"Oh, shoot," replied the other. "I completely forgot. I have scheduled exercise classes on Wednesdays. What time is it?"

"Two p.m., the last appointment for the day," the first woman replied.

They said their good-byes and went in different directions.

Almost afraid to breathe, not sure yet how she could use the information, Susan quickly jotted down their appearance and the only name—Agnes—that came up during the conversation between the two women. Only then, in euphoric disbelief, did she slowly sit on the nearby bench. The possible solution to her problem came unexpectedly fast, but she had some thinking to do.

When Susan arrived back home, Mike was astonished by the transformation. Here was his usual darling Susan—cheerful, confident, without a care in the world. "Your headache seems to be much better," he ventured, hesitantly.

"Oh, yes, it's all gone now," answered Susan nonchalantly, and Mike was happy to leave it at that.

•   •   •   •   •

Wednesday happened to be a nasty, rainy day. Susan sat with her umbrella on a bench next to the Flynns' building, well within hearing distance, still not quite sure what her actions would be. It was very unlikely she would hear anything; the rain was pouring, and more likely than not the inspectors would sprint to the underground. She would have to play it by ear. That did not deter her; she was good at improvising and quick on her feet. At 2:35, the ladies appeared in the doorway. As Susan had anticipated, they were not in the mood to talk.

"Cute teddy bear, right? And what a great idea, too," said the one whose name was Agnes. "I wonder whether they still make them; I'd buy one for my son."

"Yes, I liked it, too." The rest of their conversation was lost in the noise of the rain and the happy chatter of students entering the building.

Susan had heard enough. She stood up and confidently pressed the button of the intercom. "Hi," she replied to the greeting that followed. "I'm Agnes's colleague. She forgot to take a picture of the cute teddy bear. She thought it could favorably influence the commission. I happened to be in the neighborhood and she asked me to do it. Would it be alright if I came up?"

A beautiful, smiling woman opened the door. She was eating an apple. Two rows of white even teeth were cutting into the firm flesh with such rapturous pleasure, Susan immediately experienced a pang of hunger. She could almost feel the juicy goodness on her tongue. The woman was the very image of health and happiness. Blood rushed to Susan's face, and a dark wave of hate blinded her. She despised this type, with their calm self-assured arrogance.

The woman invited Susan to come in. As Susan already knew from the digital Yellow Pages, her name was Evelyn Flynn. She pointed to the toy in question. It stood out, indeed. "It has been in our family for a long time. I had it dry-cleaned and mended and now it looks brand-new and ready for the next generation. That's the toy my grandmother gave me when I was born. It does look cute and is obviously very special to me, but, honestly, I'm surprised that such a minor detail could have any bearing on the decision. On the other hand, it always comes to minute details when the race is so fierce. I appreciate your taking the time to help me. Is the competition very bad this year? I've heard some rumors." Evelyn was looking straight into Susan's eyes now.

She is not stupid, this Ms. Flynn, thought Susan.

"We are not at liberty to discuss such matters."

"Oh, of course, how unthoughtful of me. I apologize."

"But you touched on some very interesting ideas. I'm working on a sheet to improve our commission's questionnaire. Would you mind sparing a few minutes of your time?"

The room on her left had western exposure. The rain must have stopped by now, because her whole silhouette was glowing against the backdrop of the afternoon sun, creating an eerie effect that she was radiating light herself. Susan looked, fascinated. The sunrays seemed reluctant to leave Evelyn's body. They caressed every inch of it, lingering on every curve, every nook, and one fell under the spell of this sun-kissed woman. A sense of well-being emanated from her and she filled the room with such warmth, one felt compelled to bask in it forever. *It's a no-brainer, this one will win,* thought Susan bitterly. Since she could remember, she had to earn love and friendship the hard way. She watched every word she said, every expression of her face. In her youth, she spent hours in front of the mirror, studying the way she smiled, laughed, frowned. With people like Evelyn, everything was theirs for the taking. Everyone seemed to immediately like them. Yes, people like Evelyn could afford to be trusting. She didn't even question why Susan had to come up and take the picture herself.

Susan was not easily distracted. "Were any questions particularly bothersome?"

"Oh, no," replied Evelyn. "The ladies were very nice."

Wrong move! Susan cringed at her own clumsiness. This type was never frazzled by anyone or anything.

"What I meant was, were any questions difficult to answer and put undue pressure on you?" Susan corrected herself. "We just have to put them all in a certain order."

"Well, maybe the ones asking for the thread count of our sheets and the ones for the baby. I had trouble remembering ours. I remembered the baby's, because I had investigated the matter just recently. Otherwise, I think the questions were simple. Did we choose the name, did we buy the clothes? Were we reading any books on child-rearing? Oh, come to think of it, probably the strangest and funniest one was to list the names each of the future grandparents and parents had suggested. Now, what difference does that make?"

Oh, Susan had some thoughts immediately. The judges wanted to know whether there was any tension among the relatives, and what kind of people they were. Were they pushing the names of their ancestors or just some names they felt were beautiful or adequate for their precious offspring? It was important to note, although quite natural, come to think of it. Family dynamics mattered.

It was time to go. Susan did not want to leave a lasting impression. Ideally, it would be best if Evelyn did not mention this encounter to anyone. But even if she did, Susan took extra precautions, at the cost of feeling paranoid, and invested in a little blond wig she intended to dispose of as soon as possible.

Strolling home, Susan was carefully analyzing what she had learned. She could not believe how lucky she was. She was pretty sure she knew now how the minds of the Commission members worked. She was confident she would be able to ward off any hidden traps in their questions and fix the nursery the right way.

What a beautiful day it was! The sun was just beginning to set, and the red and purple leaves waltzed in the brisk air before falling to her feet, as if rolling out the red carpet for her. She took it as a good sign and accelerated her step.

Once home, Susan quickly voiced in "old toys" on her PAT. Orderly rows of bunnies, teddy bears, and dolls of all kinds seemed to be endless. Susan couldn't make up her mind. The idea seemed stupid to her now. Suddenly disappointed, she tossed her PAT to the other side of the couch. The VS device reacted immediately, beeping yellow stress level. For a moment, Susan felt trapped. Then she came back to her senses. *I should control myself better,* she thought, *letting go won't solve any problems.* She stood up, went into the kitchen, and poured herself a glass of water. She grabbed the PAT and started again. All of a sudden, she saw a small Mickey Mouse toy not more than six inches tall. It must have been more than twenty or thirty years old. It was not in mint condition. In many places, the paint had worn off, and the beige spongy material it was made of showed through. Susan's heart sank. Her finger twitched nervously and hit the "buy" button at the same time as the VS device's agonizing shrills announced the orange stress level. This time, however, Susan did not seem to hear it. She reclined on the couch pillows, closed her eyes, and remained motionless, as if those few minutes of browsing the GlobalNet for a baby toy had robbed her of all energy. Could it really be *the* toy? *Her* toy?

* * * * *

Susan was 5 years old. Her parents took her and her older brother Nick, already 12 at the time, to Disney World for the first time. Magic Kingdom was their first stop. She tried to remember something about the park itself, but in vain. She did not remember any of the rides or the food they ate. The only thing her memory retained from that day were laughing faces of her mother and father against the most beautiful blue sky she had ever seen. In the evening on their way to the motel, they stopped at a souvenir shop by the exit from the park.

Their parents suggested they choose one toy each. They both chose Mickey. The little mouse with big ears held them under his spell by the end of their first day. Nick liked a rubber one, so he could take him to the pool. Susan liked a small one, also waterproof, but spongy and soft, with hands and feet bending so nicely. The toy—she immediately dubbed him Mick—became her inseparable buddy, and she dragged her Mick wherever she went.

Susan smiled to herself at the memory. How could she forget this? They were a happy family. Their parents loved her and her brother so much that she didn't feel the need for anyone else in her life. She remembered them playing board games every evening, and how much fun it was. Her mother liked to win, and so did Nick, so often the game just boiled down to a duel between the two, who fought as if their lives depended on the outcome. Their father tried to reason with them in mock wrath by repeating over and over again that it was not the end of the world and it was just a board game. Usually, his words went unnoticed.

She remembered their obligatory yearly fall foliage trips, sometimes around Virginia, their state, but mostly to the neighboring West Virginia, where both sets of her grandparents moved after retiring. She remembered the chilly weather, warm apple cider, and numerous deer sightings that Susan particularly looked forward to. There were overnight stays at her grandparents, in the Allegheny Mountains, drinking hot chocolate with huge pieces of country bread and leaning against old furnaces her grandparents kept for fun, to warm up after skiing.

She felt protected and secure and not in a hurry to explore other relationships. She was not inoculated against human sins; she was living in a sterile environment of love, understanding, and forgiveness. She dreaded starting school that fall.

Other kids did not particularly like her. She became an outcast from the very beginning. The little humans had an uncanny ability to unmistakably smell fear and insecurity and single out the vulnerable. Mick was often her only companion in the cafeteria, where Susan would usually sit by herself at the end of a long table, painted a cheerful red hue, placing her loyal friend on the tray in front of her. Soon, everybody in school called her Mini Mouse. Susan was small and thin throughout her school years.

As Susan grew up, she began to see her parents against a different backdrop. She noticed the simple decor of their small house, compared to bigger and better-appointed houses of their well-to-do neighbors. Her parents were high school sweethearts in a small mountain town in Virginia. They got married right upon graduation and had Nick soon after. They both got jobs at a food megastore warehouse, working a few yards from each other, supervising the automated online order lines and fixing glitches. They lost their jobs to full automation when Nick had just turned one. For a few years they barely scraped by on their compensation checks. Then Susan's mother convinced her dad to go to college. He had always been good at math. They had no money to get degrees at the same time, so her mom worked as a nanny taking care of babies in a state childcare center and supported her husband while he studied. She was supposed to go back to school after he got his engineering degree and found a job. Then Susan was born. Her mother never got her degree and continued to work as a nanny well past her official retirement year.

Her father, smart but shy by nature—people called him a pushover behind his back—and too engulfed in his happy family life to care, was regularly passed up for promotions. Susan saw less talented but also less scrupulous people getting ahead. She felt so unhappy and lonely in her helpless anger it made her cry at night. Susan did not want to cause her parents aggravation by telling them about her misery. They were so happy and so sure their kids were happy, too. And Nick was happy. That was another reason Susan kept her mouth shut. She did not want her parents to think it was her fault. Maybe it was her fault, after all. Nick seemed to be absolutely unaffected by his parents' poor social standing. He was an average student, his grades were much worse than Susan's, but he was a kid with lots of interests and lots of friends. Susan's most vivid childhood memory was of his slim body, bent over the table on their back porch, working on a huge colorful kite, his faithful gang waiting in awe a few steps behind. During one of her sleepless nights, she promised herself to become not smart, but successful.

The next summer they were visiting her uncle, her dad's brother, at the Outer Banks in North Carolina. Susan was sitting on the shore with her inseparable Mick, as usual, watching the ocean. Mick was no longer new. The paint had lost its luster, the yellowish spongy gut was visible in many places, and a small part of its left ear was missing. Who cared? Susan still loved him. The white foam came all the way to her feet and gently tickled her toes before reluctantly receding with a soft hissing sound. She wished she could stay like that forever.

The wind was picking up. The wet tongues of the waves were becoming longer and stronger. Suddenly, she saw a conch rolling to her feet in a whirlwind of sand and small pieces of broken shells. Susan jumped up. Oh, Molly had one just like that! With big blue eyes and tight golden locks, Molly was one of the most beautiful girls of her school. Unsurprisingly, she was also one of the most popular. She had recently moved to their town from somewhere in Florida. Her dad used to be a diving instructor and regularly took newbies into the ocean on his boat. One of those divers found a beautiful conch on his first descent (talk about beginner's luck!) and having no use for it himself, gave it to Molly's dad after seeing her picture in the cabin. It was already becoming old news, but Molly still got a good crop of admiring and jealous glances from other girls when she brought it to school, which she regularly did lest her schoolmates forgot she had it.

Susan seized the shell and tried to come up with some amazing story of her own. Upon closer look, it turned out to be a beautiful Murex, all of its spikes miraculously intact. Out of a corner of her eye she saw a big wave breaking just to the right. Susan glimpsed some bright incongruously shaped object being entrained into the ocean depths. She was so enthralled by the shell it took her a few moments to realize what it was. Mick! She tried to catch him, but slipped and fell. The strong current dragged her, rolling and splashing, scraping her painfully against the roughness of the ocean floor; salted water blinded her; the sand, as tentacles of an octopus, went deep into her mouth, nose, eyes. It took her some time to stand up and regain her balance. The white-gloved hand was bobbing in the waters, as if in the final farewell, getting further and further away. Susan ran along the shore until she could no longer distinguish it amid the whitecaps.

Susan spent the remaining days of their stay combing the shore, hoping the ocean would change its mind and return her Mick. Any bright spot made her heart jump with joy, but as the days went by, her hope slowly petered out.

Soon she went back home, and in another fortnight or so school resumed. Her parents surprised her with a Mickey and Minnie set, but they sat in the same spot in her room in the same exact poses Susan's parents left them. All other efforts on their part proved equally futile. At last, they decided to let Susan be and hoped that time would take care of it.

Susan was having lunch in the school cafeteria. Trying to avoid looking at the spot where Mick used to sit, she was listlessly poking the piece of salmon on her plate. A girl from her class came up to her and asked if she could join her. Astonished and a little apprehensive, Susan nodded. Then another one came, and then another. Soon, she was surrounded by all her classmates babbling at once, vying for her attention, offering to go to the movies together, and all other wonderful things she was dreaming of for such a long time. Molly, however, outdid everyone, as usual. She slowly got her conch shell out of her backpack and placed it in front of Susan. Susan was speechless. She was afraid it was a cruel dream, and had secretly pinched her arm twice already. The girls did not disappear and seemed genuinely friendly.

That evening, when she came home after an online shopping session with her new friends, still giddy from the experience, she heard Nick talking to their parents in the kitchen. She heard her name and remained quiet for some time, to listen. It turned out Nick had told his buddies about her predicament. They took it to heart and started to plot her salvation. One of them had a younger sister in Susan's class and conveyed the message so well his sister cried.

Susan had never forgotten how the ruling of grade-school arbiters propelled her from mooks to martyrs on the wings of pity. When she started college ten years later, she made sure everybody on campus knew that her parents loved their son and all but ignored and neglected their little girl.

·   ·   ·

'She thought about her and Mike. Would they be good parents? Would their child feel the same way she did growing up? *Mike would make a great father*, thought Susan with a prick of jealousy. So kind, so calm, so dependable. He was like a rock. What about her? Did she have the maternal chops? She realized she had never given it a thought and was just handling this issue as any other that came her way, pragmatically and efficiently. Maybe she was not created to be a good mother. So, what of it? That would not in itself be surprising. Being a parent was just a job and one can very well suck at some jobs. On the other hand, it was not like any other job. It was her child, after all, and no one had the right to tell her how to raise it. *Well*, she thought, *we will have to wait and see*. She tossed her head in her usual gesture of defiance and readiness to face whatever was in store for her.

Mike found his wife lying on a couch, in a perfectly dark room, her PAT in the standby mode on her knees. She was clutching her hands to her chest, as if pressing something to her heart, staring at the wall and smiling.

CHAPTER ELEVEN

Susan was having her morning coffee on the terrace, as usual. She looked haggard and sick and felt awful. Her eyes were puffy. Her hair was unkempt and looked flat and lifeless, without all the usual styling and volumizing products. Her skin was gray, with an uneven earthy tone. Her usually so-well-put-together and coordinated body seemed to be falling apart, unscrewed at the joints. Her limbs operated chaotically, as if independent from each other. Presently, they fell on the ground in an ungainly awkward manner.

She did not sleep well that night. Her disturbing dreams woke her up several times. People from her past, people she forgot existed, were leaning close to her face, looking into her eyes, asking questions she did not have answers for, making demands she did not know how to satisfy.

All of a sudden, she was dreaming she had died, and as her soul was about to leave the body, she heard a voice. The voice said it was a mistake, it was too soon for her to die, and her soul had to return to her body. Only now, as if through a wormhole, she had traveled back in time and was trying to squeeze into her body when she was a child. It was too small, and the shape was all wrong. She kept trying and started choking; the small arms and legs were too tight and she was getting stuck, and it hurt. She got scared she would have to die after all. She woke up feeling sick.

The postal drone had just deposited a small white box on the table in front of her. She knew what was inside. It was the Mickey toy she had ordered the day before. All of a sudden, she was afraid and not in a rush to find out. She was stalling, almost regretting her venture. With terror, she looked at her VS monitor. It had been causing her too much trouble lately. Amazingly, the light was glowing a bright steady green.

Yesterday, she wanted so much for the package to be her Mick. She looked through all the pictures of the toy on the site, but the angle of the shots did not allow her to see exactly how the left ear was damaged. All the other wear-and-tear marks were inconclusive. She did not remember those exactly. Today, she was not sure anymore. At last, with her usual defiant toss of the head, as if to throw back an unruly lock, she pulled the strip. The first thing that popped out of the white packing peanuts surrounding the toy was its left ear, with a small piece missing.

It was a clear sunny morning, but for a moment everything around her became dark. Emotions and feelings Susan didn't think she still had flooded her, as if a dam broke. The protective shell she had spent many years building was blown to smithereens. Her delicate, unprotected body, exposed to the elements, squirmed helplessly. Susan started to sob uncontrollably. She quickly left the terrace and jumped into the shower so that Mike, who liked to start his day early and was already at his computer, did not notice anything. It was an unnecessary precaution, however, for Mike did not see or hear anything when he was working. When she emerged from the shower, it was the usual cheerful, confident Susan.

Susan poured herself another cup of coffee and went back to the terrace. Calmly, she put the toy back in the box without giving it another look.

•　•　•　•　•

The next day, Susan went to the interview location to check out how the other applicants were dressed. She looked around glumly. She was definitely out of her league here. The crowd seemed impressive. Susan had never worn any of the sophisticated pieces represented profusely in the interview pack. It looked more like a fashion show, come to think of it, and not your everyday garb. How could these women go about their daily routines dressed like that? They must feel so uncomfortable. Susan felt that standing out could negatively affect her chances. Still, she knew it would be too expensive to procure a whole new wardrobe; she felt she could get away with flaunting a nice bag nonchalantly with maybe just a neat pair of jeans and a T-shirt. Greta might be right on this point, after all. Susan had first viciously ridiculed the idea during their last phone conversation, but caught herself in time and conceded it was a great one, only to send Greta in the wrong direction. Last but not least, a good haircut and a manicure. A couple of old-fashioned rings from her friend Jackie, who had already agreed to lend them (Susan had told her it was for a get-together with Mike's parents and family), would clinch her look.

Once at home, Susan went straight to her closet and looked thoroughly through all its contents, piece by piece. She came to the conclusion that she had nothing to wear for the interview.

Mass production that in the past was meant to satiate the human urge to possess, was replaced by individualized production. This increased the efficiency of the economy and eliminated negative effects of product waste on the environment. Strict norms on all forms of individual consumption were put in place. By the recently tightened rule, every man or woman could acquire five outfit pieces a month, which included clothes, shoes, and accessories. Exceeding this allowance required one to pay a fine or replace the unwanted items with the new ones for a much smaller commission. Just a couple of years ago, husband and wife could bundle their allowances, but that was no longer possible, to Susan's chagrin. Mike did not pay much attention to his clothes and did not mind sharing his quota with her. He loved her to look nice.

Susan had already exhausted her monthly allowance. She even got herself a sixth item—she had an unplanned in-person meeting with an important client—and paid the necessary fine. She didn't say anything to Mike. She harangued him every day on his ways that were not frugal enough, in her view. Especially his annoying habit of not switching off the light when he was leaving the room. Electricity was not cheap, and they could save a considerable amount by being more careful. Mike thought it was peanuts (the lights went off automatically after two minutes), and he was absentminded. In a way, it was a good thing, because he didn't mind her occasional spending extravagances.

Susan went to the mirror and gave herself a once-over. She had gained weight lately and was not looking her best even in her favorite outfit—a narrow black pencil skirt and colorful frilly blouse. Being more often than not on a crusade of some kind made her especially prone to nutritional digressions. The nervous strain of the last months threw her off balance and she indulged in her favorite desserts even more often than usual. She was sure she could still pull it off by cleverly choosing the outfit and carrying herself with her usual gusto.

Upon further consideration, Susan decided it was not necessarily a bad thing and could help her make a favorable impression on the inspectors from a totally different angle. There had lately been a shift in the perception of status. Considering people had to pay higher premiums now for pounds in excess of their optimal weight, indiscriminate food consumption and the resulting obesity became financially unsustainable for most. Only very affluent people could afford to pay for deviating from their best selves. The fact did not go unnoticed, and there was a growing tendency to associate status and, hence, beauty, with heavier bodies. The bad news was that since Susan had to pay extra for those pounds, she could not afford to pay for new clothes. She would have to return a few items to get herself the bag, new jeans, and the T-shirt she had in mind.

Susan was stressed again. So many fines. She felt she was suffocating. She conceded there was something to the philosophical mumbo-jumbo behind today's policies that Greta liked so much. To thrive and not to destroy the world around us in the process, human society had to emulate nature and be waste-free. Nature is fully recyclable, in other words, one-hundred percent efficient. Susan could certainly relate to the concept. It was not unlike how she operated, herself. Only the implications of those policies didn't seem to leave any room for the freedom of choice, in practical terms. Would free will be fiction, after all?

It was not the time or place to ponder the issue. *It looks like I'm turning into Greta*, thought Susan with displeasure. Indeed, if you lie down with dogs, you will get up with fleas! Susan glanced apprehensively at her VS device and went to the kitchen for a glass of water. Well, she certainly did not want to turn into Greta. She would not give up her rights that easily, whatever the policies were. Then she took her PAT and tweaked her new measurements into the clothing account.

There were no more brick-and-mortar stores. Clothes were now fully custom-made on demand according to measurements provided by customers and stored in their accounts. There were no tremendous amounts of goods, no huge warehouses, no much anticipated regular sales; just ads of available models from various fashion houses on one's PAT and on mannequins displaying them in the lower-floor windows of most buildings. The returned items stayed on the secondhand site for a month, then, being fully biodegradable, they were recycled.

As always, Susan started by visiting the secondhand market. Women who felt the need to vary their wardrobe more than once a month quickly discovered a less expensive way to do so. They would regularly return some of their items and purchase new ones instead. They still had to pay the penalty, but it was considerably smaller than the fine for each extra item. This practice created a considerable stock of returned merchandise, which was sold at a fraction of its initial price, but it was not always easy to find a buyer for an item made to someone else's specifications.

Susan loved this market for two main reasons. First, the price. Second, it was a question of strategy. Some women devoted a lot of time to scoring the fashion ads on GlobalNet in hopes of finding some extraordinary pieces in the ocean of available models. They usually had a good, trained eye for such things, fueled by their ambitious desire to stand out. So, most of the secondhand pieces were previously fished out and preapproved by society's unofficial taste-makers. Susan had a good eye herself and was perfectly capable of doing well on her own, but the appeal of previous approval was irresistible to her. It also allowed her to save the many hours needed to search the GlobalNet. Susan was complimented a lot on her clothes. It did not prevent her from occasionally feeling jealous of Greta. Not that anyone ever noticed what Greta was wearing, her clothes having the ability to become her second skin. Somehow her eyes just got bluer, her skin brighter, her body sexier.

As much as every item was custom-adjusted, the models themselves were computer-generated. Models of various fashion houses, produced in strict accordance with the algorithms based on the values perceived as mandatory for a woman's satisfaction, tended to converge in their rendering of perfection with regard to human beauty and functionality.

Rare islands of human talent got swallowed by the digital ocean. The bastions of outstanding human gift fell under the attack of foolproof algorithms of quantum competitors. Oh, finicky human genius! Just like growing rare plants stood little chance when the produce of underground farms with artificial light and misting came into play, it was doomed in the face of the digital deluge of efficient ones and zeroes. What was affordable for a chosen few became, as a result, within reach to the masses. The elite lost its firm grip on perfectly tailored clothes. What was a poor rich girl to do? She certainly could swap items more often, but that still didn't solve the problem of standing out at any moment. True, the lack of taste or sense of measure were handled by a slew of consulting specialists whose expert advice ranged in price, but usually was beyond the means of the general public. It did help, but still, many of the affluent women became bored, gave up, and got lost in a matter of several years in the uniform mainstream. At least their leisurely lifestyle allowed them to go for fancier, unpractical pieces. The more tenacious ones, on the other hand, or those who were there strictly for the love of the game, the true devotees of the art of fashion, were not deterred by the mundane ubiquity of the sublime. They had the talent to rise to the challenge of finding their unique personal style among the impersonal, uniform perfection. Mostly, they had time.

The growing affordability of great-looking clothes made an indent in the continuous centuries-long effort by fashion gurus to challenge natural beauty by artfully concealing the faults of the human body by great design. Bio-enhancement for cosmetic purposes was strictly forbidden, albeit this law was constantly contested by mobs of women whose natural defects were made only too obvious by the ubiquitous sartorial excellence.

Susan was lucky. She soon found a smart suit, not unlike those worn by the women spotted on her reconnaissance trip. She grabbed it immediately and decided to drop her original jeans and T-shirt idea. Finding a bag was easy.

•　　•　　•　　•　　•

The manicure almost spoiled everything. She was too busy working before the interview, and never had time to dart outside to make the manicure at her favorite place. When Mike did not work from home, and that happened to be one such day, Susan would usually meet him for a quick dinner out. It would have been too late for the manicure after dinner. Her place closed early, and she was not ready to pay twice the price at one of the more expensive 24-hour salons, even for such an important cause.

Susan went to the nail salon after work and ignored Mike's messages, first indignant, then more and more worried. She was surprised by his adamant reaction, and very much annoyed with his untimely nagging. She did not expect him to understand why a manicure was so important, but he certainly should have trusted her judgment. Susan made her position very clear in the evening when they finally met, and he did not go to bed very happy. Oh well, she would deal with him in the morning. She needed a good night's sleep.

CHAPTER TWELVE

The interview was set for nine a.m., bright and early. Mike, still sulking from their fight the other night, was having coffee on the terrace, without lifting his eyes from his PAT. The day promised to be cold and muggy, so he lowered the retractable winter roof for the first time this season. The first thing Susan noticed when she came down to join him for breakfast, was that Mike, as usual, forgot to switch off the light in the kitchen when moving to the terrace. This time, however, turning off the light did not start her harping on the necessity of keeping their electricity costs down.

Instead, using her most enthralling tone of voice and smiling at him, exposing her beautiful teeth (one of the major weapons in her seduction arsenal), she said, "Please forgive me, Mikey, for being such a bitch yesterday. You know how important our baby is to me; I am trying so hard to do everything in my power to secure a contract, and the stress must have put me on edge..."

Susan was very proud of her teeth that had never known a dentist's drill, and duly so, but she was even more proud of her voice and smile. If good teeth were a gift, in her case, she had worked hard to get a voice that could translate any shade of feeling in a most convincing manner, with an irresistible smile. She could never settle for what she got. In college, she had spent long hours in front of the mirror perfecting her smile and gestures. Every day she would set her alarm clock thirty minutes earlier than she had to wake up, and walk with a stack of books on her head to perfect her posture. Later during the day, she would record her written homework to learn all of her voice's undulations and train it to convey various feelings at will. She did not toil in vain. It worked every time, without fail, at least as far as Mike was concerned.

Approaching him from behind, Susan put her arms around Mike's neck, just close enough for him to catch a barely perceptible whiff of her perfume. He made an instinctive move to follow the scent, but Susan was already sitting in front of him, exposing, but not too obviously, another great asset—her impeccably shaped legs.

"I'm sorry, too, Susie. I shouldn't have snapped at you. I know how hard it is for you. I should have known better." He tried to kiss Susan, but she stopped him with a quick movement of her hand.

"Not now, Mikey," she said tenderly. "We'd better hurry. We can't arrive all disheveled and sweaty for our interview, can we?"

•   •   •   •   •

They entered the waiting room at 8:45, exactly fifteen minutes prior to their appointment, as suggested. After registering on the reception screen, Susan started to mentally list the possible questions she compiled after talking to Evelyn, for the umpteenth time.

"Do you remember the thread count of the sheets?" she asked, anguished, in a soft voice, as if the examiners could hear her from behind the closed door.

"Yes," replied Mike.

"The titles of the books we read?"

"Yes, yes, don't worry. At this point, I even know the contents by heart, let alone their titles and authors' names. Do you really think we're supposed to read any books, though? I mean, you're not even pregnant yet."

Here we go again, thought Susan. *We talked about it only the other day. Why is it so hard to just do it and not question everything?* Aloud, she said patiently, as if talking to a child, "Mikey, honey. I don't know, but just in case. It's only two titles." She obviously did not mention her shenanigans to Mike, and he was understandably astonished at the randomness of information she asked him to memorize. Prudently, she did not mention what torture it was for her to read those books, either. She was not a great fan of reading; she preferred talking to people to get the information she needed, and reading for fun was an absurd word combination for her altogether.

"What I don't understand, Susan, is why do we have to prepare for this interview? Why do we have to lie? We want to raise the baby ourselves and we are prepared to do whatever it takes. We will love that baby, Susie."

"Love is not enough, Mike!" The words came out with so much passion, she immediately regretted saying them. She knew such a pronouncement wouldn't agree with Mike. "What I meant to say is, in an ideal world, Mike, yes, but we do not live in an ideal world."

"Sometimes I feel the more disgusting the essence, the more presentable the appearance. Maybe it's not a coincidence. You are a people person, Susan, and I won't argue with you, but there must be something wrong with our society if we have to pretend we've read books we don't feel we need to read and memorize sheet thread counts."

"There will be trick questions, Mikey."

"There may be trick questions, Susan, but I'm pretty sure there are not supposed to be trick answers. It would be cheating. Our appearance is supposed to reveal our essence, not to conceal it. What I'm trying to say is if we fall into the trap with the trick questions, that means we don't qualify. And I'm sure we do."

"This is how it's supposed to work in the ideal world, Mike. But, again, we do not live in an ideal world. If the only task were to weave out those people who lie in order to get the right to raise their kids without the required qualifications, you could be right, but even then…I'm scared, Mike, I'm very scared. What if we are perfectly suited to be parents, but because of the interviewers' or inspectors' inability, or malevolence, or even their bad mood on that particular day, we will be crossed off the list? I can't imagine how you can remain so calm. I just want to make sure we communicate who we are in the best possible way. The way I see it, we all speak different languages, right? So, for us to communicate, we have to use the Universal Communicator that translates our words into the language of the person we're talking to. But we are different in other ways, as well. We may convey our thoughts and other people, in their turn, may understand us in different ways. So, I'm trying to understand the people we're dealing with and foresee how they will interpret what we say and do, and try to make sure our intentions, words, and actions are understood correctly."

Mike rarely lost his temper, but when he did, it was like a storm. The devastation could be enormous. Susan had to find the right words that would make the unruly ocean calm and friendly again, with tamed waves clapping at her feet like little playful puppies. Susan knew her man well and was usually able to divert the hurricane and avoid the landfall just when it seemed inevitable. Indeed, one could almost see how the dark clouds dissipated from the horizon, and Mike's face, dark with disapproval just a minute ago, became serene again.

"The competition is really fierce. All of a sudden, raising children has become fashionable, for some reason." Too concentrated on toning down her gaffe, Susan did not notice the stupefied look Mike gave her. "The most important thing, Mikey. Don't forget that when it comes to the part about how well we know each other, you just pick the first answer if you put them in alphabetical order. I'll do the same, so we will take all the guesswork out of it."

"Yes, I remember," replied Mike quickly, without any comment this time.

$\bullet \qquad \bullet \qquad \bullet \qquad \bullet \qquad \bullet$

Mike had to admit that the idea was brilliant in its simplicity. He wondered if anyone else had thought of it. Then again, no one would tell, even if they did, so it was a moot question.

The interview supposedly had a section aimed at determining how well the prospective parents knew each other—the premise being, obviously, that the better they did, the better they were equipped, as a team, to raise a human being in accordance with modern standards. Each parent-to-be was given a list of ten questions about the character traits and habits of the spouse. To make tests easier to assess, the questions were multiple choice. Seven options were given. Susan's idea was to disregard the actual state of affairs altogether, even when the party knew the answer, but instead choose the answer that would rank first if all the options were put in alphabetical order. If, for example, the question was, "What is your spouse's favorite color?" and the choices were red, purple, pink, green, yellow, white, and orange, the answer should be "green." If two or more options began with the same letter, say, black and blue, alphabetical order should be used again as the guiding principle.

All of a sudden, Mike felt uncomfortable. The joy of having made up with Susan was wearing out rapidly. He loved Susan and wanted a child with her. He could not be happier about Susan's desire to take care of a child full-time. He did not, however, understand why they had to cheat so much, and Susan's explanations made the issue only more puzzling. But he trusted that Susan knew what she was doing.

CHAPTER THIRTEEN

The interview started at nine o'clock sharp. As Susan and Mike entered the room, five pairs of attentive eyes peered at them from across the long table. They were the first couple, and it was obvious they would have to bear the brunt of the interviewers' fresh readiness. *Note to self,* thought Susan. *I should avoid scheduling any test early in the day.*

"So, why do you want to raise your child yourselves?" The head interviewer looked at Susan ferociously, as if sinking her teeth into her flesh. "Aren't you happy with your careers?"

Maintaining an irreproachable poker face, affable and a little shy, Susan thought that those women probably couldn't help feeling uneasy for not grasping what could make a person choose what they perceived as voluntary seclusion, over working with peers. *I have to tread a fine line not to sound like an introvert freak,* she thought. Most of all, she did not want her desire of just taking it easy for a few years to transpire.

"I love my job and I'm very good at it," she said with pride, but no arrogance. "But I feel I still have some potential I haven't even begun to tap into. It's a pity not to use one's talents to the fullest. I'm so comfortable and secure now, I have to admit, so making the decision to move to a more challenging and demanding job was not easy. But I feel I'm ready for it, and if I want my peace of mind intact, I have to do it."

"What makes you feel you are ready? Is this just a way to satisfy your ambitions or to have thrilling experiences?" The lady was looking into Susan's eyes with such intensity as if she was trying to harpoon some hidden truth from behind her opaque inscrutable pupils.

What a way to twist her words! Susan was trying to project an image of a conscientious citizen ready to take on a task of huge importance. Who in her right mind would be a stay-at-home mom as a way to satisfy her inner ambitions? Immediately, she thought about Greta. Yes, maybe Greta.

Just the other day the two couples were supposed to go out together and were meeting at their apartment. Greta showed up on time, as always, but Greg was running late. There was some problem with one of the virus cultures. Maliciously, amused by her pun, Susan asked Greta about her own latest cultural feats. Greta told them it was *Citizen Cain*, and went on about her personal understanding of the Rosebud and then started to blabber about the creative energy she got from her exposure to art. Whatever. Susan egged her on by sceptic remarks that drove Greta up the wall. Susan could not help herself from tapping into Greta's lack of nuance and experience, and relished in unleashing her wildest insecurities. That was such a fertile ground. Everything had to be perfect to matter, to register on Greta's radar. A truly black-and-white personality.

Unexpectedly, Mike seemed interested in the topic, and they both had an agitated discussion, but Susan went to greet Greg who had finally arrived, and missed most of it. What was it that Greta said? Something like being happy was more important than being successful. Such baloney. Aha. *"Parents should not break the child, otherwise all riches are worthless."* Did she really mean that? What exactly did she mean? Greta was so full of it, it was useless to try and figure out what she meant sometimes.

"I just feel like giving back by paying it forward. I am very grateful to my parents for raising me a happy person, well-adopted to our society. They were always there for me. I want to do the same for my child." Susan tried to gauge the impact of her words, but the interviewers were not newbies and their faces remained impassive.

"Most parents would love to see and help their children more, so would you. We understand that. This is not quite what we are asking. What makes you feel you will be as good at raising your child as a qualified educator? Most parents are not well equipped for the job. What makes you think you are?"

Susan continued, "I feel very much in tune with the philosophy behind the official approach. By releasing the child's full potential, we bring about the best in a human being. I do not want my child to be anything more, or different, or less for that matter, than Nature intended. So, I'll bring all my experience, knowledge, and passion to the task."

"Why do you feel so sure you are in tune? What you say sounds correct, but it is so impersonal. Anyone can claim they adhere to the Policy. The Policy is no secret. We need to be convinced that you understand it in order to trust you with a human life. We want every candidate to succeed. We're not trying to be difficult; we want to help you. But if we leave things as they stand now, it is very unlikely you would make the cut."

"Well, maybe this is not what I should say, but here it is, as personal as it gets. I have a friend, you know, who is always on my case for being into arts and music, and finding cultural life an essential part of our existence." Mike shifted uneasily in his chair.

"What's wrong? You don't share your wife's views?" asked one of the instructors immediately.

"Yes, I do," he replied without much conviction. He realized how he must look, and his face became red.

Susan, quick on the uptake, as always, came to the rescue. "To be honest, we just discussed the matter between ourselves a few days ago, after watching *Citizen Cain*. It feels like we are cheating a bit, because our ideas and arguments are still so fresh in our memory and so easy to repeat now. I feel we have what it takes to provide a loving, nurturing environment for our child and at the same time create a happy, successful human being."

The words burst out of Mike's mouth before he could think about what Susan would do to him for his rebellion. "We will love our child the way he is, the way Nature intended. We will bring out his best, but most of all, we will cherish his uniqueness. We will let him walk his own path, live his life, and we will stand by him all the time, all the way."

The pinched lips parted in a grimace meant to show encouragement, and all the inspectors looked at each other and nodded approval, visibly impressed and satisfied by the answer. "You know, for a moment I thought you were doubting the Policy," said the head woman, "but I see now that you fully understand the meaning of the task, although you do have a peculiar way of phrasing it. You are a very interesting couple."

From then on, it was a cakewalk. Mike, as if in a stupor, avoiding thinking about the unpleasant episode, all the while feeling secure again under Susan's protection, got hold of himself and produced thread counts and book titles without messing up. The Q&A section was a breeze, too.

Susan was ecstatic. And when Susan was happy, she knew how to make Mike happy.

•　•　•　•　•

In the middle of the night, Mike woke up with a jolt. An uncomfortable feeling prevented him from going back to sleep. He crept out of bed noiselessly and went into the living room, grabbing a beer on his way. He lost track of time, sipping his beer and looking at the twinkling lights of the big city. He was thinking about an episode from his early childhood, a long-forgotten memory that suddenly came back to him as vividly as if it had taken place yesterday.

He was four or five years old, at best. It was a big family event, the wedding of his cousin Anthony. He and his bride, Matilda, were a good couple. Everybody was happy for them and celebrated fullheartedly. Mike, however, did not share his relatives' excitement. In fact, he was truly miserable. Just minutes before everybody left for the church, he was running from room to room, celebrating the event in his own way, taking advantage of the joyful commotion of the adults who left him to his own devices, unsupervised for once, to take care of a myriad of errands, forgotten or put off until the last moment.

He had gotten a splinter. He still remembered the pain and the feeling of disappointment for having messed up, for not having been able to handle his independence. It was not a big splinter. It was not an emergency that required immediate intervention of adults. Besides, he did not want to detract attention from the event and ruin the happy moment for his parents, or publicly admit that he let everybody down. So, there he was, his happiness spoiled by his secret suffering, this gnawing little pain in striking contrast with the carefree happiness on every face around him.

The episode kept playing in his mind as if it were a movie and somebody was constantly pushing the replay button, but Mike was too worn out to care. He did not know how long he stayed there, clutching the warm empty bottle, looking at the lights in front of him as far as his eyes could see. He was sleepless in a city that never sleeps, which made him feel like its secret accomplice, and this feeling gave him peace and solace.

CHAPTER FOURTEEN

Shortly after Susan's interview, she and Greta met for coffee. It was a rainy afternoon. The bright warmth of the place offered a much-needed respite. Sunk deep into the huge leather cushions of an old couch, still numb inside from the nasty weather, the two friends slowly imbibed the hot beverages in total silence, as if defrosting their ability to talk, sip by sip. The aroma of freshly brewed coffee and exotic spices filled the air along with the barely perceptible fragrances of customers past that seemed to be forever engrained in the old leather.

For a while their prolonged silence was broken only by the nervous clatter of Susan's spoon against the cup. Susan was obviously in a dark mood. She was sitting with her head down, mulling over something, obstinately stirring her coffee, as if to help the churning thoughts in her head.

Greta wondered what might have happened but just patiently observed her friend, waiting for her to speak first. At last, unable to keep silent anymore, she asked Susan how the interview went. Susan, as if waiting for the right moment, exploded. It was a torrent, a blast. Ignoring Greta's question, she ranted about the stifling strictness of the clothes and food norms.

"This is just wonderful," burst Susan into speech loudly. "I got another fine on my way here. I was in the middle of something and couldn't go to the lounge to have a cigarette. I needed it so badly—

my only one in the house for I don't even remember how long! That does it! I'll go broke if this continues! This is my fourth fine in the last two weeks. I had two pastries and one extra piece of clothing. No more freedom to do what one wants. I'll lose my sanity."

"Haven't you quit?" Too indignant to wait for an answer, Greta went on. "You complain that running to a lounge deprives you of pleasure? But you're not supposed to have pleasure at the expense of other people. It's as simple as that. You are not a callous person, Susie, what are you saying? This is pure nonsense, and you know it. You're just frustrated, that's all. You are free to ruin your health, but you cannot endanger other people's health, that's the bottom line. I know it's tough, but there it is, nothing to discuss here.

"As far as the customization of our nutritional needs, you are absolutely free to ruin your own health in that regard, too, only then you are on your own, financially speaking. You know as well as I do, that you can refuse to use your DNA tests and waive medical insurance altogether. Now that we have the technology to accurately predict future risks of any health problem, it stands to reason that insurance companies will take us aboard only if we adhere to our personalized lifestyle and healthcare strategies. Insurance is for unforeseen developments. If people ruin their health knowingly, they have to pay. And don't forget: greater predictability of an individual's potential health problems allowed insurers to significantly reduce our premiums. That makes perfect sense, doesn't it? It is not your freedom that's curtailed, but your irresponsible behavior. You cannot expect the insurance company to pay for your inappropriate behavior, or expect the State to use taxpayers' money to do it. On the other hand, if you choose to transgress occasionally, it's only fair that you should pay a fine. Your overall medical expenses would still be lower this way than if the premiums had been generated without taking your chart into account. Everything is very well structured, really."

"Yes, I understand all that, in theory," said Susan impatiently. "Why then at times does it feel like an iron grip on my throat? I don't want to do what is right. I want to do what I want. I want to live, Greta, and to feel alive! I'm not a robot. I am a human being. And if doing what one wants is a mistake, then people should be allowed to make mistakes. Maybe life itself is a mistake, an aberration. Oh well, what's the use in talking about it? I'm just not rich enough to be free, I guess."

Greta was listening attentively. Susan did not usually go into political matters. Very pragmatic, she held her hand on the pulse and was only interested in perfectioning her game to beat the system. She was not one to engage in philosophical discussions that led nowhere, either. *She must be really upset about something,* thought Greta. Out loud, however, she said, slowly, "Yes, Susan, yes, I hear what you're trying to say. It does look that way. On the surface of things, you are penalized for digressing, but in reality, you are rewarded by low insurance premiums when you stick to your optimal chart. Just look at it from a long-term point of view. If you deviate from your prescribed diet, which is strict, but does give you some slack, you have to admit, you will develop illnesses later in life that will require you and your insurer to pay a lot of money for medications and treatment. There is no way to know exactly what kind of diseases you might get, but it's almost certain your medical expenses will be much higher. Your fines, established with your personal health risks in mind, are smaller than those potential expenses. The system is fair, Susan. The high price tag is not meant for the State to profit from antisocial behavior or hedonistic self-indulgence. The goal is just the opposite. It is to curb such behavior, make people aware of the nefarious influence of it on their health, to encourage them to take care of themselves to live a healthier, longer life.

"The problem, as I see it, lies elsewhere, Susan. You do not want to pay for your mistakes, no one does. You think that if you don't pay the fine, there are no consequences, but you will pay by becoming sick later. You would just postpone the punishment. The choice is yours; the free will is there. You cannot trick Mother Nature. Man is free to make choices and to pay accordingly. You know it as well as I do."

Susan did know. She did not say anything and avoided looking at Greta. She didn't want her to see how much she regretted her stupid outburst.

"There is another side to this, too."

It looked like Greta was not about to shut up anytime soon. Susan was on the verge of leaving. "You cannot have it both ways, Susan! You can't expect to pay the low premiums that people who follow their regimen get, and not follow yours. No one is robbing you of your freedom of choice, but you are not allowed to rob other people by putting the burden of your bad choices on their shoulders.

"About the clothes...you got it all wrong. The collective impact of our behavior on the environment cannot be ignored. Look what happened at the apogee of mass production and unrestricted consumption, before the Big Crush, when people bought more food than they could eat and amassed ludicrous amounts of clothes and other goods. Humans were like a thick film on the surface of the Earth suffocating from their filth. Our planet was on the brink of disaster. Now with the circular, waste-free economy in place, it's more like a lofty bubble on the Earth's ecosystem, with a tiny footprint, operating in perfect symbiosis. People have to consume responsibly, however, to preserve this still very precarious balance. So, no need to cry foul play, no one is robbing you of your chance to stack more clothes than you need. As a matter of fact, you would pay much less for them, all fines notwithstanding, had you lived a hundred years ago."

Seething inside and having to muster all her willpower not to show Greta how close she was to hating her now, Susan was not in a rush to answer. She thought Greta had a lot of nerve telling her what to do and how to feel. Greta was full of useless knowledge leading nowhere. Susan had stopped listening to the preaching a long time ago, Greta's words becoming just monotonous noise.

Greta was puzzled. She did not expect such a violent outpour from her composed and cheerful friend, always in control and on top of her game. Something strange was definitely going on with Susan. Greta continued, "But listen, you were never into clothes. What happened? Have you met someone?" The question came suddenly, breaking the droning cadence of her unrequested homily intended to calm Susan down. It would not be the first time that Greta had handled Susan's frustrations clumsily. She seemed to be unable to find the right words.

· · · · ·

Greta's question brought Susan back in a snap. She seemed startled, and for a few seconds looked at Greta in sheer dread. Then her eyes started to close, until they became narrow slits, with two blazing beams of her stare converging on Greta's face as if they were steel blades. An ugly grimace twisted her mouth, her parted lips baring her beautiful even teeth that at this moment looked more like the jaw of an animal.

In a brief moment her face was back to its usual mocking grin, so should anyone have happened to throw a look on the two friends and witness this strange transformation, one would be inclined to doubt his or her eyes and wonder whether it was some trick of the light. As it happened, not one of the customers in the coffeehouse had any business looking at the two young women. Neither did Greta. She was looking down as she was stretching her hands across the table to hold Susan's hands in hers. "What happened?" repeated Greta softly, looking tenderly at Susan. "You know you can trust me."

"Stop talking like that, Greta, you scare me!" Susan laughed all of a sudden, lightheartedly. *Self-righteous fool,* she thought. "I was just frustrated I couldn't have one of the coffee eclairs I love so much. I am not an exercise junkie and not into health food, Greta, you know. I had too many this month already. I'll just go broke if I don't draw a line somewhere. And I bought a new suit for the interview."

Susan did not like such quick perspicacity and being so suddenly exposed. Her hands were trembling. When the facts were presented in such a manner, Susan felt like a fool and did not know what to say. She resented Greta for making her feel that way.

"Why exactly did you buy a new suit for the interview"? said Greta in disbelief.

"What's wrong with a suit?" *Damn, I should not have said that,* thought Susan immediately.

"What I mean," clarified Greta, "you bought a new suit specifically for the interview? It didn't even occur to me to buy a new outfit, frankly. It's not that the examiners have seen our entire wardrobe. Besides, you know how I am, Susan. I stick to the items I like forever." Greta smiled. "I just want to look nice and put together. But remember when we were discussing our outfits for the interview? I said I'll wear jeans with a T-shirt and you seemed to agree it was a great choice. The interview has nothing to do with our fashion sense, does it?" Suddenly, an idea came to her head. "They know how much you make and what kind of job you have. What are you trying to prove? If it were that simple, they would just analyze our tax sheets. Being a good parent is not a function of money."

Isn't everything a function of money? thought Susan, but refrained from saying it out loud. "I just wanted to make a good impression, Greta," said Susan in a small voice. "I wanted the interviewers to like me. Oh, I know it was stupid of me. It's just that I gained a few extra pounds lately and I don't look nice in jeans."

"Oh Susan, you look great!" Immediately Greta's haughty attitude and mentoring tone were gone, and suddenly she felt ashamed, realizing how patronizing her behavior must have seemed, and she felt sorry for her friend. Greta hated herself for her callousness, for going on this silly rampage about obvious truths. She was just showing off, parading her knowledge and her sensible choices with blatant disregard for Susan's feelings. Her VS device first made a warning beep and then sounded the yellow alert. "Susan, dear! Let's just enjoy our time together and celebrate your first milestone."

Greta was not inclined to give this incident much thought. She had just downloaded a new book about the joys and dangers of bringing up a child. Eager to start reading, she tried to dismiss Susan's ranting as due to her impulsive nature that had put her in harm's way before. Susan usually spent a considerable amount of money on fines, there was nothing new there.

Susan, in the meantime, suddenly remembering a dentist appointment that had completely slipped her mind, quickly wrapped up their meeting and ran out of the coffeehouse leaving Greta in a bigger state of shock than Susan's diatribe had caused.

Greta was watching Susan leave, craning her neck and twisting her body at an almost unnatural angle. She was unhappy for failing her and precipitating her departure, as if prolonging their meeting could remedy the situation. At first, Susan's walk was rushed and unsteady. Greta had a hard time not running after her to give her one last hug. In a few moments, however, Susan's gait became more poised, her high heels hit the floor with more force, and finally, with the familiar toss of her hair, she left the coffeehouse. Greta remained in her unnaturally contorted position, looking at the entrance door until her limbs went numb. Then she slowly resumed her normal pose, lost in thought and shaking her head from time to time. The incident made her circle back to the conversation she had already so hastily buried in her mind.

Having left the coffeehouse and turned a corner, Susan had to sit on a bench. She had never felt so drained in her life. Greta came dangerously close to exposing her bluff. Susan saw that Greta had picked up on her going overboard with her spending, especially on clothes, and losing her cool by talking about it. It would invariably put Greta's mind to work. It was smart to appeal to Greta's empathy and kindness by whining about her desire to please the interviewers. Susan scrutinized their conversation, sentence by sentence. No, the pain and compassion on Greta's face were genuine. Greta was a sucker for pity. She swallowed it hook, line, and sinker. Good old gullible Greta! Susan smiled tenderly thinking of many funny instances. Then her face hardened. She could not afford to be soft on Greta anymore. They were running neck and neck now, and every little advantage could become decisive and tip the scale in her favor. Greta was not her best friend anymore. For all practical purposes, she was now her worst enemy.

Despite herself, Susan felt uneasy. It was the first time she thought about Greta in such terms. She had been less than true to Greta on more than one occasion, but it was such small fry. Susan did plagiarize Greta's thoughts and nuggets of trivia picked up from her in an effort to look more erudite than she really was. Why possess such a valuable asset and not use it herself? Obviously, Susan jumped at the opportunity, her own resources scarce in this area, the interview being the latest example. She often prevented Greta from winning at their regular sport outings by distracting her one way or the other.

Maybe this is pointless vanity on my part, conceded Susan, *but this is who I am*. It was not like she purposefully deceived her or forced her hand. Whose fault was it that Greta did not take these games seriously and was not as set on winning as Susan was? It was all so benign. Susan had helped Greta on many occasions, too. Well, maybe she took it a little too far at the dance. But Greta was so painfully, so defiantly beautiful that day! Then, she remembered the college escapade.

CHAPTER FIFTEEN

College prep was a hassle. Greta—the organized, disciplined Greta—did not feel the burden. Susan was no less organized and focused on the task at hand when it suited her. Her friends could attest, not without jealousy, that she could burn a hole in metal if she wanted to, by the sheer concentration of will. This was not, however, a task Susan considered worthy of her efforts, and she felt crucified.

But then, what are friends for? She let Greta do research on colleges and compile lists of required documents. The kind and naïve Greta made no secret of the fruits of her labor. Besides, Susan made sure Greta felt indebted to her for her small favors. Greta was always so ridiculously grateful. Susan tagged along, submitting the documents to the same colleges Greta had chosen. That was not outrageous. Susan's grades were only slightly worse than Greta's.

Finally, the big day had arrived. The notifications were done by traditional mail, not electronically, to make it more special. The postal drone delivered three fat envelopes to Greta and just one to Susan. She was also notified via a curt email that she was on a waitlist for one other school, Armard; this university was both Greta's and Susan's first choice. It was also near their home town, so both girls knew about it from first grade and Greta started dreaming about it since her fifth. The Guillard, to which they were both accepted, was also very good, but no match for Armard.

Greta, her thick Armard envelope in her hand, ran straight to Susan's house to tell her the great news. She barged into the room, shouting from the doorstep, "I made it, Susie! You, too, right?"

"Congratulations, Greta! I'm very happy for you. Nobody deserves it more than you do. Go on, make a great life for yourself."

"Why, Susie, what's the matter with you! We will go there together, you and me. You did get your envelope, didn't you?"

"No, Greta. I didn't get my envelope. I didn't make it."

• • • • •

Susan could not hope to be the homecoming queen, she had never been beautiful enough, but she had her following and she spent a lot of time on the upkeeping. She congratulated herself for her perspicacity and foresight. At this particular moment she was thinking about Brandon, their school computer whiz. He had liked Susan since middle school and she was always nice to him. She masterfully cultivated their relationship, making sure it did not get outside the boundaries of an innocent friendship, but gave the inexperienced youth's vivid imagination enough fodder for hope.

It took Susan only a few minutes to make Brandon bring his computer and hack the Armard website. He poked around for more than an hour, eager to make the lady of his dreams happy, but he could not find any information regarding how admission documents were stored and protected. All the leads seemed to disappear, which was very peculiar. Unwillingly, Brandon had to relate the unsatisfactory findings to Susan. Intrigued but not deterred, Susan did some research of her own.

The Armard admissions office operated in a very old-fashioned format. It was an actual office, with standard working hours from 9:00 to 3:00, three days a week. The physical presence of the clerk was mandatory during all working hours, with a lunch break from 12:30 to 1:15. As Susan learned, the clerk, Dave, was seven years older than her and the only child of one of the professors. The legacy considerations for students had been abolished years ago, but if a child met all criteria for the job in his parent's school, he was eligible. A strong movement against this "atavism," as the activists of the movement called it, was on the rise.

After several break-ins, followed by the unavoidable purchases of ever more sophisticated anti-hacker programs, the spiraling costs made it imperative to find a cheaper and more efficient alternative. Serious measures had to be taken to protect the admission process. A drastic decision was made when new ecofriendly paper replaced the traditional one. The office went back to paper and stored hard copies of all documents.

Each of the nine admission officers had a separate safe with a personal key, where all hard copies of pertaining documents were held. In order to make alterations, one had to simultaneously break into nine separate safes, or bribe all nine officers. The contents of the safes were checked and compared by special apps every night. So, the perpetrator had exactly twenty-four hours at his or her disposal. The unorthodox approach worked.

Susan was patiently waiting in the campus cafeteria. The guy was bound to get hungry sooner or later, and this was the only option to get food, unless one was prepared to travel ten miles to the closest town or order an exorbitantly expensive takeout.

Remote learning had taken over long ago, and the main goal of keeping campuses intact was to foster socialization. First-year students were required to live on campus. Young adults were encouraged to socialize among themselves, which would provide them with invaluable skills for life. The following years were online studying only. There turned out to be an unintended bonus to that arrangement. Students who were more interested in socializing than studying would usually drop out early in their second year.

Dave walked through the door shortly after 12:30. Susan moved from her inconspicuous corner to the front and quickly ordered coffee and a yogurt pouch from one of the distributing machines. Then she approached Dave's table. "May I join you?" asked Susan in a sweet melodic voice, which she had discovered lately had a most positive effect on the opposite sex.

"Yes, of course," replied Dave, shocked more than pleased by the request. The socialization incentive was lost on him. He was not very popular among the student body and the administration alike. Soon after he had joined the university, he became widely considered a good-for-nothing scion of an influential professor, the verdict he soon finished by believing in himself.

After a few short introductory phrases—Susan knew she did not have much time at her disposal—she told Dave she had a younger sister who was considering applying to Armard next year. "But is it even worth trying? I've heard the admission process is too difficult, even the technical part of it. What is your impression? You are a student here, right?"

"No, not exactly," replied Dave. "But I am familiar with the admission process. It is difficult. As to the technical part, it's not at all complicated. Tedious, for sure, but not complicated. On the contrary." He smiled. "I guess everything that goes around comes around," he mused. Susan cringed. She had no time for philosophical babble. Dave misinterpreted her movement.

"It's just that the process is on paper now, no documents are digitized. Once you learn the basics, it boils down to a lot of unnecessary printing and shredding, that's all there is to it." He went on, with minute details.

"Really, nothing to be afraid of," he added encouragingly. He realized that Susan had not said a word for some time and her face was gloomy now, the cheerfulness of a few minutes ago having disappeared without a trace. "This way, crooks don't stand a chance."

They finished their meal in silence. At last, Susan looked at her PAT and said she had to run lest she miss her monorail. Dave made a move to say something, but then, stooping sheepishly, decided against it. No girl could stand him for more than half an hour. What else was new?

Susan was not in a hurry to board the monorail. She was slowly walking down an alley of century-old trees, her mind refusing to accept defeat. She made a wish that she would find a way to get into Armard before she had reached the last tree in the row. The closer she got to the end of the alley, the slower her pace became. "Come on," said Susan to herself. "That can't be. I always win!"

·　　·　　·　　·　　·

"*Susan!*" she heard from behind. She turned around abruptly. She recognized her at once, although her looks had changed. She had cut her hair very short, exposing her long, graceful neck. It made her look vulnerable and at the same time, rather boyish; the feeling was further accentuated by ankle-long cargo pants and military-style boots. It was certainly a sensible choice considering the muddy sleet of the final days of winter. Susan glanced at her usual high-heeled beauties—she hated being on the short side—covered with water stains. A smart camel-hair coat that perfectly matched the color of the girl's hair sealed the look.

Susan stopped and waved her hand, smiling at the jubilant figure running to her across the lawn, paying no attention to puddles and soggy grass under her boots. As the girl got closer, Susan got a better look at her. She wore no jewelry but earrings. Dainty rainbows were dangling from long, thin silver chains.

It was the girl with the shell. They had never become friends, mainly because of the age difference since Susan was five years her junior, but she was genuinely happy to see a familiar face. *What was her name again? That's right, Molly.*

"Hi there, Susie," said Molly with a smile.

"Hello, Molly, what a wonderful surprise! What are you doing at Armard? Are you a student here?"

Molly continued to look at Susan, smiling. The sun that had been hiding behind thick gray clouds all day, suddenly came out, and Molly's earrings sparkled with the colors of the rainbow, casting a shade on her beautiful neck. *Could that be?* The unexpected discovery made Susan lower her guard, and the piercing look of her eyes asked the burning question. Molly made an imperceptible bow of her head and laughed.

"You look very nice, Susie. You used to be so skinny when you were a kid, and now look at you, you're quite a bombshell."

"Oh, thank you, Molly, this is what my girlfriend keeps telling me, but I'm sure I've put on a few." Molly quivered and darted a quick look at her. The gleeful surprise in her eyes told Susan that she guessed right. "You, Molly, look great, as always. You were my hero ever since you gave me that shell. You probably don't even remember."

They agreed to meet in town the coming Saturday. In twenty minutes, Susan boarded the monorail, the master plan already taking shape in her head.

CHAPTER SIXTEEN

Molly talked nonstop. She was the youngest of the nine admissions officers. Susan could not believe her ears. Her mother had been an English professor at Armard for more than thirty years, so when Molly was assigned a job in Admissions, they exercised the legacy right and chose Armard. Molly's father had left them many years ago, she had no siblings, and mother and daughter had nobody but each other to lean on.

By mutual accord, Susan and Molly chose the coffeehouse near their high school, where they both had spent many hours chatting and gossiping with friends while cutting classes, or after school. It was a small quaint building with a tiny café on the first floor with beautiful wrought-iron tables and chairs. Cheerful multicolored cups and saucers completed the look. It was still too cold to sit outside, so Susan and Molly ducked in and took a happy trip down memory lane. After reminiscences and laughs about their fellow students, teachers, and first crushes, Susan felt ready to tackle the issue. She had already opened her mouth, but Molly beat her to it.

"So, what are you up to, Susie? Did you apply to any colleges? Maybe even Armard?" she added with a grin. The girl's crooked smile and intense stare made Susan uncomfortable, a feeling Susan was barely familiar with.

"The truth of the matter is, Molly, I have a serious problem." Molly just inclined her head, inviting Susan to continue. "The girl I care about very much did apply to Armard. And she got accepted. I applied, too, hoping I would get in, but got rejected. I don't have to tell you how hard Armard is to get into."

Susan was very much aware that Molly graduated when Susan did not care a tinker's toot about her grades. Consequently, Molly could not know about her academic achievements in high school, and Susan preferred to keep it that way, at least for now. Susan needed Molly to feel in a position of power, of superiority. Susan's solid record could ruin that. Each of her top grades was a small masterpiece of cheating, charming the teachers, or eliciting their pity, often all of the above.

"Oh, Susan dear, you must be heartbroken! What about your girlfriend, how did she take it?"

"Well, when I told you the other day that she was my girlfriend, it was wishful thinking. I really love her, Molly, but I am afraid to tell her that. I don't even know if she is interested in other girls, you know. I think so, but I'm not sure. It's all just a huge hazy blob of uncertainty."

"Oh, I know perfectly well what you mean, Susie. I know it so well, trust me."

"I just want to be close to her, see her every day in classes. I don't know what to do, Molly!" Her whole body started to shake with sobs, and her eyes that the waterproof mascara made seem even bigger, looked at Molly imploringly.

Molly examined Susan for a long time, an enigmatic disturbing smile on her lips. Susan had the unsettling realization that she had met her match and she was starting to feel like the little girl of long ago, when her fate, too, was sealed by Molly. *I won't go down without a fight, not now, not anymore.* She tossed her head, and looked straight into Molly's eyes. "Well, it was great seeing you, Molly. I guess I'd better be going now."

"Please, Susie, don't act so hurt. I'm just not too touchy-feely, that's all. More of a business lady, if you know what I mean. So, stop the deluge, Susie." Leaning across the table, she whispered the last words into Susan's ear and grabbed Susan's arm excitedly while talking.

Not a shred of sexual interest. Molly wondered if Susan could be so much into that girl to ignore her so blatantly. Susan was not as pleasant as Molly remembered her after all. She positively did not trust her.

Susan sensed a breath of cold air emanate from Molly's body. Just as Molly began to stand up, Susan burst into tears again.

"I can't! I'm a disgusting, despicable person!" Susan could not just let Molly leave. Her words came as a surprise even to herself. "I can't leave just like that, Molly. I like you. I do love that girl, I really do, I don't know what's happening to me, but I've been thinking about you ever since I saw you last week. I tried to hide it and ignore it, but here we are, it's stronger than me."

Molly's body relaxed. It was obvious that this course of action pleased her a great deal. It was also obvious she had no moral qualms about it. Susan was off the hook, at least for now. She had won herself a little time.

It was a chilly March day and it was rather cold in the coffee shop, but Susan felt sweat drops run down her back. The cold beads on her forehead were masterfully eliminated with a napkin while Susan was burying her face in her hands for more drama.

"Let's go," said Molly. They left the coffeehouse and headed toward the monorail.

What was expected of her? Should she try to hold Molly's hand? Should she try to embrace her? Susan considered herself straight, although she had experimented with boys and girls. This was a totally different matter, though. It was presumed to be devoid of any romantic fluff; they were just exploring and getting to know their sexuality. Now she was supposed to like this girl. How was she supposed to go about it? She had no idea. Susan had never liked anyone. She felt like that desperate little kid again, looking up to an older girl, so smashing and intimidating with her gorgeous long golden locks and beautiful bows. Only now this girl had her hair cut very short and drop rainbow earrings were dangling from her ears on long silver chains. That girl was still in control, however, and Susan did not have a clue what to expect.

They entered Molly's apartment. It was a small unit, a studio, in full accord with the norms for a single dweller. It was on the top floor of a high-rise building situated in the south part of the campus with an unobstructed view of the ocean, and was full of light, even on such a gray day. Susan liked how the room was appointed. Molly certainly had a knack for home design. It comprised a wall unit with a Murphy bed in a beautiful gray-grained wood that practically blended into the gray walls, a slick convertible leather couch in a brown-gray color, an intricately carved Spanish armchair, and a huge coffee table with many drawers (a smart find for such a small space). The kitchen's chrome and nickel appliances were sparkling clean and the space was devoid of clutter. Molly was either not very much of a cook or exceptionally neat. Probably the latter, for there were no personal objects in view anywhere, except for rows of books on the wall unit. A gray, long-hair sheepskin rug covered the area between the couch and the armchair, and a throw of the softest beige cashmere was lying on the couch. Two tall leafy plants stood by the window in matching comedy and tragedy mask planters.

Molly motioned Susan to the couch and took a seat near her, playing absentmindedly with a loose strand of her hair.

"So, what's the deal, honey? Do you just want so badly to get into Armard or is there some other equally compelling reason behind this farce? It's obvious you are not into girls and I doubt you have even been with one before."

Susan was not altogether surprised by Molly's remark. Moreover, she had half-expected it. She was well aware that she was failing miserably. Both girls sank deep into the cushions. Their bodies were leaning against each other, and this proximity was burning Susan's body and made her feel trapped. Molly was enjoying herself. Her mischievous and contemptuous grin was driving Susan mad.

"Not everything is lost. I think I can help you. Oh, and get back at my pain-in-the-neck colleagues, too, for good measure. But it's going to cost you," Molly went on. Susan's body stiffened. "My usual price is thirty packs of cigarettes or its equivalent in insurance fines. For old times' sake, however, I'm ready to give you a discount. Besides, I do have a sweet spot for you, honey. So, let's make it twenty-five packs. You don't have to give them to me all at once. But you'll have to bring me five by next Thursday. The cutoff date is next Friday, so we have to hurry. And now let me teach you a few tricks on how to make a girl happy. That will give you a leg up in all your dealings. I think you're still very raw, but you have great potential."

Susan left Molly's apartment shortly before midnight. When she finally came home, everybody was already sleeping; she sneaked into her room and went straight to bed. Her PAT rang. Greta was leaving her another message. "I'm going mad with worry. Are you okay? I have been calling you all day, but you're not picking up." Susan was very much aware of this fact. She had counted eleven missed calls from Greta while travelling home on the monorail.

CHAPTER SEVENTEEN

Susan stayed home for three days. She did not pick up her PAT and she kept off social media.

Molly told her that her name was first on the waitlist. It sounded like great news at first, only no one had ever turned down their acceptance to Armard. The PAT rang. It was Greta again. She had not heard from her in three days and was wondering whether Susan was alright.

Stupid Greta. So needy.

"Frankly, not so good, Greta. This Armard business is killing me. It's not that I want to go to Armard so badly, but being without you! I just can't stand the thought of it. Oh, I'm so sorry, Greta, I can't talk anymore, I'm about to—" Sobs interrupted her speech. Whispering weakly, she said, "Let's talk tomorrow, Greta, dear." Susan hung up. Then she ran to her mother's closet and ferreted out a pair of black leggings. Her mother was taller but two sizes thinner than Susan. On her way back to her room Susan grabbed some flour from the kitchen—thank God her mother was very old-fashioned and liked to bake—and darted into her bathroom grabbing some crayons on the way.

The doorbell rang ten minutes later. Those were the longest ten minutes in Susan's life. It was Greta, pale, her lips shaking. She cowered, noticing the change in Susan's appearance. The self-asserting plump girl with peachy complexion looked much thinner and frailer than just a few days ago. Her big shiny eyes, presently two dark murky lakes, exuded misery and suffering; her unkempt hair, dull and devoid of its usual luster, hung down in shapeless strands, and her skin appeared gray and lifeless.

Susan's sufferings were not all pretense. Her mother's leggings were killing her, but Susan tried to think only about how it was helping her cause by contributing to the image of utmost despair she was trying to project, and apparently, her toils were rewarded.

"Susan, dear, I can't take it anymore. I can't live a normal life knowing how much you're suffering, all alone. I'm going mad. Let's go to Guillard together."

"What are you talking about?" Susan, aghast, clutched Greta's arms and looked eagerly into her eyes.

Greta—so beautiful, so compassionate, so righteous. How happy, secure, or just loaded must a person be to throw away something many would stop at nothing to get? What made her so generous? Whatever it was, she must have a lot of it, to give up such a big chunk so cavalierly. Or maybe she was just foolish? Susan caught herself abruptly. This was not a good time for pointless musings.

"I already made my decision, Susan. First thing tomorrow, I will send in my acceptance letter to Guillard and turn down Armard."

Susan's heart leaped from joy. She threw her arms around Greta's neck and started to cry.

"Oh, Greta, what are you doing? Why? No one has ever been so good to me. I will never be able to repay you."

"You don't have to repay me, Susan. It just feels like the only way to handle the situation. You are my best friend; I can't let you down. Just forget all about Armard; go to bed and rest now. Let's go and celebrate tomorrow, what do you say?"

Forget about Armard? Fat chance! Celebrate? Absolutely! thought Susan, saying meaningless niceties to Greta while seeing her off to the front door.

The moment she closed the door behind Greta, she peeled the leggings off her numb body and sighed with relief. She took a quick shower to wash the flour off her hair and white crayon off her face. She deserved some rest now, but she would have to repeat the act tomorrow.

Susan called Molly and said she had to see her urgently. Molly did not mind. They agreed to meet at Molly's apartment early next morning, before classes.

Susan spent more than an hour applying makeup and figuring out what to wear. Finally, she stuck to her usual clothes, just chose a tight sweater. She did not mind if it looked like she had tried, but not too hard. It had to be at least somewhat spontaneous. She grabbed the two cigarette packs she managed to save so far by cutting down on her own smoking and left the house while everyone was still asleep.

Molly met her in light gray cashmere loungewear and a cup of coffee in her hand. The smell of freshly brewed coffee was blending in with the smell of an exotic candle that lingered in the house, probably from last night, and was still sitting, now extinguished, on the familiar coffee table.

"What happened, Susie? You couldn't wait to see me?"

Susan seemed caught off guard. She looked at her feet, then around the room and then, covering her face with her hands, turned slightly to make sure Molly had a full view of her beautiful legs. Staggering slightly, she said, "It's useless to try to hide anything from you, Molly, you see through me. Maybe nothing has happened yet, but it's about to. Nothing is the same since I met you. You were right, of course, and the girl I talked to you about is just my best friend. I have never been into girls. But I think I'm falling for you, Molly. Please don't say anything," she added quickly, as she saw Molly's head jerk. "Please hear me out."

Susan related how she had stayed home for three days, under the spell of her encounter with Molly, shocked by her new feelings. She carefully omitted the fact that she avoided Greta to make her feel guilty and give up Armard, at which she had brilliantly succeeded. She presented the fact as an unexpected boon.

"Oh, Susan, you're good. You're even better than I thought. I'm impressed."

"Trust me, Molly, this was not my intention. This is only messing things up, at this point. Just think for yourself. I didn't want to see anybody. I admit, I was also afraid she might sense something was happening with me, and I didn't know what to say to her."

"But what seems to be the problem? Now you'll get her spot legally. Isn't being in Armard your ultimate goal? What else do you need?"

"I feel so bad, Molly. The girl gave up Armard for me, and I resent her for that, instead of appreciating it. But I still don't want her to hate me when she finds out that I would basically take her spot and not give it up, as she did."

Molly was sipping her coffee, her usual crooked grin gone, revealing a beautiful face that could be called delicate if not for the hard, penetrating gaze and bitter crease of her mouth.

"Yeah, I guess that makes sense, when you put it that way. So, what do you want from me? How do you suppose I can keep her on the list if she is sending her letter as we speak?"

"Well, I was thinking...What if there were a mix-up? Dave doesn't seem like the sharpest tool in the shed..."

"Oh, you know Dave?"

Susan bit her lip. How stupid of her. "I just met him in the cafeteria the day I met you."

"Alright, so what happens next?"

"What if the girl I substitute is not Greta, but some other random girl?"

"But this is pointless! When this girl doesn't get the follow-up documents in a couple of days, she will surely start inquiring, and the whole thing will blow up. It is possible to put the blame on Dave, and none will be the wiser, but Greta will be expelled anyway," Molly said.

Susan continued, "This way, I get a few days to accept Armard and turn down Guillard, so when the mix-up becomes exposed, I will have no place to go. Remember, I will not be a victim, Greta will. So, she will probably still get her spot at Guillard, but frankly, I don't give a damn about her anymore. I just don't want her to hate me. If I don't have a place at Guillard, she will accept the situation as an ironic twist of destiny, she's that kind of girl."

Molly sat there, nodding her head from time to time, as if going over every step of the plan silently in her head. "Yes," she said finally. "I think that can be done."

Susan stood up, slowly approached Molly and sat on the couch beside her. Molly felt a hot wave of desire engulfing her from head to toe. Soft, yet impatient and demanding lips were looking for hers. Susan's fresh breath was caressing Molly's face, as she whispered, "I'll repay you, Molly, I promise."

CHAPTER EIGHTEEN

Greta came to get Susan the next evening, as they agreed.

Greta did not belong in Armard if she didn't want it enough to sacrifice her friendship, to give up a little of her oh-so-cherished peace of mind. Doing the right thing was more important to her; so be it. Let her be the good one. In fact, she was just a coward. She deserved to stay behind. She was more afraid of sullying her reputation than of actually getting somewhere. Susan would accept a little soot on her name. But she would do it from Armard. Susan tossed her head and stepped out of her house into the night.

The next day, Susan told Greta she was accepted to Armard. The timing could not have been better. Greta, perplexed, had just shown her some follow-up documents from Armard.

"Your letter must have gotten lost in the mail, Greta. What an amazing thing to happen. I mean, what are the odds? This is a sign, Greta! Your extraordinary selfless act got rewarded. We will both go to Armard, Greta, isn't it wonderful?"

It did not take her long to convince Greta. She was ecstatic as it was. Greta did not feel any remorse, but the good deed did cost her a few sleepless nights and occasional bouts of dejection.

Susan was already completely back to her normal cheerful self, assuming her usual patronizing attitude toward Greta, with constant biting remarks and incessant teasing, especially in public. Greta could not help feeling annoyed, but she couldn't tell exactly what it was that she expected. Both girls quickly turned down Guillard's offer and happily proceeded with the Armard acceptance routine.

·　　·　　·　　·　　·

The scandal erupted in two days. The wronged girl stormed in the Admissions office accompanied by her parents. Things got ugly. The administration was accused of rigging the admission process. The university tried to hush things up, but the family would not hear of it. Just as Susan predicted, a scapegoat in the face of Dave was quickly found and severely reprimanded. The parents wanted blood. Dave got fired.

Inspired by her success, Susan was brilliant. When the news of the mix-up broke, she was inconsolable. She cried for hours, and a few mutual friends even heard her mention suicide after getting drunk. Greta, who was about to storm into Susan's house and ask her why she was not doing anything, after literally taking her spot, was stopped in her tracks by the barrage of Susan's tears and lamentations and the sympathetic behavior of others toward her predicament. Even the teachers were harping on Greta, trying to convince her she was the stronger of the two.

In the beginning, Greta thought it peculiar that Susan was the victim in both situations, but finally her ability to think and act was crushed by the enormity of Susan's suffering.

Greta, exhausted by this emotional offense, ended by being more scared by Susan's mental state and her overwhelming presence than concerned about her own destiny. Greta was ready to say anything just to stop the torture of this constant display of suffering. Susan followed Greta wherever she went, like a ghost with huge black eyes, filled with sadness, gaze unfocused, her body wavering. Greta started to have nightmares. She could not, however, shake Susan off; the latter seemed to grow bigger and taller every day, filling Greta's visual field completely. Her words to Susan were half-hearted at first. Who could blame her? She had lost a spot at the most prestigious university in the country. As the days went by, she became more feverish with her pleas, and by the end of the month, Greta ended up believing her own made-up arguments. Susan was keenly following the metamorphosis. She wanted to catch the moment of utmost sincerity before it died out and a new crop of doubts and self-pity took root.

They met for a coffee in their usual spot. It was a warm April day and they sat outside at their favorite wrought iron table in the corner.

"Go, enjoy, you've deserved it!" Greta said in earnest. "I'm the one who turned down my acceptance. You did not force me to do it."

"But you did it so that we could stay together! And now I can't even repay you. I have already given up my spot in Guillard. So even if I turn down Armard now, I won't be able to join you. I will have no place to go!" As Susan anticipated, Greta was given back her spot in Guillard, as the mix-up occurred through no fault of hers, and it was deemed unfair to make her pay for it.

Greta's tormented soul felt that something was off in Susan's words; there was some inconsistency, some shadiness. Something, somewhere did not add up, but she was too tired and too afraid of more drama to try to figure it out. She did have a vague disturbing feeling occasionally that Susan was not prepared to make the same sacrifice for their friendship, but it was so painful, she preferred to chase it away. Susan had nothing to do with it. Greta did turn Armard down of her own accord, and Guillard was a great school, after all. She should put the whole thing behind her.

•　　•　　•　　•　　•

Susan and Molly were lying in bed, chatting lazily. One of Molly's favorite candles was burning. Susan hated the heavy, imposing smell, but chose not to say anything. She ventured instead, "I can't believe the school year starts in less than a week." She was secretly studying Molly's face. It was so beautiful now that the bitter crease of her mouth had gone and a soft smile was playing on her lips. Eyes half-closed, Molly was fiddling with Susan's hair, something she had loved to do since their first encounter.

"It will be so wonderful to finally live close to each other. We won't be able to move in together right away, but no more monorail trips for you."

Susan just smiled in reply. Molly! What an arrogant contemptuous piece of work. Well, everything in due time. It was, all things considered, a very productive summer. Susan learned a lot about Armard and the campus life from Molly. Nothing prevented Susan from seeing her as she pleased. Greta left for college early, planning to find a job on campus or the surrounding area. They parted on a good note, but she needed some alone time to get back on track, as she told Susan, and the latter was relieved to comply.

"Well, your meeting starts in an hour. I'd better be going," said Susan.

"Damn that meeting! Why did they have to schedule it for six in the evening? What is so important that it can't wait until morning?"

"I know, Molly, I know. This is so annoying. Thank God it's just one evening. We will see each other tomorrow."

"You know what?" Molly sat abruptly. "I'll take a quick shower now and we'll walk to the office together. I'll go to the meeting and you will take the monorail back. Get ready, I'll be quick."

The new arrangement meant Susan would have to walk about twenty extra minutes to get to the monorail from the Admissions office. She would have rather avoided that, as she preferred to limit her walking to the bare minimum. Her high heels made the endeavor not only painful, but at times hazardous, especially on the unpaved paths of the campus. She said nothing. She made a languid movement with her hand, meaning for Molly to go ahead, and smiled again. As soon as Molly disappeared behind the bathroom door, Susan closed her eyes and listened.

At first, she heard Molly fumbling with some containers over the sink, then, when the steady sound of the water stream changed into a choppy one, signaling Molly had finally stepped into the shower, Susan quickly jumped to her feet. She started to nimbly and methodically go through all the drawers. Her face was pale with concentration; her thin, agile fingers swiftly lifted and felt every item, following its contours so precisely they seemed to be devoid of any bones, and deposited it in the exact same spot it was taken from. Table. Nothing. Wall unit. Again, nothing unusual. Built-in closet. T-shirts, underwear, nighties, socks. Susan paused in bewilderment looking at rows of socks rolled into neat, almost perfect spheres. What a neat freak. How does she do it? Susan picked one such sphere. It felt heavy. Careful not to undo the folding, Susan peaked inside. Keys! Regular keys, practically identical. Eight of them. At that moment, Susan heard Molly turn off the water. She carefully closed the drawer and got dressed.

Molly made copies of all the keys for the individual safes in the Admissions office just for fun. It had all started as a game, to add some excitement to her life. She was waiting for a good moment to make the mold of every key, and got the last made just two weeks before she met Susan. It was the first time she realized she could get some practical use out of it.

So, this is how she does it! She has spare keys to all the safes. All she has to do is print the new document and put copies into all eight safes when everybody has gone home. I wonder how she managed to get the keys. Well, Molly is smart, I have to give it to her, and she had a lot of time to wait for the opportunity to present itself, thought Susan on her way back home. Now she had to find the best way to use the information. She tried many times, after she had managed to make Molly particularly happy, to whizzle out how she managed to rig the admissions process, to no avail. Molly slipped up big this time. Well, it was about time. Susan did not need this relationship to carry over into the new school year. That would lead to unnecessary confusion as to her sexual orientation, let alone prevent her from exploring other possibilities. Susan intended to use her one year of social bonanza to the fullest.

Two days later, the head admissions officer found an anonymous letter on her desk, stating that the junior admissions officer, Molly Brown, was in possession of spare keys to all the safes in the office. A search of Molly's apartment confirmed the information. Molly was expelled and banned from working with confidential information.

Susan came to say good-bye. Her face was exhausted from a sleepless night and her eyes were puffy and red from crying. Molly did not have much time. She had to finish packing by the end of the day; the movers were coming at eight a.m. sharp the next morning. She could not even stand the thought of staying in town another day. Molly was efficient and distant. The bitter crease of her mouth was more pronounced than ever. "I knew it was too good to last," she said. She was too proud to ask Susan to come visit her at her new place when she settled down. And Susan pretended she was too shaken to think straight.

When she was already far from Molly's building, she suddenly stopped and looked back, trying to locate her windows. "I'm a quick study, Molly, honey," she whispered. Then, with a resolute toss of her head, she turned around and walked quickly to the monorail station.

CHAPTER NINETEEN

The second year of college was the best, when studies became virtual and students were no longer required to live in close proximity to the university. Susan reached out to Greta toward the middle of the first year. Greta was doing great, and was back to her usual self. Susan brought up the idea of moving together to New York. Greta was gravitating toward the idea of trying to make it in the Big Apple herself, so Susan did not have a lot of convincing to do.

Susan and Greta became roommates. Greta was excited to have a space of her own, the necessary concessions and adjustments to the needs and preferences of her roommate notwithstanding. She spent a considerable amount of her savings on room decor and all the trappings of college life, from frivolous to indispensable. Susan's approach was more sober. She felt it would make more sense to invest in clothes and beauty products. Susan had always been very particular about her beauty regimen. She felt she was not beautiful enough to rely on nature alone and needed to secure any help she could get.

A few days into their new living arrangements, Greta, an early riser, went to the nearby library early in the morning to study. She claimed she concentrated better in a reading room. Susan did not understand the logic behind such behavior. She wouldn't dream of showing up in a library at the crack of dawn, strands of her hair still wet after a hasty shower, eyes not properly made up, looking homely.

You were not supposed to mix work with pleasure, and libraries were certainly meant to be places of great fun.

Susan, however, did not mind how things panned out. It gave her a perfect opportunity to go through Greta's stuff. She ransacked it not so much with the intention to steal, though she was not above that if she felt she could get away with it; rather, she was convinced it was a great way to know Greta's hidden side, if there was one.

It took her just a few minutes to check through the room. There was nothing worthy of Susan's attention. Greta's clothes were too boring for her to borrow. It looked like the girl had never heard of sex appeal. Besides, Susan was shorter and plumper, but she preferred not to focus her attention, or anyone else's, on this fact. A few items in the bathroom, however, had caught her attention. Greta, as Susan was well aware, did not use a lot of makeup, so Susan did not anticipate finding anything of interest. She did find some expensive face creams and shampoos. Immediately, she jumped into the shower and used Greta's hair products and lavishly applied some of her creams. The covert operation successfully completed, Susan leisurely applied her own makeup and carefully styled her hair. Only then did she deem herself ready to join Greta at the library.

Susan had to stop using those products every day after Greta voiced her surprise and concern at how often she had to refill her supplies. Oh well. Twice a week was good enough. She did not forget to graciously offer Greta the use of hers anytime. Greta was so moved. What a godsend.

•　　•　　•　　•　　•

She called it upon herself. This is all her fault, thought Susan angrily. Susan knew she was not being quite honest with herself, but this time she let it slide. *Greta should have known better than to compete with me.*

Susan remembered how close she had come to blabbering out all her hard-won interview tips and ideas. As was only too clear, although not entirely unexpected, Greta could not be bothered to do her own groundwork for the interview. Obviously, she was opting for an ingenue style. Susan caught herself. Greta *was* an ingenue. There was nothing artificial about her, for better or worse. *Well*, thought Susan with venom, *hopefully, for worse.*

Susan stood up. Looking under her feet and treading gingerly, careful not to ruin her new suede boots in the huge puddles, she started for home.

·   ·   ·   ·   ·

Greta finished her coffee. She was not in a hurry to get home. Greg told her this morning that he would be in a conference until the very end of the workday. It was just past two now, so she had almost one hour to herself. As much as she tried to dismiss her feelings, Susan's behavior had disturbed her a great deal. If someone had asked her why, she would not have been able to explain. She wanted to sort things out in her head.

The strain effects of precision genomics on the individual have been all over the GlobalNet. Why did Susan, who was very familiar with all the discussions and arguments, and pragmatic as she was, get so adamant all of a sudden? So much passion and revolt from a usually sensible woman. Somehow, it just didn't add up. Her demeanor today was so out of character. The Susan she knew would take her transgressions in stride. She knew what she wanted and would not usually mind the consequences. Susan's eventual change of heart did not sound altogether genuine either. Besides, Greta could swear she felt animosity toward herself. That was definitely a first, and most disturbing. Greta had always felt she could depend on Susan. She had always had her back. She was not so sure anymore.

Greta left the coffeehouse and slowly walked home. The weather had gotten much better. The sky had cleared, the wind subsided. The merry afternoon sunlight was jumping in the puddles, flirting with mannequins in the windows that managed to remain spotless after the morning torrents, and livened the gray facades of the buildings along the straight, wide avenue. Usually, they looked so uniform and boring, but now that their texture was put in relief by the mischievous rays, Greta was amazed to notice that no two were alike. The city was so clean and beautiful. Dazzled, Greta lost track of time, slowing her pace without realizing it. It was almost four o'clock when she finally got home. Greg was already free, and noises of clacking dishes were coming from the kitchen.

She was so happy she could share her doubts with him right away. "What's gotten into her? She does splurge on sweets often, but that's it. Extra clothes? Willing to pay a smoking fine? She managed to quit after more than fifteen years of smoking without a peep when the fines were hiked the last time. She's so pragmatic the rules don't even affect her that much, they kind of go along with her own ways. Thrift is her second nature."

"You know I have never liked her very much and I don't trust her, Greta."

"You are not being fair, Greg." Immediately, Greta jumped to her friend's defense. "She had a difficult childhood. Her parents did not openly mistreat her, but they loved her older brother more and didn't make a secret of it. It scarred her for life."

"All I know is my personal danger sensors go off full blast in her presence."

"She is ambitious and knows exactly what she wants, but that's no reason to dislike her."

"That's precisely the reason. More often than not, in my experience, very ambitious people have their moral values conveniently skewed in their favor. Susan has no constant beliefs, only her selfish interests, to paraphrase the famous quote. You and Susan exist in parallel worlds, that's why you don't collide. In a way, you are not real to each other. You operate by different sets of laws. You want different things, or for different reasons, and you go about it in different ways.

"I don't understand what you see in her, but, frankly, I understand even less what she, the self-serving woman she is, finds in you. You are not very well versed in the ways of the world, Greta. Susan is, only too well. I'm afraid she is just using you."

"That's fantastic, Greg! What a way to add insult to injury. I'm stupid because I don't agree that my best friend is a bad person?"

"You have to agree you are not street-smart, Greta. Anyway, I would avoid talking to her in such a manner. She may resent you for it—"

Greta interrupted him. "Are you implying I am just book-smart? Do you think I'm that naïve? What does it even mean, book-smart? What's the use of being full of knowledge that you can't even use to your own advantage? What am I, an encyclopedia? I can hold my own, as you very well know!"

"I know, Greta. I never thought you were stupid or naïve. It's different. You are somehow pure, pure as a child. I guess people like you have some magic power in them; they turn everything they touch into gold. For Susan, on the other hand, anything she achieves, no matter how difficult, loses its luster the minute she gets it. I wonder if this isn't precisely why a person like Susan would want to be your friend. She's probably hoping that some of this gold will rub off on her."

"I didn't know you were such a poet, Greg." Greta laughed, pleased against her will and even forgiving Greg his new dig against Susan.

"You're not flashy, oozing attraction, but the more I learn about you, the more I see how priceless you are. A hidden gem, indeed."

"Thank you, Greg! And the more I learn about you, the more shocked I am! So, I'm not oozing attraction. What a nice way to put it!"

"Well, I'm a scientist, Greta. I guess I'm not oozing attraction either," he said and laughed.

"This is not funny. I don't know, Greg. Maybe I don't ooze attraction to you, but I have to say, and it will probably come as a surprise to you, that many men find me very attractive."

"Oh, Greta, you are the most beautiful woman I know! It's just a bad choice of words. I meant *poisonous* attraction, like insect-eating plants luring their victims."

"The next thing you'll say is that Susan is that kind of woman."

That was precisely what Greg was thinking, but he decided it was enough honesty for the day and full disclosure was not the way to go.

"By the way, why do you think Susan may resent me?"

"For this very reason," said Greg after a moment of silence. "You can be happy, Greta. You are an organic part of this world. You are truly free—because the world's laws are your laws. You embrace these laws, they're an integral part of you. Susan bumps against them. She will take your high-mindedness and lofty principles for hypocrisy. She would not believe you speak in earnest, and will resent you; and if she does believe you, she will hate you."

Greta jerked, remembering that she did feel some animosity coming from Susan.

"Enough of that," he added quickly, misinterpreting her movement for unwillingness to see her friend being disparaged even further. "Let's have dinner, Greta, before everything gets cold. We wrapped up our conference a little earlier than planned today, so I already ordered us your favorite pasta primavera. I love you, Greta, and I will choose you every day of the week, and twice on Sunday."

It had not been a satisfactory day. First, Susan's strange outburst and the very disturbing way she had left the coffeehouse. Greta tried to fight it, but she knew the feeling that was slowly creeping into her heart. Susan had not been fully honest with her. Greta may try to fool herself, but that was no use. It was only a matter of time before she found out she was right in the first place. That was the first crack.

And Greg, too. Sometimes she felt he did not fully understand her. One thing was certain. He used his precise merciless mind of a researcher to analyze her. He seemed to examine her like one of his viral cultures, with keen scientific interest and insight, but it seemed devoid of any emotions. Could a loving human being be so detached and objective in his judgment? Wouldn't one be tempted to twist the truth ever so slightly? Moreover, it seemed he did not think about her outside their home. Was his mood, his life even, governed by the successes of his lab? She wondered.

Maybe Susan was right. The best unions were not based on love, but something more stable, less ephemeral, and more practical. But what? Susan told her a long time ago that she envied their stability. Susan's impetuous nature always caused trouble. Passion is destructive. She cared too much. She all but said it outright that Greta was a cold fish and Greg was married to his viruses. Greta laughed it off then, but the thought had been haunting her ever since. She started to have doubts.

Was she boring, simplistic as Susan had implied on many occasions? Even worse, unjust and intolerant? But can one be more or less moral? Does virtue come in increments, or is it indivisible and absolute? *Oh, no,* Greta begged herself. *Let's not go into those depths, not now. It's not helpful to go to such levels of abstraction.*

She had tried to never nag and make her point when she knew her counterpart was set in his ways. So, she did not want to pursue the conversation tonight, but she hated his pronouncements! Not "oozing attraction"? At least, he retracted that, in a way. But not "street-smart"? That was obnoxious. It sounded disparaging, somehow it implied she was inferior to Susan. That was unsettling. Quite bright academically, Susan did not like to study and always had some kind of aversion for the written word. She could spend hours trying to figure out a way around it rather than opening a book. She amply compensated with her quick wit, laser-sharp ambition, and tenacity. Susan was one of those people who probably have their eye on the ball even when they sleep, and Greta admired her for it. Susan also had a lazy side, what with sleeping late on weekends.

Sidetracked from her grim thoughts and smiling suddenly, Greta remembered their college years. Almost every time before exams, Susan would float into the library around noon, perfectly fresh and immaculately made-up, and would make fun of Greta who was usually already into her fourth or fifth hour of studying. Her complexion would be gray and eyes puffy from lack of sleep, a stylus sticking from her unkempt hair. Susan would immediately start nudging her to make a break and go have lunch which, in her case, was actually breakfast. It took her a few hours just to warm up to the thought of opening a textbook. Yet she had always been a solid student, her results consistently higher than one would expect considering how little she studied.

Later, lying sleepless in bed long after Greg was fast asleep, Greta kept wondering why it was that although she had worked very hard, people thought she had it easy and often attributed her achievements to some silver bullet, whereas Susan projected an image of a hard-working woman. Greta knew for a fact that Susan was not above cutting corners and even cheating on occasion. *Oh, well, it's useless,* conceded Greta at last. *I got distracted from my plans enough as it is. I haven't even started reading my book!*

CHAPTER TWENTY

Greta woke up with a jolt. Her PAT must have been buzzing for a while now. It was Susan.

"Hey, good morning! Are you still sleeping?" heard Greta. "Come on, look out the window. It's a gorgeous day out there. I could hardly wait until a decent hour to call you!" Greta looked at the clock. It was eight a.m. She could hardly agree with Susan that eight o'clock on a Sunday morning was a decent time to call, but what was the use of saying anything?

"What's up, Susie?" she asked.

"I was thinking, since it looks like such a gorgeous day, why don't we go ice-skating today, you and me? The rink is already open, you know."

"I don't know, Susie. It's supposed to be very cold today." Greta shivered at the thought. "Besides, we have our interview tomorrow. I should think at least a little about what to say."

"Oh, please, how cold could it be?" said Susan cheerfully. "And you will definitely be great tomorrow. You're so smart. Please don't make me go alone. Mike is busy this afternoon. What about Greg?"

Greta, groggy from sleep, tried to concentrate. What was it that Greg had told her yesterday? Right, he had to stop by his lab today. "It looks like I'll be alone this afternoon, Susan."

"Great, it's all settled then! See you at the rink. Would around two work? Or maybe three is better? Whatever time works for you, Greta."

"Three will do," answered Greta in a feeble voice, and then she hung up. Anything for more sleep. All four of them attended an outdoor rock concert yesterday and went to bed well past midnight. Besides, she had to have a clear head for the interview tomorrow. *Susan!* thought Greta with a smile. *Always so full of life!* And fell back to sleep.

. . . . .

Greta spotted Susan right away. Her spiffy red hat was bobbing back and forth among the spectators gathered along the rink's edge. They were there to cheer on the beginning of the new season, despite the biting cold. The statue of Prometheus, presiding over them as the master of ceremonies, seemed to shine more brightly than usual as if to brag of its imperviousness to the vagaries of meteorological conditions.

Susan noticed Greta too. She waved happily and moved to a quieter spot to wait for her. She had already picked up the skates for both of them, and they were dangling from her shoulders. She also held something that she was gingerly moving from one hand to the other. Ice cream! Greta could not believe her eyes. "Susan, it's minus ten degrees. What were you thinking?"

"Oh, Greta, please! You know I love ice cream. And you love it, too. Let's have fun!"

Oh, whatever, thought Greta. It would be easier to just eat the stupid ice cream than to explain to Susan that she didn't mind ice cream on a hot summer day, but not today, when the only advantage was that the ice cream wouldn't melt in her hands after a few bites.

She knew something was wrong right away. It felt like she opened the front door of a well-heated house and let a blast of freezing air in. She nearly choked on the ice cream and started to cough spasmodically. The icy sensation, once inside, gushed from her throat to her entrails and into her very bones. She glanced at Susan, as if to look for help in-between her cough attacks, and bumped into a pair of cold watchful eyes. She had another vicious bout of coughing. When she looked again, Susan, eyes full of terror, just froze and held a barely bitten ice cream in her awkwardly stretched hand. *I must be losing my mind,* thought Greta.

"Hold on, I'll be right back." Susan dumped her bag and the ice skates on the bench beside Greta and disappeared in the crowd of onlookers. Greta had stopped coughing by that time and was sitting there, hunched miserably in her smart ski jacket that was so useless now. Susan emerged in a few minutes with a cup of hot chocolate. "Here, that will take care of it."

Greta took a small sip of the burning liquid. The heat traveled throughout her body, reaching every corner of it, down to every one of her fingertips.

"You really scared me, Greta! I didn't know what to do. Thank God I saw this man with a cup of something steaming hot and he showed me the chocolate stall." Susan radiated happiness. "Let's go ice-skating now! You look alright," urged Susan.

Greta did not mind. A memory flashed through her thoughts. Whether it was Susan's chocolate or the one of long ago, she was not sure, but it did the trick. Greta felt fine.

•   •   •   •   •

Greta was 11 years old when her father got his first overseas assignment. Her parents had never left their home country and were hoping, someday, to save enough money to live a few years in Europe. So, when her father was approached by the top management of his company about heading their small European branch in Salzburg, Austria, he agreed without a moment's hesitation.

A team of hefty robots packed their belongings, loaded the neat identical boxes into a huge truck, and took them to the airport. In those times, the zip two-hour flights over the Atlantic Ocean existed only between major cities. So, Greta's parents, instead of taking a slower, nonstop flight to Salzburg, decided to take a zip flight to Vienna to see the city and then take a regular one-hour flight to Saltsburg. Her mother spent hours researching travel guides and putting together their walking tour. Even Greta couldn't wait to get acquainted with the dazzling European capital.

It was early December, and they were excited to see Vienna during Advent. They had heard so much about the famous European Christmas markets with their stalls brimming with Yuletide gifts and culinary specialties. There was something for every member of the family to whet their appetite and pique their interest. Roasted chestnuts for all, glühwein for both parents, smoked sausage for her father; Greta's mother was collecting Christmas ornaments; Greta wanted to try the apple strudel and was looking forward to the Christmas cookie-making class at City Hall.

Greta's mother researched the improvised side trip in depth. The more she read about Vienna, the more irresistible the trip became. The last-minute decision proved to be serendipitous. It turned out that the forerunners of the Christmas markets went back to 1298, when Albrecht I granted Vienna's citizens the privilege of holding a December Market. So, that December, Vienna was celebrating the 800th anniversary of the tradition and intended to do so with particular panache.

"How lucky we decided to visit Vienna this year. Now we will get to see the special festivities," kept repeating Greta's mother.

They took the one a.m. flight to have as much time as possible in Vienna before their six o'clock flight to Salzburg, the last one for the day. The time difference with Vienna being six hours, they were supposed to arrive there at nine a.m. In the plane, Greta was bundled up in two blankets, feeling drowsy. She hated waking up in the middle of the night. It was also so cold in the plane. She was already fast asleep when it took off.

She woke up the very moment the landing gear touched the tarmac. She checked her watch. It was nine o'clock sharp. Greta looked out the window and uttered a small cry. It was snowing, and everything around her was already white. Huge fluffy flakes were hitting the illuminator and slowly gliding down. They left wet streaks, as if the city was crying, which was in stark contrast with the festive decorations at the airport. All of a sudden, Greta lost all desire to go into this cold weeping city. She felt weak and had but one desire—to curl under the blankets and be left alone. Greta looked morosely at her parents who seemed to be in the opposite mood. They had already retrieved their bags from the overhead bins and were impatiently waiting for permission to get off. They resembled two hunting dogs having smelled their prey, pulling at the leash and looking ahead, toward the front of the plane, as if trying to speed up the process, laughing and chatting with fellow passengers all the while.

Just as their taxi bot approached City Hall square, all aglow with thousands of lights, Greta's VS device, a hip novelty at the time, sounded an alarm. Her mother touched her forehead. It was burning. In apprehensive silence, they ducked into the coffeehouse in front of them to read the first diagnosis. Just a regular cold. Her parents looked at each other in relief, and then both reached to hug Greta, bumping their foreheads. All three laughed. Greta took the medication, and the fever started to subside. She was still very weak, but nice and warm in her corner from the hot chocolate and a warm woolen throw thoughtfully provided by the owner in every booth. They were two hundred yards away from the stalls, abuzz with lavish activities. So close yet forbidden, unreal like a fairy tale, a mirage, they tantalized and beckoned.

Greta refused to go to a hotel. They spent a few hours in that warm cozy coffeehouse looking at the beautiful City Hall square, their imagination providing the rest.

The owner, a gracious old man with a splendid moustache, offered to stay with Greta while her parents went to take a peek at the market. "It won't be the same next year, you know," he kept repeating. They refused; neither did they take turns. They did try the coffeehouse version of gluhwein, and it did not impress them much, probably because most of the essential ingredients, like frosty air, laughing faces of children and adults alike, caroling around the huge Christmas tree, and hundreds of lights glowing over their heads, were missing. The owner unearthed some archaic board games from his youth which they had never heard of, not even Greta's parents—Uno, Jenga. They laughed and played until it was time to leave. They rescheduled their flight to two p.m. Just when the coffeehouse started to fill up for lunch, every new customer bringing in, along with cold air, divine aromas and fragments of Christmas tunes and carols, they ordered a taxi bot and went to the airport.

Indeed, this family doesn't need to see the Christmas markets to put them in the Christmas spirit; they have it inside them, murmured the owner when they said their good-byes. He was shaking his head and smiling into his thick mustache long after the family was gone.

The medicine kicked in amazingly fast and by the evening, Greta was fine. They had dinner at their Salzburg hotel, not to exhaust Greta, and Mom and Dad joked that it was the hot chocolate that cured her.

CHAPTER TWENTY-ONE

During the days after she got the official interview notification, Greta tried to figure out what the questions would be. They obviously would have to do with what was perceived as good parenting. The zeitgeist values would probably call for caring, nurturing, kind people that would not interfere with the regimen designed for the child. On the other hand, they should be able to foster the child's development in every possible way. It must be difficult to find the right balance. The slogan last year was, "The child knows best!" What does it mean, exactly? Tame, permissive parents? That could hardly be true. What, then?

After ice-skating, wandering aimlessly about town, unwilling to go back to the empty house, she was mulling over the issue again, still not sure what the answer should be. You love your child precisely the way he is, for his uniqueness. And you help him in uncovering his unique talents. You get a precious bundle, as a work of art, in a crate, with plenty of packing material to be carefully removed, layer by layer. The biggest challenge is to accept a child that is not absolutely the best even at its best. It takes a lot of humility. But really, just love.

Lost in thought, unaware of her whereabouts or the direction she was heading in, she happened to come to the Independent Parenthood building. There was a line, but not a huge one. It was mostly just future mothers. The hopefuls more often than not were all clad in black, carrying vintage Chanel or Birkin bags. Scents of exotic perfumes emanated from the line. It was becoming more and more fashionable among the upper crust to apply. Pushing a stroller had started to bear a certain cachet, signal an elite status. No one talked; women just darted surreptitious looks at each other, full of guarded animosity.

Greta immediately felt uneasy and self-conscious. All those immaculately made up and put together women intimidated her. She felt out of place in her expertly cut, but still hopelessly sensible pants-and-sweater outfit, and even the smart jacket she was so proud of did not seem to save the day. Her choice of outfit for the interview appeared all wrong all of a sudden. What was she thinking? Jeans and a T-shirt! So plain! She must have gotten something more sophisticated. Wait a minute. Isn't that why Susan bought herself a suit? Susan knew! And she intentionally had hidden it from Greta. Or was it a mere coincidence? After all, Susan did not conceal the fact that she bought a suit. Confused and disturbed, she turned back abruptly and rushed home.

• • • • •

The next morning, Greta had a stupid tiff with Greg about the color of their future nursery's walls. She asked Greg whether he liked her choice. The timing was far from perfect. Greg suggested waiting until they knew the sex of the baby and paint the walls accordingly. Greta thought that so much common sense robbed the whole venture of its charm. She accused Greg of being an insensitive pragmatist. He, in turn, said he never suspected she could invest so much time and effort in such trifles and was short of calling her downright brainless. She stood behind her choice—mint green—which she insisted would be perfectly fine for a girl or a boy. The issue still unresolved, they darted out of the house not to be late, both still fuming. Looking back, she couldn't understand how such a small issue could provoke so much passion and fury, especially considering she and Greg rarely fought at all.

That was not the right way to begin such an important undertaking. The interview was scheduled for 2:30, but the fight made her lose her footing right from the start and she had trouble concentrating on the task. She did not have enough time to style her hair after the shower; her makeup, although minimal, was done hastily. More likely than not, no one would notice, but it weighed on her mind just the same. On top of these pesky annoyances, now she felt pathetic and underdressed in her jeans outfit. It spoiled her mood, made her feel less in control. Brooding and unhappy, she was walking silently along Greg's side, looking gloomily around her. They entered the park at the end of which stood the Independent Parenthood building. The last leaves were waltzing around them in their final moment of glory, reluctant to land, blown apart or thrown at each other by sudden gusts of wind.

She saw an old couple, then young parents with a stroller, heading toward a playground. Two small children on scooters were chasing each other and shrieking in delight. Greta involuntarily slowed her pace and watched them, mesmerized by the sight, smiling. Then she stopped in her tracks, when a thought hit her like a bolt. She had to snap out of this mood. This was the most important decision of her life; she could not mess it up. So, who cares if her eye shadow was not perfectly blended and she had no time to put on those new earrings? She fumbled with them, unsuccessfully, for several minutes, but finally had to settle for her everyday studs. Only she knew how sick she was of them. She had to concentrate on the interview. How could she allow herself to get so side-tracked and lose perspective? And what did the color of the walls matter, at the end of the day? She firmly caught up with Greg who was walking two steps ahead of her now and resolutely but tenderly put her arm under his.

"I'm so sorry, Greg," she said, with feeling. "It was so stupid of me, really. I don't care a single bit about the color of the walls, choose any color you like. I love you and want you to be happy."

"How funny! I was just thinking the same exact thing," said Greg, clasping Greta in his arms and laughing. For a moment they just stood there, lost in each other's eyes, oblivious to the world. A little girl, zooming past and all but bumping into them on her tricycle brought them back to reality. "We'd better hurry," they uttered at the same time in dismay. They had twenty minutes left before the interview, and were cautioned multiple times to come early. Laughing and holding hands, ignoring the walking lanes, they ran straight across the lawn in a motley swirl of leaves they kicked back into the air.

They entered the interview room just in time, still smiling and a little out of breath. They brought in the cool freshness of a nice autumn day, their youth, strength and happiness, in stark contrast with the stifled atmosphere of the place. The stern look of five people behind a long desk in front of them quickly brought them back to reality. The interview started with the usual questions— names, ages, occupations, address, even though they had access to all the information they were collecting prior to the interview. Obviously, it was just a stalking horse, to distract the parents and lull them into relaxing their vigilance. Or maybe they just wanted them to feel more at ease. After completing the routine, the woman at the center of the table suddenly shot the most important question in a sharp, almost shrill voice.

"Why do you want to take care of your child yourselves? Aren't your careers fulfilling enough?"

Why, indeed? Greta expected this question. Greta and Greg had spent months discussing it before coming to this decision. Greg was more than a little apprehensive and downright scared by the daunting task, but Greta did not have to convince herself; it looked like the natural choice to her. She had no thread of doubt in her heart that it was the right thing to do, but it was still so hard to put into words. She wrote and destroyed dozens of drafts in preparation for this interview, but she was still not sure how to best answer this question.

"Oh, I love my job. As I have just said, I work for a big food company whose stance on social issues is very appealing to me and so—"

"Yes, yes, Greta, we are aware of that." Now the examiners sounded truly annoyed. "More to the point, please. What makes you both think you have what it takes to raise a happy child and what made you consider this path in the first place? Greg?" This was asked by the same thin, middle-aged woman with slightly pinched lips that gave away her fastidiousness, and who was obviously the head of the commission.

"We just feel this is the right thing to do!" blurted out Greg, all their long hours of preparation and eloquent speeches going to the dogs. He immediately regretted his remark and hurriedly proceeded with their long spiel about why they felt on par with the best educators and child-rearing specialists.

"I see," said the same woman, giving him a long pensive look and scribbling something on her tablet. "You certainly understand the policy very well. More importantly, your own vision is in tune with it. Do you have something to add?" The woman was looking at Greta now.

What was there to explain? Greta just wanted to be with her child; wasn't it natural, anyway? Somehow, she felt the question weird, inverted.

Greta felt defiant all of a sudden. The stuffy atmosphere and stiff people made her crave some fresh air. Greta looked through the window. The wind picked up, and the leaves were now frantically whirling in the air, pushed toward each other only to be pulled away the next moment. Her eyes followed two leaves interlocked in synchronized moves as if they were two passionate lovers. A sudden rush of wind threw them apart, and Greta, mesmerized by the sight, was almost sure she saw both leaves extend their points in a desperate attempt to stay together. Greta had a sharp poignant pain in her heart. Suddenly, she knew.

"Have you ever observed the leaves fall, esteemed members of the commission?" asked Greta. Greg looked at her in scared disbelief, forgetting how easy it was to disconcert her. Greta's gaze was wandering among the interviewers, singling no one in particular. She continued. "Have you seen leaves from the same branch, sure they were destined to be together forever, being torn apart by the wind? I just know I won't be able to let go of my baby."

"You certainly have a vivid imagination and a peculiar way of describing things, not without its merits, I must say," the same lady said slowly, looking at Greta with sudden interest. "Anyway, I think you have told us all we need to know, that is, unless my colleagues have any additional questions."

The other members shook their heads to signal they were satisfied with the answers. "Alright, then," said the lady. "Thank you, you may go now. You will be notified of the next steps." She stood up, signaling the end of the meeting. Greta and Greg did not have to be asked twice. The couple thanked everybody and left the room.

On the way home, they were still holding hands, but instead of running, they were walking slowly. They did not talk, but they did not need to. They knew they were thinking the same thing. They had started a process to win the right to raise their child at home, and it was out of their hands now. The intangible idea felt very real now. By the look on the lady's face, they could, in all likelihood, talk the talk. But were they able to walk the walk? They would have to take it one day at a time.

The wind had finally calmed down, laying the leaves neatly on the ground. They muffled their steps and seemed to whisper something, their soft murmurs providing much-needed support. Or they just read too much into it.

Just before setting, the sun reappeared from behind the clouds and let its loyal rays run loose for a few brief moments before diving behind the horizon, entraining its guard with it. The most stubborn ones lagged behind, jumping from one treetop to the next, playing in the newly bare branches like rambunctious children, but soon even they followed suit.

There will be a day, there will be food, thought Greta. Aloud, she said, "We can do it, Greg. We will do it." Greg smiled at her and gently squeezed her hand, hugging her closer to him.

CHAPTER TWENTY-TWO

The next day, Greta had a conversation with her colleagues that almost ended in a heated brawl were it not cut short by an all-staff meeting. Her office hours were from one to three that day. Usually, she put on her VR goggles and tuned in at the very last minute, but today she finished her lunch early and joined her coworkers. New food places were being discussed. One of the guys mentioned a new restaurant, Carnivore, that had opened just last month. In defiance of all traditions, it served huge slabs of wild game meat, obviously artificially raised, on sloppy mounds of mashed potatoes, disheveled lettuce leaves and other equally messily presented greens, as if to conjure images of primitive hunters enjoying their prey of the day. Despite its jarring lack of refinement and subtlety, it was all the rage among the foodies and the followers of the nascent back-to-nature movement. Greta jumped in immediately.

"I like new trends in food, but it seems to be an idea fraught with many potential dangers. It caters to our wilder instincts, Bob. It's a slippery slope for regression into renewed dependency on wildlife for food, and with all the dire consequences, including modern viral pandemics. It may be like the smell of blood for a predator, and may set our instincts back in motion. It's been only three years since the last spillover. Although, hopefully, the situation is now getting under control; still, it's a force to be reckoned with. It took such a long time to curb and then eliminate meat production, alter our tastes, and make our diet much more plant-based. Why play with fire? When our impact on the biosphere was minimal, our irresponsible behavior was not so apparent—"

"What do you mean, 'irresponsible'? Is eating what I like irresponsible? It's obvious you just don't like meat, Greta, otherwise you would be less cavalier about the issue."

"Let me finish! Yes, it could be irresponsible, believe it or not! And yes, I do like meat on occasion and I love seafood, to which my reasoning fully applies. When our impact on the biosphere was minimal, we could get away with ignoring the laws of nature. We were concerned only with obeying the human, often inhumane, ones."

"I still don't see how—"

"For a very long time we could get away with polluting our environment, destroying our forests, accumulating indestructible waste, killing wildlife, and driving scores of species to extinction. All this in full conformity with men's laws. Now, lest we set out to destroy our planet and perish ourselves, we cannot ignore nature's laws anymore; following them is imperative to our survival. That's the challenge of our times—to change our mind frame, become less arrogant, and respect nature's design, including wildlife.

"It may seem that it doesn't apply since we don't use real meat from wild or domesticated animals anymore. All Carnivore does is replace our oval-shaped cutlets from meat substitutes with something that looks like the real steak of long ago, but I feel this approach may open the door to dangerous trends. We may decide to allow growing animals for slaughter in limited quantities at first, but who knows? Human nature being what it is, I think it's better not to tempt us. So, in my opinion, the answer is no, Bob. You cannot eat what you want." *What's gotten into them?* mused Greta. *First Susan, now Bob.*

"That may very well be the case, Greta, but I still believe we have the right to make our own decisions, and we should have access to all choices. I have the right to decide for myself, I'm a free man! I often have nightmares, you know, how I keep running through an endless tunnel with no light at the end."

"You should take some wellness and relaxation classes," chimed in Gabriella, a small girl with hair neatly parted in the middle. "I don't think you should take up knitting, as I did, although I personally think it's a lot of fun and does wonders for my nerves, but maybe you would love puzzles or pottery workshops."

"Okay, Gabriella, thank you. I don't think doing puzzles like my in-laws will cure my anxieties."

"I agree with Greta," started a lanky, nerdish-looking young man.

"Of course, Richard, what else is new? You always agree with everything Greta says, and besides—"

"Greta made a very good point," went on Richard, paying no attention to Mary's biting remark. She was a tall, lean, slightly stooping woman known for grabbing the bull by the horns and not being very diplomatic about it. "Our elimination of meat industries and wildlife commerce certainly gives us legitimate reason to hope we have quenched the spillover incidents for good. But the situation is very precarious, the barrier still weak, and making it easier for our millennia-old meat-eating and loving culture to sneak in through the back door, like a Trojan horse, would be a great mistake. I think...humans are an integral part of the biosphere. We have the unique possibility to transform it due to the size of our population and technological advances. The human impact has reached planetary scale and scope, which is why we can't afford to act irresponsibly. Our impact on the planet may be strong enough to destroy the medium that nourishes and sustains us. This is of course, a well-known fact..."

"Precisely! Don't feed us truisms, Richard!"

"But maybe the planet has ways to defend itself? What if these pandemics are just a way for wildlife to take care of itself?"

"This is such a far-fetched idea, Richard. You definitely need a relaxation class; you're nuts."

"If this is so important to you, Bob, why don't you consider joining the community on the Moon? Food Mecca and Gourmet Paradise advertise their food as no match for anything you can taste on Earth. No wonder, I'd say! Anything goes on the Moon, otherwise who would be foolish enough to live there? There are shuttles every two months, I believe. Why don't you go and check?" said Mary.

Contrary to everyone's expectations, Bob did not protest, but became visibly uneasy and even blushed slightly.

"Ah," quickly said Mary. "I have caught you red-handed, haven't I? Have you gone already, or are you considering?"

"Yes, indeed, I have been considering it for a while, what of it? I'd rather be free than paying by constant humiliation for the conveniences of a more developed society. I feel like an animal led to slaughter myself, with fences to the left and right of me, and doomed fellow animals trotting in front and behind me."

Mary opened her mouth to say that he didn't seem to mind terribly if animals were slaughtered in this manner just to satisfy his fancy, but Gabriella, outraged, outpaced her, for once ignoring Bob's obvious double standards.

"But it is in your best interests!"

"I want to be the one who determines what is in my best interests!"

"Well, if this is how you feel, you should definitely check out the Moon colony."

"Free? What nonsense! Absolute freedom is an illusion, Bob!" persisted Greta. "You must eat, you must sleep, you must die. You call that freedom? To be free from subjugation by other people is one thing, but no man is free from the laws of nature. Don't be ridiculous. Our planet will die if we do as we please. We have to be law-abiding citizens of the planet Earth. To preserve our home is one of our responsibilities."

"Exactly!" intervened Richard. His body, wiggling more than usual, resembled a noodle on a pasta spoon, making one wonder whether he had any bones in his body at all; his weak, badly shaven chin was shaking. "The biggest fallacy of all times is that man is the king of creation. We are obsessed with our self-importance, our power, and our freedom; in truth, if someone examined us as a species from afar, we'd resemble a growth run amok." He turned to face Bob. "It looks like you want others to take care of those annoying problems and spare yourself the aggravation. You want to be more free than others, Bob." Richard laughed at his allusion to *Animal Farm*, which he himself found very witty and to the point.

At this moment their group leader tuned in and the conversation stopped. The meeting began.

The COVID-19 pandemic of the early twenty-first century gave the incipient meat-replacing industries a powerful boost. As most epidemics spilled over from wild animals, domestic ones often serving as a breeding ground for mutations, the spillover (the cross-species transmission from wildlife) was finally in focus of the general public. In just a few decades the millennia-long cultural traditions underwent a critical transformation, fueled to a great extent by fear of a pandemic of equal or greater caliber. Zoos of all kinds were eliminated by the same token, with the additional push from animal-rights activists. Circus animal acts died out shortly thereafter.

• • • • •

That day, Gregory stayed in his laboratory until dinner. Greta was waiting for him impatiently. The office discussion disturbed her more than she was ready to admit. The minute she heard Greg opening the door, she ran into the lobby.

His brawny, rugged physique was in such contrast with Greta's idea of a scientist. Greta still had trouble seeing him among neat rows of petri dishes, powerful microscopes, and sophisticated computers. He was such an outdoor type. She could more easily picture him as an explorer, forcing his way through frozen landscapes or climbing mountains, starving, exhausted, but inching to the top nonetheless.

Even now, she could bet he had brought in with him the freshness of pristine wilderness and not just a breath of cool outside air.

"Hey, Greta, you look upset, what happened?" asked Greg the minute he saw her. He paused for a moment to hang his coat and empty the contents of his pockets in the catch-all on the small table by the entrance door.

"Oh, it's nothing serious, how was your day?" Greta laughed, lifting on her toes to kiss him.

"It was an okay day. I missed you so much," replied Greg. He encircled her in his strong embrace and carried her to the couch by the window. "And now, on with your story."

"How do you even know I'm upset?"

"Oh, Greta..." It was Greg's turn to laugh. "You are not exactly good at keeping a poker face. Now, do I have to torture you to hear what happened?"

"Oh, it's just a conversation we had at work. Let's talk after dinner. I just can't stop being surprised at how different we all are. It's a long story."

"Sure. Don't forget, we have our inspection soon, and you should not let anybody or anything upset you. And tomorrow, we will celebrate our successful interview at Carnivore. This is a very trendy new restaurant. I made a reservation three weeks ago. I wanted to surprise you."

"Greg, that's fantastic. I can't believe it! This is exactly how it all started today."

"Shush! Not a word about what upset you! Let's enjoy our dinner."

That night they chose a VR dinner at a remote Tuscan village restaurant. They loved this application Greg discovered when Greta turned 30. It allowed you to choose virtual lunch or dinner settings at various restaurants around the world. It was still a bit pricey, but they didn't mind the extra expense once or twice a week to spice things up; it was also a great alternative to going out if they were too tired or just lazy.

After dinner, when they were comfortably sitting on the couch, Greta finally related the office conversation to Greg.

"I fully agree with you, Greta," said Greg, thoughtfully sipping his wine. "I also think Richard made a very good point. Earth did turn its immune system on maximum. Granted, we have come a long way in our fight against viral calamities, to stick to my field of expertise. Think about the pandemics of the last two centuries. The completion of the Global Virome Project and our antiviral vaccines, to say nothing of the digital immunity passports, certainly allowed us to implement a very efficient and secure pandemic preparedness plan. We have effective schemes to protect our economies. We have enough hospitals and protective equipment. All these measures allowed us to deal with the latest viral outbreaks better than in the 21st century. 'Viruses are, however, a perfidious enemy, Greta; there is no way to know exactly when, where, and how they will get loose. And if another pandemic strikes, we may be doomed to fight the last war, to a certain extent. We will have to tweak the existing vaccines or maybe develop completely new ones. And it takes time. I certainly hope that in the future, a universal vaccine will be found. This is what I work on, as you well know. But for now, this is our weak spot. Should some virus get out of control, and it's always a possibility, we may not be much better off than during the COVID-19 pandemic. After all, humanity had one hundred years to prepare for it after the 1918 Spanish flu, and look what happened. Even with a few lesser ones in between, COVID-19 caught us unprepared. There is no guarantee it won't happen again according to the same grim scenario. So, before we ruin the planet, the planet may very well ruin us. We can only do so much.

"Our best bet is still prevention, that is, to keep and strictly enforce our ban on wildlife commerce and strict adherence to meatless food. This way, we have a good shot at effectively preventing a spillover. Any unnecessary interaction with wildlife has to stop. We may pay dearly if we don't. I came across an archaic slogan the other day—'If you can't beat us, join us.' It made me think about humanity's place in the universe. It's better to live in harmony with nature than to declare a war on the universe. We are not likely to win. Is this what made you so upset, Greta?"

"Yes, but there is another aspect of the pandemics or any other global problem that our discussion made me aware of," said Greta slowly, then paused.

Greg smiled at her encouragingly. They both enjoyed their after-dinner unhurried quiet talks. They dubbed them "philosophical" discussions, which allowed them to exchange ideas and bond. "I was thinking about the concept of individual freedom. More specifically, about the absurd situation when people perceive public acts serving to protect them with animosity and fight against them. This distrust for institutions must stem from times past when authorities were promoting interests of groups in power.

"In prehistoric times, the environment presented danger. In order to survive, people had to join their efforts. Their concerted efforts were indispensable for survival. As human society developed and became stronger, the pressure of the natural environment eased its grip. Men acquired the ability to change it to their benefit. Now, humans could afford to fight among themselves for power and riches. The law of man was born to keep the fight more or less civilized and to enforce the status quo favorable to the ruling elite. The first governing institutions were thus authoritarian. So, public mistrust in governing institutions ensued.

"As democratic rule started to prevail, the role of the government began to change, and so, slowly, did the old perception of its nature. People increasingly started to consider the government as their ally, an institution serving to promote their interests. Now, full circle, authorities are to promote interests of humans in their struggle not so much against each other, but against natural disasters. They lead research, organize prevention, and deal with consequences in the aftermath. The authorities also make sure we abide by universal laws, as our ability to affect our planet becomes commensurate with powerful natural forces. In other words, the State has to carve an optimal niche for humanity in our biosphere, which translates into men getting the most out of our biosphere on a sustainable basis, without hurting or destroying it. Which made me think that maybe Bob is not so much off the mark. Greg, has it ever occurred to you, that the more developed a society gets, the less free we become? Bob is not the only one to feel we are being duped and lulled into submission. But I don't see it that way. I see the objective necessity of such measures. They are not created, just voiced by the State. And does being so law-abiding make people like me boring?"

"Not to me it doesn't." Greg's answer came quick as a shot. Then he paused. Greta waited. "Maybe marriages are made in heaven, after all, Greta. I can see that for Bob you may be a boring, self-righteous person. But by virtue of my everyday work, I realize very well the price of freedom he talks about". He fell into silence again. Greta did not rush him. "As a teenager, I read in some novel, I believe, about the plague epidemic in Middle Age Europe. Two men were curious whether rumors that victims' bodies became black after death were true. One evening, they mounted their horses and went outside the city wall to the place where corpses were deposited, to find out. The next day, their bodies joined the pile. Everyone is free to dispose of one's life as one pleases. With viruses, a person may be contagious without feeling sick. That means he or she should exercise extreme caution and be responsible to avoid infecting others, even if this particular person does not mind taking risks for his own sake." He paused again. His gaze, usually kind and full of bonhomie, became cold as steel. Greta had never seen him like this. "Under the circumstances, such freedom is not suicide, Greta. It's murder."

CHAPTER TWENTY-THREE

Susan and Mike were sitting in the living room, waiting for the inspectors. They got the latest appointment for the day, at 2:30 p.m. Mike was excited. It was Susan who did all the planning and purchased everything for the nursery, and Mike admired her taste and creative prowess, never ceasing to wonder how she could achieve such stunning results with so little money. Under her guidance, he contributed a few cute shelves and picture frames in the shape of wild baby animals. He was a do-it-yourself kind of guy, pretty handy around the house. He particularly liked his latest creation—a small shelf for Susan's childhood toy Mick. He found the story so endearing.

Susan was quiet. She was more pale than usual, and her hair was drawn in a simple tight ponytail, which made her look years younger. She was wearing black pants and a cashmere sweater with intricate design. Having caught her reflection in the mirror, she grimaced. Her image reminded her of Greta. She had copied Greta's idea for her inspection outfit after duly nixing the very idea to her face. *Okay, it's time to snap out of it!* She shook her head with such force her ponytail hit her painfully on the face. At that very moment the intercom buzzed, announcing the arrival of the inspectors.

The inspectors loved the apartment and were impressed with the future baby's room. Susan did her homework and coached Mike well. There were no surprises.

"Did you come up with a name?"

"No, we want to see the baby and try to find a name that would suit her or him best."

"Did you consult your parents about their preferences?"

"We love our parents and don't want to hurt anyone. We thought it was just not realistic to find a name that would have a special meaning for everybody, so we decided we would choose the name ourselves, and as we've already told you, take the cue from the baby. Our parents loved our approach. We didn't want anyone to feel left out."

Susan felt like she had successfully avoided falling into the trap of creating the impression that she was catering to her tastes and fancies rather than the baby's needs. Every item or toy was chosen upon careful research of the latest developments in the field.

"What an unusual wall color! It looks so nice, but I don't think I have ever seen this particular hue in a nursery."

As much as she was itching to paint the nursery the palest, most delicate shade of pink, Susan knew very well that it would be a great mistake, for the inspectors would rightly assume she wanted a girl and would not be happy if she got a boy. The paint had to remain neutral, then. When perusing the returns site, she accidentally came across this light green shade that was 75% off, and she could not resist the temptation, although she was originally leaning toward a mint green hue. Obviously, that was not what she told the inspectors. Instead, she fed them a soppy story how it was the color of the walls in her great-grandparents' guest room where she used to sleep, and how this color calmed her down. She was debating between grandparents and great-grandparents, but finally went with the latter, to be on the safe side. She doubted it was possible to check data on houses that far back. She could always claim she had made a mistake, should the truth come out; anyway, she was such a little girl at the time.

Mick, whose bright though considerably faded colors were in jarring contrast with the room's subdued color scheme, begged for a special question. Susan's reply was a studied combination of personal excitement and parental resolution to do whatever it took for the child's well-being, while firmly remaining on scientific ground without being carried away into pure nonsense or superstition. Susan felt it would help reinforce the image she was going for—that of a modern couple, solid and trustworthy, but not too stuck-up—and should the interests of the child so require, ready to explore new ideas with a good dose of humor.

Mick the Mickey Mouse was her favorite toy in childhood, a present from her beloved parents. She fortuitously retrieved it while shopping for a baby shower present for her pregnant girlfriend. She thought it was a sign to start her own family. It would remind her, every time she entered the baby's room, of her happy childhood years and encourage her to be the best mom she could be, just like her mom was to her. The energy of her parents' love encapsulated in the toy would protect her own child. Susan's eyes shined, and her cheeks became pink. Every time she mentioned her parents, tears glistened in her eyes.

Mike was standing behind the inspectors so they could not see him. He looked at Susan pensively. He was not surprised anymore at the stories she came up with. He could not fathom how she could sound so sincere. If he didn't know for a fact that all of her stories were pure fiction, he would not have the slightest doubt. But then, what was really true, as far as Susan was concerned? Where did the false Susan end and the real Susan begin? Who was she? Was there even a real Susan? Mike shivered. A chameleon, always busy blending in and seducing her victim. Had she ever stopped in her tracks to think what she liked? Yes, he bet she did. She liked to win.

Susan was satisfied with her performance. She felt that she had nailed it again. She was also relieved because she decided not to coach Mike this time after their disturbing conversation before the interview. She had just told him to leave the talking to her.

Mike did not feel like asking questions. After a celebratory toast and a quick dinner, Mike said he had a deadline that he didn't mention earlier not to put extra pressure on Susan. *What a dear,* thought Susan warmly.

· · · · ·

Susan did not mind that Mike was busy. She didn't feel like celebrating. She was satisfied she had carried out her plan. That was it. Full stop. No elation, no feelings of triumph. Nothing even close to her emotions after the interview. She felt tired and drained. A scene from a movie they saw with Mike a long time ago came to mind. She felt like a hunter who was chasing her prey through the woods on a cold rainy day, trees trying to grab her by their gnarling arms to throw her off her horse, wet leaves hitting her face. She would only bend lower, clinch her teeth tighter, and persevere without paying attention to any inconveniences, ignoring wounds in the heat of the chase, only to realize at a much later time that the prey was just a mirage, a play of light and shadows in the trees she was not aware of because her sweat and the rain were blinding her. She would stretch her hand but it would only grab emptiness. *Nonsense,* thought Susan. *I'm just tired.* She went to the fridge. She deserved a treat. Ice cream should do her some good. She still had a small container of her favorite flavor—double dark chocolate. She knew that tomorrow, her snooping VS monitor would report the consequences of this digression to the central office, but today she didn't care.

Susan finished the last spoon of ice cream. She peeked in the container, making sure she had scraped every morsel. She had. She sighed. She remained motionless for some time, her blank stare glued to the blinking red lights of the ferry landing on the other side of the river in front of their building. Eating ice cream made her feel even worse. What a waste. Not deterred by the ice cream fiasco and not quite ready to call it a night, Susan stirred impatiently. What was Mike up to? He rarely worked that late. Maybe they could watch a movie together, some brainless comedy to cheer her up. She was about to call Mike to ask him whether he would join her, but then decided to have a look at his computer, to first check how his work was progressing. By now she knew the telltale signs of his wrapping things up. She did not want to look needy. She opened the camera application and accessed the camera data.

Susan was a curious woman, which was duly noted in her psychological and moral portrait on file with the HR department of her company. But it neither fully nor correctly explained the overwhelming urge to know everything about Mike's whereabouts. However, since Mike's wanderings on the GlobalNet were more numerous and diverse than his physical ones, Susan had to find a way to get into his computer. Mike being a computer programmer, she knew better than to embed any spyware into his equipment. She realized it would be very short-lived. Susan was not afraid of the complexity of the task. She was good at finding ways out of seemingly hopeless situations.

Mike never worked in armchairs, in his bed, or on the sofa. He claimed that he could concentrate only while sitting in his state-of-the-art ergonomic chair at his huge desk with many computing devices on its immaculately clean, dust- and clutter-free surface. Susan put decorative mirrored panels in the doors behind Mike's chair at an angle to guarantee an unobstructed view of the computer screen and a camera recording its reflection. Trust, but verify.

Her first thought was that the camera malfunctioned. Prepared to see pages of code, she did not grasp right away what was in front of her eyes. All this time, Mike had been staring at a blank screen. Susan felt suddenly very cold. *How dare he!* Her VS monitor beeped a short warning. Livid with rage, she grabbed the armrests of her chair with such force, her knuckles whitened. *I can't deal with this now. I have to sleep on it,* was the only thought that shot through her head. She stayed in the chair for a few more moments. Back to her composed self, Susan finally left the terrace and went to the bedroom, wishing Michael good-night in her usual cheerful voice. Without lifting his eyes from the screen, Mike mumbled in return that he still had something to take care of. Had he lifted his head to look at Susan, he would probably have failed to recognize his wife. Her vivid brown eyes, peering mockingly and confidently from under long eyelashes which softened her gaze and gave her face a slightly scared look, were now two blazing fires on an ashen face with hollow cheeks.

Late at night, she took the white box Mick came in from under the bed, affixed the return label, and took it to the mail room. The mail was picked up at nine a.m., but Susan didn't want to take any chances.

•   •   •   •   •

The following weekend was their tennis outing. Both couples were looking forward to it. As usual, they had two options. A tennis court about a hundred miles away from the city, or an underground one that was part of the latest state-of-the-art sports complex in the city center, or rather, under it. Saturday was supposed to be a great day, weather-wise, sunny with just a slight chance of snow later in the afternoon. Susan was the only one unwilling to leave the city, so they opted for the former, although the use of flyways was heavily taxed on weekends to avoid congestion. The flight was supposed to take no more than thirty minutes.

As most people of their age and older, they still missed tree-lined streets and city flower beds. Now, trees remained only in specially designated parks; most of them could not survive in the shade of modern buildings, which rarely had less than 150 floors. Besides, they were thought to interfere with the new communication networks and were considered an eyesore by city beautification authorities for disrupting new patterns and proportions. To compensate for the disappearance of oxygen-producing units, most of the tall buildings had special greenery on their facades and gardens in the lobbies and on the roofs, arranged in accordance with the new urban standards and needs. It was still mostly an acquired taste. Those who yearned for the unruly vastness that contradicted the new human vision of effectiveness and beauty, not yet locked in the tight grids of perfect geometric shapes, found relaxation and solace on such expanses of terrain as the tennis compound. It did not feel like mere square feet of prized real estate and the eye required a few seconds to wander from one object to the next, which was rest in itself. Its indolence and apparent inefficiency were therapeutic. Susan just liked their chicken wings.

They agreed to meet at ten in the morning, in front of the equipment rental building. Greta and Greg, as usual, came a few minutes early. Susan and Mike were a few minutes late.

They rented the balls from the machine while the rackets were being printed to their specifications, and headed toward the courts. Susan wasn't prepared to let her friends forget that they dragged her out to the country against her will.

"It's really too cold to play, guys," she kept nagging. "My hands are frozen, I'm not sure I'll be able to keep my winter gloves off. Now the wind is picking up. And look at these so-called woods! Those ugly crippled dwarfs of the trees that make an awful grating noise in the wind. And the stench, pardon my French, of those rotting leaves!"

"Oh, come on, Susan, it is such a peaceful morning; nature is just getting ready to take a snooze," said Mike genially.

Ignoring Mike's remark, Susan stopped suddenly. "Look! Oh, no! Even the food counter is closed for the season. I was hoping to at least get myself some chicken wings."

They had finally reached the courts. Susan cut short her diatribe and immediately took matters into her hands. She was all business now. First thing, she ran around the court and chose the side, not to play against the sun. The court was positioned so that the players never faced the sun directly, and the tall trees around the court were supposed to protect from the sun even further, but this was useless now that the trees stood bare, a fact that Susan did not fail to mention. Greg quickly acquiesced that it could very well be, that's why to make things really fair, they should rotate after each set.

Susan bit her tongue and refrained from further comment until the game started. She quickly kicked off her coat and gloves and started her warm-up, giving occasional curt commands to Mike.

As far as their technique, they were all pretty much at the same level, so things got heated right from the start. Greta did not play to win, she did not like the game that much, but she considered it a means to an end. In that particular instance, it enabled her to see her friends, with an added bonus of getting out of the city.

The men kept playing, concentrating on their game, but Susan did not close her mouth for a second, disputing every serve and claiming the ball was out whenever she had the slightest opportunity, the electronic scoring system notwithstanding. Greg and Greta were leading at first, but toward the end of the game Greta could hardly bear the incessant outpourings, and worn out at last by all the shouting, just let go. Immediately, she messed up her serve and sent the ball out. The victory went to Susan and Mike.

·   ·   ·   ·   ·

They were walking slowly back to the building, their minds and bodies, kicked into high gear by the tough competition, at ease at last. They were all laughing and talking at once, reliving the most dramatic and exciting moments of the game. Susan was smiling broadly, her vanity appeased. It was one of the rare moments when she could allow herself to let go and during which she was particularly attractive. She was a hit, eloquent, funny. Her carefree mood little by little engulfed everyone. Even the usually reticent Greg dropped his guard and fell under the spell of her effervescent quips.

Presently Susan was making fun of Greta's lamentable finale with an unusual acerbity. Mike visibly cringed, but Greta didn't mind too much, remembering how frustrated she herself was with Susan on occasion.

Greta was game for any kind of creative talent, be it a new theater production, new movie, a piano recital, or an artist retrospective. She did not neglect the gastronomy either. She gave new stars on the culinary firmament the same amount of attention. She was craving this vibrant, powerful energy, consuming it by gulps, and it filled her with life, as if she were drinking from the Fountain of Youth.

But then she hated going with Susan, who volunteered to keep her company a few times. Susan wouldn't stop talking and whispering during the performance until hushed by their neighbors. That was embarrassing and a pity. Greta would have enjoyed discussing the experience with her, but Susan was bored by such conversations and would usually squash Greta's efforts in that regard.

It looked like it wasn't going to snow, at least not anytime soon, but the air was heavy with humidity and late fall smells. Greta slowed her pace and fell slightly behind. She made a few steps off the road and ventured into the bordering woods. It had been a while since the trees had shed their leaves that had by now lost their bright colors and were the uniform shade of brown. They were lying on the ground like a thin layered cake, the hardiest ones glued together by the moisture and mush that recent rains had turned the more fragile ones into.

Greta preferred the straightforward, eager smells of spring to the saturated, complex aromas of fall. Today, however, she relished the bittersweet smell of decay that enveloped her from the moment she put her foot on the soft soddy ground. It did not feel sad to her, for it already held the promise of a future life. Suddenly an odd thought occurred to her, as if she were trespassing, invading Nature's privacy and spying on it, as it was quietly preparing for the salubrious slumber after a mighty feat to gather strength for another one, come spring. After a short while Greta fell in tune with it and at peace with herself, ready for her own big test and accomplishment.

Greg's voice brought her back to reality. He was asking if she would like a round of mini golf. There was a new eighteen-hole miniature golf course adjacent to the rental building. "Do you want to give it a whirl, kiddo? You like mini golf."

Greta was winning. Susan, so jubilant just a while ago, looked preoccupied. Suddenly, sounding as if she just had an epiphany, she proposed, "Why don't you take some pictures of us? Who knows, maybe next time we come here we will have kids in tow."

Greta jumped at the opportunity. She loved taking pictures. She readily took out her PAT. She would have to pick up her tempo, however, if she wanted to keep up with the game. Greg was definitely going for a hole-in-one. She did not want to mess up a unique shot. She ran around the enclosure to position herself closer to the hole, with Greg facing her. She wanted to capture his expression when the ball fell into the hole. Hole-in-one it was. She pressed the release button. The shot must be great. The sun was right behind her, Greg's blue ball—he always picked the blue, Greta liked green—perfectly matched his navy sweater. He threw his arms in the air, roaring victoriously.

Excited, she tripped on the border and would have fallen if it weren't for Mike who caught her just in time.

"Just like her," uttered Susan under her breath.

"Are you alright?" asked Mike with concern.

"Yes, yes, Mike, thank you. Let me see whether the shot came out okay. Oh, where's my PAT?" Mike picked up her PAT that she dropped while falling. It fell smack on the tiled path. Luckily Greta had just purchased a novel anti-shock protective cover for the screen that made the PAT practically indestructible.

It took Greg two giant leaps to land right by Greta. "Is everything okay, Greta?"

Greta nodded, anxious to get her PAT back. As Mike handed Greta her PAT, it lit up. They both looked at the screen, hoping the shot wouldn't disappoint. Mike's hand twitched, as if he had touched a burning stove.

"What's the matter, Mike?" She followed his gaze. She saw nothing out of the ordinary. It was her latest wallpaper. It was a picture of her toy giraffe in their nursery.

"What's this?"

"It's my favorite childhood toy," replied Greta, shocked. "My parents gave it to me when I was four. I'm probably stupid, Susan definitely thinks so, but I feel that the energy of my parents' love is emanating from it." She looked defiantly but at the same time questioningly at Mike, as if yearning for his support. "What's wrong, Mike?" Mike's face seemed to have frozen. His lips became white, his eyes devoid of expression. At this moment, Susan, who was sulking alone at a distance all this time, joined them and hugged Mike. Greta did not repeat her question and just looked at Mike. He smiled and gave her a thumbs-up.

They went on with the game. The magic of just a few minutes ago was, however, broken. The spirit of their joyful unity had evaporated into thin air. Mike became taciturn and disengaged, for no apparent reason, concentrating only on his game. Susan became more and more aggressive and nervous, making one mistake after the other. Her every effort to snatch the lead from Greta had proven unsuccessful. She was now hanging slightly apart from the bunch, brooding, chewing on a twig, and leaning heavily on her putter. Greta was on a roll and leading by a considerable margin. She was usually very good at this game, but today her great photo of Greg seemed to have given her extra confidence, and she was euphoric and ignored the party's dynamics. Greg was his usual calm self, and in all likelihood, the only cementing presence at the moment. Like a good host, he was working the group, saving it from complete disintegration. A few words to Mike here, an encouraging smile to Susan there. Greta, perceiving everyone through the lens of her camera, was lost to society for all practical purposes. Greg knew her too well to even try. She was in her own world now.

Encouraged by the success of her first photo, Greta kept shooting. She did not have time to get a good look at her pictures during the game, which was becoming more fast-paced and intense by the minute, but she did manage to capture a few dramatic moments. She hoped she didn't mess up the focus and the pictures didn't come out blurry.

They were at the seventeenth hole now, a water hazard. It was her day. The ball flew neatly over the water expanse and landed less than a foot from the hole. It was a beautiful shot. The noise of a broken putter got lost in both Greg's and Mike's roars and cheers in pure recognition of her mastery. They were not exactly spectators rooting for their favorite team and forgot for a moment that this shot had probably sealed Greta's victory. Greta ran closer to her green ball, happy as a child. The men followed her.

"You are a true ball whisperer," said Mike in awe.

Suddenly, Susan uttered a sharp cry. Startled, everybody looked back at her. Susan was sitting on the tiles, her right leg extended forward at an awkward angle. In front of her lay a small round piece of wood.

"What's the matter, Susan, what happened?" They all seemed to shout at once, running to her.

"I tripped on this stupid log!" exclaimed Susan. "Oh, my foot hurts so much. And I broke my putter, falling."

Immediately, there was a commotion. Mike, yanked out of his revery, was trying to find a cold stone to prevent swelling, and Greta was folding her coat for Susan to sit on. Greg did not participate in the hubbub. He was standing a few yards away, looking pensively at the piece of wood in his hand.

The party cut the game short and carefully walked Susan to a bench near the closed food counter. The drink dispenser was still operational, and they bought some coffee and hot cocoa.

The day turned out to be nicely warm, after all, especially toward the evening. The air was fresh and crisp without the unfriendly prickliness of the first chills. It seemed the sun's rays were giving away the remainder of their warmth before Earth turned to present her other side to their vital radiance. No one was in a hurry to leave.

Even Susan was smiling again, upbeat and chatty as usual. Her foot had not even swollen, and she was thanking Mike, loudly and profusely, for hauling cold stones and putting them on her ankle.

Greta was sitting with her back to the table, scrolling through the pictures she had taken. Every one of her happy interjections was immediately followed by three simultaneous sounds of a received message from the PATs of her friends.

"Oh, Greta, stop that already, you can do it later," snapped Susan.

"Yes, indeed, Greta, there's no need to send us the pictures right away. They are great, though; nothing new here, of course. Thanks for the trouble, that was so nice of you! Why don't you drink something?"

"I'm good, thank you. You know it's no trouble for me, Mike. I love taking pictures. Better tell us more in detail how the inspection went. Any tips for us?"

"It was all pretty straightforward, right, Mikey?" cut in Susan.

"You know I'm not an authority on such things," replied Mike slowly. He was visibly ill at ease. "I don't even see the need for all this fuss. In my opinion, a few pictures of the nursery would be more than enough. I think even the inspectors were hard-pressed to come up with relevant questions. They went into a ten-minute discussion about Mick, you know, Susie's childhood toy that she had miraculously recovered after so many years. Can you believe it?"

Greta was about to say something, but Susan cut her off rather unceremoniously.

"That's because you had work to finish, Mike. You just wanted them to leave as soon as possible, and everything seemed unimportant to you. I think those questions about the furniture arrangement were quite to the point."

"I don't know...I still think the Mick discussion was the most interesting part." Mike looked straight into Susan's eyes.

"What old toy?" This time, Greta was able to squeeze in her question. She looked at Susan, who suddenly stooped a little under

Greta's inquisitive gaze. *I have never realized how short Susan is!* thought Greta in bewilderment, rather irrelevantly.

"The toy Susan's parents gave her when they first took her to Disney World, hasn't Susan ever told you that story?" Greta looked at Mike, then at Susan again. Mike was calm and amiable, as always. "It's a small rubber Mickey Mouse. Nick dragged my parents to the gift shop, and he liked a huge stuffed Mickey, so of course they bought it for him. They bought me a toy too, after the sales lady asked them what toy the cute little girl had chosen, meaning me."

Susan looked defiantly at Mike, who just kept looking at Susan with a strange expression and did not comment.

"I liked it a lot, not surprisingly; it was the only toy they ever bought me. I usually got hand-me-downs. Anyway, I lost it soon after. It was almost thirty years ago. You can imagine my excitement when last week, while shopping for my friend Miranda's daughter's tenth birthday (you remember Miranda, Greta, right? Her girl is already turning ten, unbelievable, isn't it?)"

Greta did not remember Miranda, or her daughter.

"So, quite accidentally, I saw this Mickey toy, that looked so much like my old Mick. I purchased it, of course. It turned out to be the wrong toy, and I kept it in the box and left it on the table in the nursery and forgot to put it away for the inspectors' visit. It was practically the first thing the inspectors noticed. I went through all this trouble to prepare the room for our baby, and there we were, talking about a random silly toy! It was so frustrating. I got so worked up, and because I was not prepared for the turn the meeting was taking, I freaked out and instead of calmly explaining that this toy was not intended for our baby, I blurted out your theory about good vibes, or whatever. Are you very mad at me, Greta?" asked Susan.

"Don't get upset, Susie, dear. It's really no big deal. I know your parents were not exactly there for you, and you thought my attachment to the old giraffe sentimental and silly, so of course I got confused!" She laughed.

•   •   •   •   •

On the way back, Greg and Greta remained silent. Greta was thinking about Susan. She did not buy her story about Mick. It did not make any sense. Why did Mike get so taken aback upon seeing her phone screen? Why was he so unpleasantly surprised that she had a favorite toy? Even if Susan did not tell him anything about it, most children have a favorite toy. There is nothing extraordinary about it, so it must be something else. *Susan said today she used my good energy idea. So, Mike should have known I have a toy, too!* That's it. Susan claimed it was her idea. Of course, maybe it just didn't come up at the time, and they were just happy the inspection went well.

Wait a minute! Greta realized something. *She must have ordered her toy way before I told her about my giraffe. And, come to think of it, she was appalled, but then she explained that it was because the idea seemed too outlandish. Nothing makes sense! I'm probably just imagining things. She must have just kept this giraffe story from Mike to hide the fact that she got so nervous during the interview she had to repeat what she considered pure nonsense. Yes, that must be it. Susan lost her cool. And she hates to lose her cool. She has to always be in control.*

It did seem like the most reasonable explanation, but Greta was not completely satisfied with it. The familiar nagging feeling remained. Mike was strangely persistent and talking as if urging Susan to come up with an explanation in front of everybody, as if he was trying to expose her. And Susan's speech was too garrulous and she was talking faster than she usually does.

Why did it have to come to this? Vague dissatisfaction gave way to a sadness she always felt when stumbling upon shady dealings. She was sure something was not right.

Only when the skyline of the city filled their front window, Greta spoke slowly, after taking a few shots of the imposing sight that had never ceased to amaze her.

"I haven't heard my VS monitor for a while. I wonder whether it's broken? When did it go off last time? Ah yes, when I spilled water on Susan's skirt. No, there was one incident after that. In the coffeehouse, where I was with Susan after her interview." She paused, pondering something. "Greg, do you think Susan really twisted her ankle today?"

Greg thought for an unusually long time before answering. Greta knew his habit of considering his answers carefully, but this time she thought he probably didn't hear her and was about to repeat her question when Greg finally spoke.

"You know I don't quite like her..."

"You seemed to enjoy her company today when she was making fun of me for botching that serve and sending a ball out." Greta could not resist the urge to taunt Greg a little and shatter his composed shell. Greg did not fall for it.

"Susan can be pretty charming when she gets what she wants," he said simply. He ignored the jibe, trying to find the right words to present his thought in the most precise manner possible. "It's not like I don't want to share my thoughts with you, Greta; it's just that when I'm not sure about something, I don't want you to come to the wrong conclusions because of my rash words...

"When I think about something, my thoughts may roam unrestrained, in any direction, tackle any dubious ideas, venture into dark corners. I don't have to double check myself; I don't have to be responsible. When I talk to you, or to anyone, I have to make sure that what I say is correct and I can prove my idea."

"This is a scholar talking, Greg! I understand now why virtue is considered boring by many. What happened to good old gossip?"

"You know I'm not one to gossip. Boring it may be, but I do not want to falsely accuse someone, even in a seemingly innocuous conversation."

"Oh, Greg, on with it already! Don't be such a pretentious ass!"

"Okay, I think it was a bluff. She just couldn't stand losing to you. She just can't stand losing, Greta."

"She is pretty unique that way, isn't she?" It was the first time she did not jump to Susan's defense when Greg uttered unkind words about her friend.

"I wouldn't put it past her that she broke the putter out of frustration and it gave her the idea of a broken ankle. The woman is nuts."

"I don't know, Greg. It's just that if someone could go to such lengths over a stupid mini golf game, what would she be capable of when something much more serious was at stake? I'm scared, Greg."

"I'll protect you, don't be!" replied Greg jokingly, but his eyes remained serious. "Frankly, I did not expect this question from you, Greta. I guess I underestimated your woman's intuition."

"I don't think you did, Greg, dear. You may have overestimated your male intelligence."

Greg laughed heartily, but with a faintly perceptible note of surprise, duly noted by Greta. "I think I underestimated you, period. You have no receptors to attract evil. It slides right off you. You usually don't even register it. And you don't have any mechanisms to fight it. Your aloofness is your protective layer, like a film of oil on the water's surface helping smooth the waves, at least to a certain extent. So, I'm surprised. Now I have to be especially careful about what I say."

"Why is that?"

"When you defended Susan no matter what I said, I felt more secure expressing a different point of view. Now you yourself have doubts. I have to be extra careful not to sway you in the wrong direction."

"What makes you think I can be so easily swayed?"

Now it was Greta's turn to fall silent. "I don't think people fall for tall tales. You need hard facts to prove your point. But then, people rarely listen with their head, more often than not their feelings are involved. Charismatic but unscrupulous leaders with a special gift of persuasion often hold millions under their spell, manipulating them by tapping into good or dark corners of their nature, while some dorky genius doesn't stand a chance to convince anybody. That's why there are so many Cassandras."

"Exactly. People believe what they want to believe, Greta. If I reinforce your idea, you may be inclined to be less scrupulous about collecting adequate evidence."

"True. But if we both came to the same idea, there is a strong chance it's a correct one. I know you're not trying to deceive me. You are not a manipulator, Greg."

Greg remembered Susan's big shining eyes, full of good-natured happiness, and how she timidly put her hand on his arm to attract his attention when she saw a bird she was unfamiliar with and thought that he might know. Indeed he did, and she was delighted and impressed by his knowledge. Maybe Greta was right all along, after all, and Susan was just an unfortunate kid trying to make something of herself. "We will wait and see, Greta. We are home."

•   •   •   •

They docked the planocar and entered their apartment. Greg did not feel like continuing the conversation and pretended he had an article to read by the next morning. Greta wondered why Greg's behavior was suddenly so ambivalent. But then, she was not her usual self either and was having conflicting feelings about Susan. I guess Greg is right, we will have to wait and see. That night, she dreamt about the mini golf course. She was talking to Greg, who was looking at her, smiling, then suddenly his face started to stretch, morphing into Mike, looking at her with admiration and encouragement.

Greg was also not quite pleased with himself. He liked to know exactly what was going on, to have everybody and everything securely pegged and in their places. He liked to be on firm ground; today, he felt like the ground was shifting under his feet, and that made him sick to his stomach. For the first time in his life, doubt crept into his mind and he did not like it. His system of values risked being eroded and going to the dogs. At least he had the advantage of not being surprised at the thought that teamwork did not preclude competition. It just evolved and took new forms. He had seen so many new modalities.

So, he was not surprised by Susan's shenanigans. He witnessed the likes of those every day. Bullying, demoralizing the opponent—check. Diverting attention and impeding concentration—check. Hard core seduction—check! Those were the usual suspects, the black- and-white figures of his daily life, and he preferred it that way. Grays were not his forte. When Susan timidly touched his hand today, he did not feel virtue or sin. He felt passion, desire. Not entitlement, but desperate desire to belong. Who was he to judge? Her methods were not straightforward, granted, but they were not criminal either.

He could not concentrate on the article. His thoughts got hopelessly muddled. He stood up and went to the window. The twilight city lay in front of him, as far as the eye could see. He could not see any black or white. Black and white, safe heaven. No mistakes, no doubts. No living. The city was an exquisite study in shades of gray, darker and well-outlined buildings in the front and fuzzy, barely discernible off-white forms on the horizon. Where would Susan fit in? What about Greta? Yes, what about her?

Susan looked so genuinely frightened, vulnerable. It was such a visceral cry for help. She touched a chord that was going rusty in Greg's soul. He felt Greta did need protection, too, but Greta was so elusive. If he was not swift enough to catch her attention, she would run away into the vastness of her intricate mind and he would be left grabbing emptiness. Susan was a force of nature, a tsunami coming at him, engulfing him and entraining him into her depth, pulling with a strength that made him powerless, at her mercy and scared but at the same time exulted. He was yearning for both, unable to choose.

He remembered that he wanted to buy the antique black-and-white bookends he had no time to complete the order for that morning. He clicked them and was about to proceed with the purchase, but stopped midway. They suddenly seemed too straightforward to him, lacking in elegance and sophistication. Angry with no apparent reason, he closed his PAT with force.

• • • • •

"How could you do a thing like this? This is unbelievable. The same inspectors are coming to their house in less than a week. Now they are going to think she stole your idea!"

Susan's eyes became two glaring slits. "What makes you think they'll believe me, and not her?"

"You were first, and people tend to believe the one they hear first. But it's not only that. I don't know...Greta is too genuine to be believable. She is so artless, so vulnerable..."

"That's exactly my point," said Susan coldly. "You should not talk into a void; you have to talk to your audience. I made sure to talk to those people so they would believe me."

"You crossed the line, Susan. You stole from her." He thought for a moment and smiled all of a sudden. "Greta is like an exotic musical instrument, maybe something like a sitar? People don't recognize the instrument and the melody sounds too foreign and fancy to them. They would rather stick to the tried and true than to give her a chance. Yet her melody is so warm, so vibrant, so full of life...Greta's not being equipped to defend herself when wronged by her best friend has nothing to do with stealing others' ideas in order to look more suitable for the role of a mother. The point is, Greta doesn't have to lie to pass these tests, Susan. You do." Hit by a sudden thought, Mike looked at Susan in dismay. "Are you even fit to be a mother, Susan, if you have to go to such lengths to prove that you are?"

Stunned, Susan was listening to Mike with her eyes closed. She did not want him to know what was brewing in her gut right now. The bitter venom of rancor, hot and sticky, was filling her being, shooting to every part of her body. *He has lost his mind!* Shedding instinctively all pretense Susan replied, "I don't know, Mikey. Sometimes I wonder myself." Then she added with the usual toss of her head. "But I want it." And having left the room, she whispered under her breath, "And I always get what I want."

All her superb intrigue, the jeweler's precision of her gestures, gazes, words, her stellar performance! It must have been her day, and to hear that Greta, the dead fish, who could not even secure a victory when it was coming her way, was vibrant and exquisite. What a cruel joke!

"Your VS beeper is going bananas, Susan!" Susan heard Mike's words, as if in a fog. "It must be broken." Susan looked at her monitor. Red alert was blinking. *My back is against the wall. There's no way out,* thought Susan, petrified. She was too exhausted to start another battle.

"That must be my foot, Mikey"—her tone became instantly plaintive—"It hurts something awful." Limping a little, she went into the bedroom. Mike said nothing.

CHAPTER TWENTY-FOUR

Susan was sitting alone on the terrace, mulling over what to do next. Greg had clearly wavered, but there was no follow-up. Moreover, he avoided staying alone with her or just being close to her during their get-togethers. It annoyed her, for it meant a hindrance and the necessity of finding other ways to proceed with her plans. She was tapping the table with her fingers, as she always did when the needed solution did not come right away, thinking about Greg and Greta. Susan felt jealous of their relationship. It seemed they connected on some deep level; Susan could not make out which. Was this love? Susan wouldn't know. Whatever it was, she refused to believe that his feelings toward Greta made him devoid of weakness. *He is not a philanderer, okay, he overindulges himself in his work instead*, thought Susan angrily. Stop. His work. If not another woman, then his work. Maybe Greg wouldn't be so impervious to temptation if his precious work was at stake. She did not know any of his work acquaintances, though. They didn't seem to be of use anyway. Judging by Greta's remarks, they were mostly Greg's close coworkers, none of them prominent enough. She had to think.

The day was cold, but the warmers, built in along the perimeter of the terrace, made it fresh but pleasant. A thin thermal jacket would have been an ideal choice, but instead, she opted for a soft bulky sweater that did nothing for her figure, but felt wonderful. She deserved a break now and then, didn't she? Mike was working anyway, as he often did lately. Susan was monitoring the situation closely and checking his screen regularly, but she had never seen him staring at a blank screen again. She still couldn't believe he would get mad at her over Greta. She was not even his type...if she ever was anybody's type. One would not have time left to love her, having to make sure not to commit some moral impropriety. Greg could live with her because he had eyes only for his microbes, dry stick that he was. They were the same, maybe that was what brought them together in the first place. Susan could not forgive Greg her unsuccessful stint.

Two outcasts! Anyone would suffocate with either of them. The Moon is where they should go. The Moon. Of course! What do we have there? Susan took out her PAT. The Moon branch of the Institute for Viral Research. Its most prestigious branch, as a matter of fact, located on the outskirts of the Moon colony due to the extremely dangerous nature of their work. *Who is the director, I wonder? Unbelievable. Look and you shall find!* Susan sat up straight in her chair. A face she recognized immediately was looking at her from the bio's picture. That was the man Greg had a falling-out with at the charity event they sponsored and where Greg and Greta met for the first time. John Drake, that's it. He did seem like a guy determined to go places. Sure enough. Director of the most promising branch of the Institute, for more than three years now.

She sent John a message. How was he doing? Did he remember the event her charity had sponsored a few years back? Would his Institute be interested in something along the same lines, maybe just on a slightly more modest scale? Her foundation would be honored to be of help and told him to shoot her a message should he be interested. The year was drawing to a close, and Susan did have some funds at her disposal, so it could actually work out quite nicely.

He was interested, and replied within an hour, without any beating about the bush. Susan deduced that she was correct in her assumptions that John may have satisfied his vanity and was looking for another position, preferably on good old Earth. Susan offered to meet him virtually, in the setting of his choice, to discuss the details.

By the evening of the next day, the new scheme was already set in motion. During the chitchat after the business part was over, Susan adroitly brought up Greg's name. After a minute-long vituperation, he, exhausted at last, asked about Greg's whereabouts. Susan obliged, adding casually that he and his wife were planning to have a child, and as far as she knew, they were set on raising the child themselves and were ready to go to great lengths to keep the kid close. At the present time, they were going through the selection process which was coming to an end. Hoping to win was, of course, very foolish and unwise, considering the slim chance of getting such permission.

The look in John's eyes told her unmistakably that his mind had started working in the anticipated direction.

• • • • •

Greta was looking at the inspection appointment notice on the cocktail table. The inspection was supposed to be in three days. On the one hand, she was thrilled by this tangible proof that the process was in full swing. On the other hand, it had caught her almost unaware. To begin with, they had to move to a new apartment after they had officially declared they were ready to have a child within a year. They were so lucky they found a bigger apartment in the same building. It could have been a huge hassle, otherwise.

The nursery was painted and furnished, but Greta was still feeling like she was not quite ready. She was so happy taking care of everything, of every little detail. Nevertheless, knowing that her choices were about to be subjected to public scrutiny was giving her cold feet. She stood up and went into the nursery. She flipped on the light switch, and a soft amber-colored glow filled the room.

She was very proud of the way she had decorated the baby's room. She did not want to use the obvious gender colors—pink and blue— and stuck instead to her original mint green (Greg having withdrawn all his objections), gray and white, with small splashes of navy. For as long as Greta could remember, Susan made fun of her for buying matching kitchen towels and expensive scented soaps. Now she was on her back for spending too much money on the nursery and baby clothes. "What does it matter, anyway, the child won't even remember anything," Susan would repeat in sincere amazement. One could very well pull it off on hand-me-downs, now that so many of their friends had children. She did not care what the brand was, as long as it was free. She was probably right, too, but Greta couldn't help herself.

Greta remembered every thought, every feeling behind each piece, and she loved the result. The shade of green she chose for the walls looked so soothing. The cloths, sheets, blankets were of the finest, softest cotton. The toys for the crib were cute and cuddly. There was no way the inspectors wouldn't be satisfied.

She especially loved the giraffe, her favorite toy when she was a child. All the perfectly beautiful new things, although undoubtedly gorgeous, lulled the eye, so this old faded creature instantly drew attention and became the focal point of the room. It was evident that it had seen better days, but, in Greta's eyes, its bold imperfection gave the place a special charm. She was not certain that she should keep the toy in the crib for the inspection. She was afraid it could ruin their first impression, but she was sure she would keep the toy for the child. She was convinced that the good vibes would safeguard her little one.

Greta loved family heirlooms. She believed these objects emanated some kind of protective energy from her ancestors. She could feel this energy and liked to surround herself with such things. It was not easy under the new anti-clutter rules that stipulated every individual was only allowed five keepsakes. Greta had a hard time choosing among the many mementoes she accumulated, but she absolutely could not let go of her favorite soft toy. She also had to cut her monthly new clothes and household items allowance in order to keep some of the things that had been in her family for generations. They were her lucky charms, her amulets.

Greta was not exactly sincere when she told Susan not to worry about the toy incident. She felt robbed, as if her home was physically ransacked, her privacy violated. Moreover, it seemed that if it weren't for Mike, Susan would not have told her about the incident. Decidedly, highly inappropriate behavior. The very idea now felt sullied, and Greta didn't feel like going with it. She decided to keep the giraffe out of the nursery for the inspection. Greg didn't mind one way or the other. She stood up, went to the nursery, and put the giraffe in one of the crib's drawers. There was still plenty of room there. The minute she had hidden her special giraffe out of sight, she felt relieved and cleansed.

•   •   •   •

Greta and Greg were waiting. The inspectors were already five minutes late, and Greg was slightly annoyed by their tardiness and by the whole procedure. Why waste so much time on things like wall color? His team was working on a new type of antivirus vaccine, and this time, they were weeks, if not days, away from a major breakthrough. Yet here he was, wasting precious hours on stupid inspections. Absentmindedly, he examined the nursery. Greta had done an amazing job. He was about to tell her, when the buzz of the intercom notified them that the inspectors had arrived.

Greta stood up, ready to greet them. The doorbell rang. The inspectors were interested in everything. They examined every nook and cranny of their nursery. They left no stone unturned. They enquired about the wall color (a random ad), the names for the baby (they had not thought about it yet), why they chose this particular room to be the nursery (they wanted Eastern exposure). Finally, the inspectors zeroed in on the crib.

Having apparently exhausted all possible questions, one of the inspectors—Greta heard her colleague call her Agnes—pulled the knob of one of the crib drawers with the words, "Oh, these must be really roomy,"—she stopped in mid-sentence—"what's this?" She pulled out Greta's giraffe.

For a moment, Greta just stood there, petrified. She had realized too late that the crib was probably not the best hiding place for the toy she didn't want anyone to see. "Oh, that was my favorite toy when I was three or four," said Greta without enthusiasm.

"So, why did you keep it? You must have given up some other item, under those new anti-clutter laws..." One of the inspectors was particularly inquisitive.

Greta immediately felt filthy. She did not want to answer. The words stuck in her throat and refused to come out. She curled herself into a small fuzzy ball, hugging her shoulders with her hands and burying her chin in her chest. *Disappear, disengage at all costs!*

She heard the door of the apartment across the hall close. There were two apartments per floor, and their neighbors were a young family with a little girl of three or four. *This must be the time she spends with her parents. The family must be in the hallway now, waiting for the elevator*, thought Greta automatically. Residents rarely used the elevators, unless they really enjoyed walking the streets, the old-fashioned way. The convenience and efficiency of the planocars converted all but a few die-hard wanderers into modern city dwellers zipping from place to place in their small slick vehicles. *They must be going to the swimming pool on the roof or to the playroom on the ground floor.* The little girl was running in the hallway, laughing. Her voice resonated across the huge space like a little silver bell.

Greta woke from her stupor. Her body that resembled a closed bud just a minute ago, started to open up. Her back straightened, her arms gracefully unfolded and firmly grabbed the side of the chair.

"I kept this toy for my future child," she replied, looking straight into the inspector's eyes, her chin slightly up.

"But it's pretty old and unsightly," pursued the same inspector, Agnes. She seemed genuinely intrigued, or maybe just happy to encounter something outside of the usual boring routine.

"I don't anticipate my child playing with it that much. Frankly, I don't think the poor toy can withstand any rough handling."

"Why, then?" Agnes kept pushing, now absolutely dumbfounded.

"I believe this toy holds my parents' love, the positive energy of all our times together, their glances, hugs, kisses. And when I place it in our baby's room, it will release those good vibes." She fell silent for a minute.

At that moment, she resembled one of the figureheads on the bow of an old ship, ready to enter proudly and fearlessly into unfamiliar waters.

Every time Greg looked at her, he could not help admiring how beautiful she was, standing against the background of mint-green walls, in her light-blue sweater, her blue-green eyes glowing fiercely. The sun played in her long blond hair forming a shining halo around her thin face. He remembered his fantasies of a few days ago with a shudder. Madness, pure madness! What was he thinking? He smiled at Greta.

"What a fantastic idea!" exclaimed both inspectors at the same time.

"May I ask, how did you come up with this idea? Did you read about it or hear it from some of your friends or acquaintances?"

Of course, it had to come to this. There was no way the inspectors could have forgotten their talk with Susan less than a week ago. "No, the idea is mine, but I did share it with a couple of my friends who also want to have babies soon."

"But why did you hide the toy?"

Greta began, a little hesitantly at first, but gaining confidence as she went along. "A while ago, I came across a riddle: 'Does a falling tree make a sound even if nobody hears it?' How arrogant of us to even briefly entertain the thought that our perception might make a difference! Please, bear with me," she added, feeling everyone tensing up. "Anyway, this is not what I want to say. The riddle made me somehow think of ordinary people who go about their duties, making our lives brighter and better, one day at a time, not expecting praise and glory for their accomplishments, big or small, in return—the unsung heroes. No one knows their names, maybe no one is fully aware of what they do, but the results of their actions live on, and they do make a difference. So, well, if I talked about my special toy, or even worse, if I tried to score off it, it would have lost its magic."

CHAPTER TWENTY-FIVE

"Unbelievable, Pat, don't you think? Three women with childhood toys in this year's quota. That can't be a coincidence."

"No, Agnes, I suppose you're right. It can't be." The two inspectors had just left Greta and Greg and were now slowly heading toward the underground. "The last two, Susan and Greta, are friends, according to our charts. So, nothing really surprising there. The issue must have come up, and one of them copied her friend." Pat paused for a minute. "I did not like Greta that much. So full of herself. Putting on airs of great academic knowledge. All this talk about falling trees. Such nonsense."

"I don't think she means to put down other people, Pat. She probably has no idea people can feel put down by such musings. It looks to me like she has no bad intentions toward other people, no malice. She has nothing to hide. So, she is not very careful about choosing her words. She is ingenuous, not arrogant. Extremes meet, they say."

"I don't think it matters, Agnes. You always defend the weirdest types. For practical purposes, as you said yourself, opposites converge. Whether Greta is a fool living in her own world or an arrogant bitch, I feel Susan is better suited to be a mother. She seems to be a warm, nurturing woman, attuned to people and their needs. Do you remember what we were taught at our latest refresher course?

The qualities we need most are those of respect and good-natured kindness toward other people."

"Yes, of course, I do; you, on the other hand, always fall for the conniving type, Pat! The ones who sing the nicest tune, which may not reflect their true self. That does not mean Susan wasn't the one who came up with the idea. Greta, a consumed introvert, also seems to be a socially awkward type, in the sense that she doesn't know how to approach people to get what she wants or prevent them from using her. Do you know what I mean?"

Pat answered, "You are too good to her. I'm not sure she's as genuine as you think. She just doesn't give a damn about other people and what they think. She thinks she's smarter than everybody else and is always right. Pretty much the same as the first one, Evelyn. Only Evelyn is older and has been around more. It is her second child, I understand."

"That's what I'm trying to say. Greta is too young and inexperienced and says just what she feels because she thinks everybody would be delighted with her epiphanies. She believes there is just one absolute truth, and she has uncovered it. She must have grown up in a loving environment. One can only envy her. Anyway, such people can be jarring, but also refreshing. No, I believe she is sincere, to the point of not always acting in her own best interests. Her best friend is quite the opposite. Very socially smart. That does not make her a liar, either, but of these two, I think Susan has a better chance of pulling it off. Greta seems to be a better candidate to come up with such an idea in the first place. The Susans of this world are not sentimental. Rather, they can't allow themselves to be sentimental."

"Even if Susan stole her friend's idea and is such a good actor, she will raise a down-to-earth person who will know the ways of this world much better than any exulted woman, too absorbed in abstract knowledge to learn to care for the real people who surround her. What if her child is completely unlike her? She has to learn how to listen."

"You make a good point there, Pat, I agree. I just can't stop thinking about her words. I don't think it's nonsense. Wouldn't you agree that Greta had summed up the essence of motherhood?"

"You are right, I guess, but it's so counterintuitive, somehow."

They had reached the underground entrance at this point and had to part ways. "Listen, it's not our decision to make anyway. Let's put all the information in our reports. We will submit separate reports, since we tend to disagree on some points, and let the Commission decide."

CHAPTER TWENTY–SIX

"That was a narrow escape, Greta," said Greg the second the door closed behind the inspectors. "You were so beautiful at that moment, though. Your eyes shone in such a mysterious, alluring way, as if you were a siren. Why did you go into all this highfalutin mumbo-jumbo anyway? That was suicide. It's appalling how you can complicate the simplest things. I doubt inspectors have the time or inclination to ponder philosophical riddles. Besides, you got it all wrong. No matter. I think you navigated the tight spot brilliantly, in the end."

"I know, I know! That's the beauty of great words. They can make your thoughts go in so many different directions. I was not talking about the meaning of this riddle, not exactly. I just said that it made me think of unsung heroes; that sometimes the only way to make a sound is to not make it your goal. I just didn't know how else to explain what I felt. Sometimes, I feel there are no words to express my feelings."

"Nonsense, Greta, there are always words to express one's feelings."

"You must be right, but I'm very bad at communicating my ideas. People always assume the opposite of what I'm trying to say. It was so unexpected. Now, in hindsight, I understand how stupid it was of me to keep the toy in the baby room, but oh well, what's done is done."

Greta was not inclined to share Greg's enthusiasm. She was not at all sure they had aced the inspection.

"That's your problem, Greta, but this is what makes you so unique, too. You always say what you think. You don't make any adjustments for your audience."

"What do you mean? You're not suggesting I should lie, are you?"

"No, not at all. It's just that different people might understand the same words differently. You have to try to keep in mind whom you are talking to. Look, if you came into some casual diner and said, 'Would you be so kind as to pass me the salt?', people might think you were making fun of them. This is just not how people talk in a place like that. On the other hand, if you said something like, 'Pass me the salt, hun,' in some posh surroundings you would definitely raise quite a few eyebrows, don't you agree? It's not enough to understand for yourself. You have to know how to communicate your thoughts to your specific audience. Some people are so good at communicating, they don't even need to understand what they're talking about. They get to hear the trees that never fell, in a way." Greg chuckled. "I'm joking!" he added quickly. He expected Greta to laugh at his clever example, but her face became serious.

"It's just that I do not want to win independent parenthood at any price, Greg. I want only the best for my child. If I'm not good at being a mother, I would rather the State raise him or her. But I so want to be good, Greg!"

"You will be, I have no doubt about it."

"You are right, of course. There are many ways to communicate the same thought. Those who are good at this craft have such an advantage over the rest. What good is it to have something to say if you don't know how to say it? Especially, and how ironic, considering I'm a journalist?"

"And a great one, at that," said Greg, and he was not being a hypocrite. "People need someone like you to tell them the truth. You are authentic and sincere, and most people feel it immediately with their gut. When you need to get something in return, that's another story. But then again, it's always easier to give than to get, for some."

$\bullet \qquad \bullet \qquad \bullet \qquad \bullet \qquad \bullet$

Greg told Greta he would join her in a few minutes. "I decided to buy those bookends, after all. I had been eyeing them for quite some time." Just a few days ago, he had dismissed them as too simplistic. Today, he decided they were exquisite in their simplicity. Oh well, who needed justification, he loved them.

"Good for you! They are beautiful."

"Don't you think they're a little simplistic?"

"No; rather, dramatic. Maybe just a little tragic."

"Tragic? Why? It never occurred to me to think about black and white as tragic."

"Well, if something is black or white, no halftones, it means no compromises are possible. And inflexible ones break but don't bend, as they say."

"So, you find the bookends beautiful?"

"Well, an object is not exactly beautiful in itself. It has to fit the design of the space it is placed in, and the design has to fit the person, don't you agree? Maybe something truly exquisite has the power to transcend, maybe even transform, its surroundings. To a certain degree, at least. Just as with people," she added after a moment's silence.

"You are amazing, Greta! Never a dull moment with you!" Greg laughed happily.

"Why is that?" Greta smiled.

"You keep me thinking, inquiring, wondering. I will never tire of you. I love you so much, Greta. You are my object of sublime beauty."

Greta laughed. "I know I should shut up and not say anything, but I just can't let it slide, Greg! I'm sorry, darling, you contradict yourself. If I am *your* object of beauty, that doesn't mean I'm a universal sublime object of beauty." She added quickly, "I will be completely satisfied if I'm an object of beauty just for you, Greg. I don't need to excite and please everybody."

"You got me there, I admit."

"Besides, your test tubes steaming with viruses must be no less intellectually stimulating for you, are they not?"

"Well, none of them are as beautiful as you are. Let's go to bed, it's getting late."

Greta smiled to herself. She didn't want to point out that she thought Greg was contradicting himself again. Besides, it looked like he wasn't in the mood to continue the philosophical discussion. Neither was she.

CHAPTER TWENTY-SEVEN

Greg did not expect to hear from John.

"Come on, man, I know our last encounter left a bad taste in your mouth, but we are not children, for Chrissakes. I'll be straightforward—I need to get back to Earth. The job is captivating. But you know this yourself. The life—to die for. The VR job on the landscape is breathtaking, and there are no devices that spy on you and constantly report your slightest transgression to the insurance companies, or worse, the Public Order Ministry. You can eat and drink whatever you want, buy whatever you want, and as much as you fancy. You can smoke wherever you please, man! But I turn forty in a month, and it just hit me—if I don't get married now and have a child as soon as possible, I may just as well put the idea to rest. And one thing that's difficult to find here is a young beautiful girl interested in starting a family and living happily ever after, you know. The local atmosphere does not agree with them. Ha-ha. Pun not intended."

Greg assured him that he was interested, but had an important meeting at noon. He would get back to him in the evening. Just five years ago he would have grabbed this opportunity on the spot. Now the situation was so different. Now he had Greta. She was so intent on winning the contest, they both were, and to raise their child themselves on Earth. They had no trouble reducing their consumption and complying with the nutritional guidelines.

Moreover, they shared the views and principles behind those policies. They loved their beautiful planet and wanted to protect and preserve it even if that meant certain personal sacrifices. Those were not even sacrifices, just responsible behavior.

Right. Quite so. But what if they did not win? He had not followed the subject closely; it was Greta's department. He reached for his PAT. The figures were pretty depressing. A tiny percentage of all applicants made the cut, and applications were on the rise. *Why on Earth?* thought Greg. But he had neither the time nor desire to go off on a tangent, although his curiosity was piqued. *I should ask Greta.* An acute pang of pain quickly brought him back to reality. To accept John's offer to swap positions without saying anything to Greta would be immoral.

He had always considered high moral principles the cornerstone of his character. One precise blow, and his personality was crumbling. To tell her now meant to admit he did not believe in their victory, even worse, that he had a personal interest to wish for their defeat. He got a sense from John that his mind was set and he was not inclined to wait another week, let alone a couple of months. John was a great scientist, and he and his talent would be up for grabs. He would find another position without much trouble, although Greg's laboratory was definitely his first choice. What a conundrum, what temptation, what torture.

Greg's life, a roller-coaster of victories and setbacks, proceeded in fits and starts. Yet he was inching forward, day in and day out. His life was more of an expectation of a life than a real one at present. He did not hedge his bets; everything was hinged on the ultimate outcome. If he failed to make a breakthrough, all the trials and tribulations of the last years and all his sacrifices would have been in vain. Was it a mirage, was he really on a wild goose chase? One way or the other, the Moon offered enormous opportunities for independent research in the area of his dreams.

Five years ago—no, less than two years ago—before he offered Greta to start a family...oh, he spoke too soon. He stopped in the middle of the thought. How he hated himself at this moment. He was nothing but a phony, a travesty of an honest virtuous man. He felt real pain, as if torn apart, as if it were not his moral beliefs, but his body enduring the torture.

The sad truth was that he realized he was faithful to Greta not because he loved her. He did not want to make his life more difficult than it had to be. Like recently with Susan. He rejected Susan's advances not because he loved Greta, but because Susan was unpredictable, disruptive. He did not choose love; he chose control.

He could live without other women. He could not live without his work. *I wouldn't be myself anymore. Something vital would be killed in me. How will I be able to give if the source of my ability to give were dry? But Greta has the right to know. I have to tell her. What a painful awakening. No matter how beautifully I camouflage it, Greta will see through all this bunkum.*

Greg ordered a bottle of scotch. Gloomily, he poured himself a drink. The way he saw it, either he was a scoundrel, or he would pass up the opportunity of a lifetime. He knew from the very beginning what choice he would make. It was better to hate himself for secretly accepting the offer than to hate Greta for making him do it if he rejected it. Did that turn him into a monster? Or did Drake just conveniently provide him with a flashlight to see his true nature? As it was, he had reached the farthest and darkest corners of his soul, in all its ugliness, and was shocked. So proper, so fastidious. He did not avert his gaze. He was staring straight into its cold mocking eyes, feeling its foul breath on his clean-shaven face. The more he looked into the deepness of his soul, the more he drank.

Greg believed that in human affairs, things operated along the same scheme as with viruses. The virus has to bind to a human cell. So, the cell has to have a receptor the virus can sink his hook into. Evil needs the same kind of receptor in a human being, a predisposition, however small. There are no unaccounted for transgressions. Everything you do gets a separate life and grows bigger with years. And then there comes a moment when it returns to haunt you. He should not have consented to independent parenthood. It was a weak, foolish act on his part, which meant he should not have married Greta, who would not be happy if she couldn't raise her child herself. He was not betraying her now; he betrayed her the day he married her.

He wrote John and proposed a VR meeting the next morning.

•   •   •   •   •

John gave him a comprehensive tour of his facility. Greg liked what he saw. Now he had no shred of doubt that he made the right choice. After the institute, John showed him around the neighborhood and the center of the colony, which was the size of a small town but growing fast. Its skyscrapers were much taller than those back home, and the towering grandeur of the buildings overwhelmed and even slightly depressed him. They resembled bristles from afar, which made the colony look even more unfriendly, but as far as Greg could judge from his short VR excursion, John was right. The combination of Earth's technology and the local entrepreneurial spirit, bursting with creativity as yet uninhibited by ecological restraints, produced extraordinary results.

As John explained, the town was enclosed in a bubble of artificial atmosphere matching the one on Earth. Food warehouses and consumer-goods production facilities, fully automated, were outside the town, forming a tight circle around it, working at full capacity to satisfy the voracious appetites of the colonists. The competition for proximity to the town was fierce, steep premiums notwithstanding. Waste, in huge amounts, was accumulated further still, forming the second circle around the colony. This vivid testimony to excessive, bordering on chaotic consumption hit Greg unpleasantly.

The stores were online only, but they all had a presence in the city via interactive screens of various sizes and priced accordingly. The streets gave the impression of overzealous peddlers touting their merchandise from every square foot of the sidewalks. Every facet of human needs, real or imaginary, was carefully studied and attended to.

This feverish, disorderly, colorful mess was appealing and repulsive at the same time; most of all, frightening by the sheer abundance of goods and the urgency with which they were thrust upon you. Greg imagined Greta on those streets and recoiled at the mere thought. On the other hand, it could be a fun experience, useful for her work. Greg decided to investigate the living conditions more in depth later on, for Greta's sake; he did not care about them. He was not exactly ascetic, but not prone to self-indulgence either. Just too busy to care.

His mood went south irreparably. He cut short his tour, mumbling something about his promise to be home for an early dinner and hurriedly disconnected himself. In the evening, he confirmed his decision to swap positions with John. They did not anticipate any problems with the authorities. They were correct in their assumption; their arrangement was approved within a week. Both Greg and John needed a few weeks to wrap things up. Greg agreed to take the last shuttle of the year to the Moon; John would leave the next day, by the same shuttle on its way back to Earth.

CHAPTER TWENTY-EIGHT

Susan was smoking in the lounge. Her body was absolutely still, but her mind was racing, considering and rejecting one plan after the other. Now that she and Greta were approved for the next series of tests—Friends and Family—she was panicking. She never volunteered with the Service, as Greta did. Having a child of her own seemed like such a fantastic idea at the time, but she helped her out for four hours out of six during Greta's second week with the Greens.

At the time, Greta and Susan were both just toying with the idea of becoming mothers. Susan especially did not pay much attention to this topic. Whenever Greta brought it up, Susan became visibly bored and would laugh it off and say it was not in her New Year's resolutions yet. Greta was a little intimidated and put off, so she finally stopped talking about it. She was thinking more and more about becoming a mother in practical terms. Greg was still not quite ready. Greta felt he would need some time to adjust to the idea, and she would be able to nudge him in the right direction. In the meantime, she investigated the subject in depth. She did not want to follow the traditional path. She could not fathom being satisfied with visiting rights. The more she read and thought about it, the more she was leaning toward trying to raise their child themselves.

There was no childcare for working parents, obviously; the institution was abolished when the State took over child raising. The "independent" parents had no right to hire nannies full-time.

Considering the scientific basis of the new child-raising and educational system, the State needed strict accountability that could be achieved only if parents were the sole care providers. Whenever they wanted time to go out or time to themselves, they could, however, use the Volunteer Service. Families with young children were encouraged to volunteer in a pilot project designed to familiarize potential parents with taking care of young children. The service was free for parents and the volunteers were working pro bono as well. Parents were allowed six hours a week for such services. It was considered that more time off the strict regimen would result in failing to meet monthly goals. Parents were free to use their close relatives as babysitters for additional hours, but they would do so at their peril. Should the child fail to meet the monthly developmental goals for three months in a row, the State had the right to take the child from the parents.

Susan had not taken it seriously. She usually took everything seriously, even the smallest things, but there it was. She made a mistake. She had to find a way to undo that mistake.

Susan remembered she had not yet checked her calendar. That was unacceptable. She should not become sloppy with such important things. She had all her friends' birthdays there, as well as those of their husbands, wives, and kids, together with their names, favorite foods, drinks, colors, toys, and whatever information she had ever come across. As a matter of fact, she kept a file on everybody of importance in her life. That way, she could whip up a nice personal message in a matter of minutes. She also jotted down all the likes and dislikes of the people she deemed important enough to put in her files, and was actively regifting presents, relying on those records. She became so good at it, no one ever suspected foul play. Strictly speaking, it could not be called foul play, considering how skilled she was at satisfying people's needs with other people's gifts.

Presently, she saw that it was Lisa's birthday. They were meeting Lisa later in the day. She sent her a nice card and shipped the bottle of champagne she had taken at her own thirtieth birthday. *I knew it would come in handy someday,* thought Susan happily. *I bet Greta doesn't even remember it's Lisa's birthday today.* She would crush Greta, that dreamy weakling. It would be a piece of cake. She shifted uncomfortably in her seat. *Oh well, too bad.*

Susan was not a weakling.

•   •   •   •   •

The huge ice cream cake in her favorite flavor—double dark chocolate—was a work of art. Greta ordered it from the best city bakery, six months in advance. The elaborate tower was covered in butterscotch frosting that required a whole week of work. Susan could be very sentimental about certain things. Her thirtieth birthday was one of them. So, Greta went all out. She thought about every detail. Greta wanted her best friend to feel loved and let her creativity and spending soar without restraint. Foreseeing greater expenses than she could afford, she cut her clothing allowance to three items a month, starting in January. Any voluntary reduction of consumption was encouraged by considerable monthly bonuses, so by early May, when most of the payments were due, she had a nice sum stashed away.

She rented one of her friend's favorite venues. She was hesitating between two of Susan's favorites—the Old World and Seventh Heaven. Then, upon probing Susan for her preferences, she settled on the Old World. The Seventh Heaven was a modern joint, with tables for two floating in midair on white panels in the shape of clouds. Greta got a kick out of it when she attended the restaurant for the first time. Granted, the idea was appealing, but the food was nothing special, and now Greta considered the whole affair rather tacky.

Greta picked Susan up after the latter's hair appointment. Greta told Susan she would like to take her to dinner at Old World to celebrate her birthday. When they arrived, everyone was already there, waiting for them. The surprise worked wonderfully. It was clear Susan did not expect anything on such an extravagant scale. The surprise was genuine, there could be no doubt about it, but Greta was slightly taken aback by Susan's initial reaction. In all of the surprise parties Greta had attended, the birthday girl would radiate the pleasure of being the cause and the center of such splendor, giving out fake "you shouldn't have," and "I did not expect this," although it was clear that everybody should have and it was more or less exactly what was expected. Susan, on the other hand, looked like a robot that had encountered a situation it had not been programmed to deal with and was just going through the motions.

Susan did not like surprises for exactly that reason; she did not like not knowing how to react. She needed time to calibrate her enthusiasm to the perfect level between the ingratitude of a spoiled brat and the excessive neediness of a wallflower, not that she had ever feared being accused of the latter. She immediately ducked into the bathroom under the pretext that she had to freshen up. In a few minutes, having peeked out to be sure the crowd had finally left her alone, she sneaked into the kitchen. She opened the fridge and took out a bottle of her favorite Becks that she knew Greta would have for her. She drank it slowly, her gaze lost somewhere in the depths of the petal jungle of the lonely peony on the counter in front of her that must have been left out in the heat of the moment. Beer did not match the atmosphere of the venue or the pink color scheme (Susan's favorite) of the party. To accommodate the birthday girl's taste Greta ordered two six-packs of her favorite beer, Becks, and kept it in the kitchen fridge with one six-pack of raspberry beer she ordered just for the color.

Susan was now calm enough to examine the contents of the fridge and grab two bottles of the rosé champagne she found there, as well. It would make a nice birthday present, everybody appreciated it. The bottles were obviously taken out of their packaging before being put into the fridge to cool. Susan looked around. Nothing was lying on the counters. Her eyes continued to search the premises, suddenly concentrated on a mission. Her gaze stopped on two huge garbage bins. Susan lifted the top of the one closest to her. Sure enough, she found two perfectly preserved boxes under some disposed wrapping paper. Two boxes did not fit into her bag, so Susan had to limit her bounty to just one packaged bottle, but not without trying to shove both of them in her bag. The bottles were designed to take any shape, to save space in the stores' refrigerators, which served her purpose wonderfully.

The boxes, on the other hand, hadn't changed much in the last centuries, except probably for the addition of a built-in speaker which allowed recording of personal messages. It had been introduced more than a century ago, and was not exactly a novelty anymore. She thought the house must pay a sky-high waste premium to keep using those huge cardboard boxes, biodegradable or not. In the end, unable to let the empty space in her bag go to waste, Susan decided to settle on one packaged bottle and one without its box. She stopped by the bathroom again to adjust her makeup and joined her friends who were beginning to wonder what could have possibly kept her so long.

Susan was born in May, a very fortunate occurrence as far as fresh flowers were concerned. Greta ordered peonies, Susan's favorite flower, in bulk. It was not possible to have them delivered the night before the event, the only available slot being two days prior to the party, and so Greta had to keep them in her bathtub, making sure they didn't wilt. The aroma and the responsibility gave her an awful headache, but she managed to keep the flowers in top shape.

A huge vase with peonies adorned the mahogany-clad hallway, reflecting in the many Venetian mirrors that walled the hall. It was an intimate party for twenty-five guests. The long communal table was decorated with pale and dark pink peonies and pink candles in silver candelabra. Rosé wine and rosé champagne in heavy antique silver coolers were placed on a small mahogany side table with beautiful intarsia. Susan preferred beer to rosé and champagne, Greta knew that, but pink drinks matched the flowers and the venue so perfectly, Greta just couldn't resist the urge. It also matched the food much better than beer. The menu was rather traditional, not surprisingly, considering the old-fashioned flair of the venue. The waiters looked like noiseless flocks of birds in their black uniforms.

The most spectacular element was the cake. Greta spent many hours examining various designs and flavor combinations, before settling on one of the most elaborate ones that she figured matched Susan's tastes. The three-tier cake had a band of thirty pale pink flowers and mint-colored leaves winding from the bottom to the top with dark-pink birds on them, each flower holding a candle instead of stamens and pestle. Susan cried when she saw the cake. Still, after the party, she did slip to a few of the guests that the wine pairings were odd, in her opinion. That remark fell on deaf ears, for everybody was absolutely in awe. One simple soul emboldened by the very wine in question, no doubt, even ventured a question as to how Susan figured that, considering she had nothing but beer the whole evening. Her observation got equally lost in the happy tumult of the exiting crowd.

CHAPTER TWENTY-NINE

Greta woke up in a great mood. She felt happiness before she realized its cause, before any conscious thought entered her mind. It was one of those rare days in the city when you could just open the window a crack and not use the heating or cooling systems. Fresh warm air was entering the room and caressing her cheeks and forehead. It was September 17th, and it was her birthday.

Susan asked to see her in the morning for a quick coffee. She probably had a few last-minute questions to run by Greta about the surprise birthday party she had planned for her. A thirtieth birthday was a big milestone, and was celebrated accordingly. Best friends were supposed to spearhead the celebration. Susan was always so thoughtful, so attentive to detail. She would probably grill her about the minutiae of the menu. Full of pleasant anticipation, Greta smiled and jumped out of bed.

In an hour she was already sitting with Susan in their favorite coffee place more or less equidistant from both of their houses. Susan was not particularly cheerful. She avoided eye contact and was playing with the edge of her napkin. Greta knew her friend only too well. That was not a good sign. What could the matter be? The bakery messed up the inscription on her cake? The wrong brand of champagne got delivered? Oh, what did it matter? Surely, it could not be very important. Just as Greta was about to offer some words of encouragement, Susan said, "I'm so sorry, Greta, I messed up big time."

"What's wrong, Susie, is it something about the party?"

"That's the problem, Greta, I did not plan any party."

"What?" Her VS device leaped to red and started to beep hysterically. Greta just sat there without hearing.

"The timing really sucks, too. Early September is usually a very busy time for me, you know. I had a very important fundraiser two days ago, remember. I wish your birthday were a couple of weeks later. As it was, I didn't have a free minute."

"But Susan, why didn't you tell me? This is my thirtieth birthday, it's more than just any party. I would have organized it myself!"

"Oh, please don't make it worse than it already is! I'm devastated! I didn't realize it was that important to you, Greta! It is such a childish attitude, you have to admit."

"Childish attitude? All our friends had parties for their thirtieth birthdays, and you seem to have enjoyed yours, too!"

"You don't have to rub it in. I told you I was sorry. But if you want me to feel guilty for putting my job ahead of pleasure, please feel free. I can't really feel more upset than I am. This fundraiser was extremely important to me, really, Greta. You know how hard my job is, I can't afford to make mistakes. Your accusations make my heart bleed."

"I'm sorry, Susan, just forget it." Greta backed off. "You're right, it's only a party, after all."

The way Susan presented the facts, she did not do anything awful, as Greta felt at first. Susan's job was demanding, and of course she could not attend to her personal business. Yet at some level, Greta was not fully satisfied. She started planning for Susan's party months in advance, taking care of things and tweaking her work schedule accordingly.

Some of their friends were shocked, some did not care much, others agreed tacitly with Susan. Susan did not ask Greta to throw her a lavish party, it was strictly her own initiative. If she wanted to show off, that was certainly her right to do so, but what did Susan have to do with it? She was a hard-working woman with no money to burn, and she said she had been working on a very important fundraiser.

Susan played her cards well. Many agreed that one should not force others to respond in kind by spending money the person may not have. Most of their friends would not feel comfortable wasting such an amount on a stupid party anyway. Susan cleverly made them think that Greta came from money and she was not used to worrying about such things. Susan could not afford this luxury. She had to worry all her life. Susan was good at starting rumors; no one was ever able to trace them back to her. In this case, it was not difficult. Greta somehow looked the part.

The way Susan saw it, she had absolutely no reason to invest her time or money in Greta's party. Greta was under her thumb and there was no one among her friends Susan needed to impress. So, she made sure to look overworked and exhausted and act jumpy as if she had spent hours working on a project. She even invested some of her special occasions money in theatrical makeup that had served her well in the past.

Susan was able to hush the murmurs of disapproval. Only a few stalwarts of virtue were still skeptical, but sticklers for high morals, respectability, and such did not usually have the guts to stand up to her. Susan was not afraid of them, for she knew by experience that high moral principles only took you so far. She held the self-proclaimed defenders of virtue in great contempt and thought those were just spineless dreamers who spent the better part of their lives disgusted by the world's vices and lacked the courage or the smarts to get what they wanted. As a result, they were limited to their own world at the base of the mountain of human achievements, admiring their own perfection. Their indignation would subside over time for there were many things to object to in this world, and life would soon provide them with enough fresh fodder to be indignant about. She turned out to be right.

Greta was not upset that she did not get a party *per se*. For her, the main point of the party was to know she had people who would try to make it a special day for her, show that they cared. Greta wanted to make Susan's birthday special. She was prepared to make certain alterations to her life plans and professional schedule. She would have acted differently in Susan's situation. In fact, she did act differently. Susan not only did not want to do the same for her; she did not even feel compelled by gratitude.

But was it even fair to expect people to feel and act the same way in similar situations? Maybe Susan did dismiss the party as a childish luxury she could not afford. Susan was a matter-of-fact woman. Greta wanted to believe and to forgive, and believe and forgive she did, but the tiniest worm of doubt had found permanent abode in her heart. A tiny worm of sadness, for the world wouldn't be the same anymore; less perfect, less shiny. A tarnish. A small gray area.

·　　·　　·　　·　　·

Susan turned on the light in her walk-in closet and stood there indecisively. The shelf in front of her held numerous gifts and other objects earmarked for regifting. Now she needed something to make Greta feel truly special. She meticulously went through the whole stash. She frowned, imagining what her friends would think if they ever saw this bounty. Susan had mastered the ability to stretch her buck to perfection. She thought the notion itself must be unfamiliar to those coming from money. If they happened to hear the expression, the knowledge would still be purely theoretical. They would have to stretch their imagination to come up with things to spend their money on. She did not allow herself but a few moments of weakness. With the usual defiant toss of her head, she was back in the saddle. *Whatever. It is what it is.*

The idea of giving joy to those you cared about, especially the ones who could use some help, had slowly transformed itself over the centuries. The growing prosperity and abundance of merchandise made it difficult to choose the right gift. The custom started to degenerate into an exchange of things of equal value, and more often than not, of equal uselessness. Registries remedied this to some extent, but could not prevent gifts from ultimately succumbing to cash-giving, which made the custom meaningless. The anti-clutter laws excluded gifts from the monthly allowances, while allowing their exchange for other items for a nominal commission. The custom of gift-giving started to get its second wind.

Nothing quite fit the bill. Susan sighed. She wouldn't be able to get off easily. It looked like she would have to buy something, which was her last resort, but the situation certainly warranted it.

Her gaze fell on her jewelry box. She had bought a bold silver necklace with emeralds on her trip to India with a bunch of friends after her junior college year. Greta could not join them; she had to work as an intern, which was a prerequisite for getting her degree in journalism. Susan purchased this necklace in a small place after two hours of haggling, for very little money. Actually, so little she doubted those were real emeralds, but she preferred not to dwell on the thought and did not share the details with Greta. Greta commented on it in delight many times. It suited Susan's features and made her look even more striking. That would be perfect. She had already gotten a lot of mileage out of it; it was time to retire it. Their mutual friends knew the exotic piece and would immediately credit Susan for making such a generous gift. Everyone knew how much she loved that necklace. *And it won't serve Greta that well, either.* Susan smiled maliciously. *This is so not her style.*

· · · · ·

Greg tried in vain to make a reservation at a decent restaurant. It was to be expected, considering the last-minute character of the request, and that it was a Friday. That was when Greg decided to try the new app that became enormously popular in the wake of the last pandemic. For a rather steep monthly fee, you could make several reservations a month and have dinner at a VR restaurant of your choice in any location. You obviously had to cook your dinner, but the VR surroundings were of astounding quality, and could have fooled a local. You were under the impression that you were sitting in a coffeehouse in Florence, in a bistro in one of the backstreets of Paris, or a restaurant on the Amalfi coast.

Greg ordered a nice bottle of wine and cooked an unsophisticated pasta dish—he had no pronounced culinary gifts—and chose alfresco dining in one of the restaurants of the Cinque Terre area. His effort, along with the novelty of the experience, made it special and remedied the situation perfectly. After the meal, Greta went to the terrace to finish her wine while Greg was checking his lab results for the last time before going to bed.

She saw a delivery drone from afar, while it was still a small dot in the sky. Soon she could clearly see multicolored balloons, many of them. *Some kid will be so thrilled tonight.* Greta smiled to herself, approvingly. *What a great thought.* The drone was moving in her direction, and soon Greta could discern a small package beneath the colorful balloons. Out of curiosity, she started counting them. It was a challenge, doomed from the very beginning. They constantly changed their positions and she could not see the ones in the back, but it gave her an excuse to keep looking. They were a festive sight that matched her mood perfectly. The drone made a slight turn and landed on the terrace right in front of her. It was a gift from Susan. Having oscillated between "cloudy" and "rainy" ever since the rough morning, Greta's barometer resolutely jumped to "sunny" as far as Susan was concerned. Greg did not comment. Greta assumed he was still resentful, and did not try to make him change his mind. She considered it wouldn't look right after all his efforts.

The next day, Greta mailed the necklace back to Susan. In the enclosed note, Greta thanked her best friend for such an exquisite and valuable gift, but said she couldn't accept it knowing how precious it was to her. Susan was not surprised.

CHAPTER THIRTY

They were sitting in an old-fashioned bar, another nod to times of yore. These were becoming very popular with the young crowd and old folks alike. Greta, usually opting for modern design in food and entertainment venues, felt like this one would be a lucky exception. There was something so bewitching about its dark wooden panels and huge mirrors gleaming mysteriously in the dim light of the crystal Old World chandeliers. Susan was always on her back for being so fussy. She did not favor any particular ambiance, as long as the company and price were right. Not that Greta paid more attention to the curve of the chair than to the person who filled it, but it did matter to her and she had preferences. The ambiance could ruin or save her mood.

It was Susan's idea to celebrate the successful completion of the inspection and getting clearance for the next stage of the parenthood exam, the so-called Family & Friends test, with a few of their closest mutual friends. Susan and Mike were running late, as was often the case. Greta, Greg, and the two other couples were already at their second round of drinks when Susan and Mike finally showed up. Although Susan was laughing and chatting as usual, Greta, who knew her better than anyone else in the party, sensed right away that Susan was not herself. Susan's foul mood escalated as the evening progressed, along with the number of consumed drinks that were more frequent and stronger than usual. Her voice became louder and harsher and the jokes less benign, but no one seemed to mind.

Greta was seriously worried, however. She grabbed the first opportunity to inquire in a low, concerned voice, "Why are you so on edge, Susan?"

"Me? Why on Earth would I be on edge?" Susan's pretty face twisted in an ugly grimace. "It's you who should worry, Greta, not me!"

"Worry? What about, Susan?" replied Greta. She was astonished by her friend's words and even more so by the rudeness and aggressiveness of her voice.

"You are the one who got complaints from neighbors when you were babysitting for the Greens." The party fell immediately silent and listened closely.

"What are you saying?" Greta gasped. "No one has ever complained! Wait. Wasn't it—" Susan suppressed her words with a hoarse laugh. She was visibly drunk now. Her voice became shrill, and Greta could see ill-concealed hatred in her eyes.

"Don't you remember how scared the Greens were that the neighbor might file a child abuse complaint? Screams and noises were coming from their apartment for hours every day you were taking care of the what's-his-name child of theirs?"

"How can you say that?" Greta asked. Red blotches covered her cheeks as was always the case when she got nervous. She jumped up from her seat, almost in tears; she faltered. "It was when you were taking care of little Jimmy while I was taking the two-hour refresher course twice that week. The Greens okayed the arrangement, as long as it was only for one week, which it was. And there was no question of neighbors complaining. Meagan, his mother, was just very upset."

Oh, Susan remembered only too well, and was scared now that other people, the aforementioned Greens, first and foremost, might remember, too. That little rascal! He had just learned to walk at that time and it seemed he had to investigate every nook and cranny of the apartment. Whenever he got tired of this fun activity, he would eat, or poop, or just cry for attention. Susan was itching to read the latest tips on the makeup palette for spring that were coming en masse on her favorite blog, "Tides of Times." It seemed like such a good time for it. When else would she have a whole two hours to herself? She tried in vain to interest Jimmy in toys and some snacks, not exactly the paragon of health food. She was aware that his VS device would record the unauthorized nutritional deviation, but she was sure she would be able to pin them on Greta. The fact that the child did not talk yet surely was a boon. The spoiled brat would not sit still for two minutes. Of course, she had no choice but to let him cry. The child had to learn to wait. Nobody would have known, anyway, were it not for the emergency that made Meagan come home one hour early.

"Oh, of course I can say that! After spending time with you, the kid was just impossible. He refused to nap or eat regular food! Were you feeding him cookies or something so you could finish the article you were falling behind on?"

"Okay, Susan." Greta's voice was suddenly firm. Her friends looked at her in surprise. Even Susan was momentarily taken aback, her eyes losing focus and flickering. Greta seemed absolutely calm now, only her bright blue-green eyes were gray and murky. "You are way out of line now. I can't believe it had to come to this. No one has ever complained while I was taking care of Jimmy. I have it on record that I had my refresher course twice that year, dates and times. The agency can confirm the dates I was volunteering for the Greens. All the complaints are meticulously documented, so it will be very easy to establish that none were filed while I was taking care of Jimmy. And although I doubt the Greens remember the days I asked them to replace me, they certainly would remember it was you whom I named as the person who'd take care of their son while I was gone. So, if there were complaints on your watch, it will be easy to establish."

•   •   •   •   •

Greta had volunteered for the Greens for two months. Her babysitting experience was a rocky road. After the first day with eleven-month-old Jimmy, she felt she would never have children of her own. She was drained of all energy and barely made it home. She had to take a taxibot, a luxury and absolutely futile waste of money, considering the effectiveness of the mass transportation system and the slightly more expensive convenience of private planocars. Little Jimmy was delightful, but he seemed to be a representative of another species. Greta had no clue what he wanted, and why and when he wanted it. She was afraid of him.

Babies must be equipped with fear sensors, for as Greta's agony and frustration grew, the kid became more demanding. Feelings of failing at her task greatly contributed to her purely physical exhaustion. Hungry, barely on her feet, ears brutalized by constant whining, Greta was on the verge of tears. That was not how she imagined kids to be. She had no idea how to approach the little alien, who was scrutinizing her with his smart watchful eyes that showed unequivocally that he knew he was in control of the situation. That evening, she said nothing of her experience to Greg, who was too frustrated by the disappointing results of his latest experiments. He asked her perfunctorily how her day went. She was relieved she didn't have to lie, as she was not prepared to tell the truth. First, she had to figure out what and where the truth was.

The next week was a nightmare. The lack of understanding and cooperation was absolute. The kid would start fussing the second Greta voiced any suggestion. By the end of the first week, having exhausted all her ideas of engagement, she was sitting beside Jimmy and absentmindedly pulling at his legs just to make sure he was not going anywhere. All of a sudden, his face broke into a funny crooked smile, and a little laugh that seemed to come from his belly, followed. Greta felt a jolt. A bond, finally! It did not last long; in just a few moments the little human was back to his usual tricks and Greta was relegated to her role of running after little Jimmy, trying to fix the mess he left behind.

Greta, however, was so elated by her success and suddenly refreshed, she started building him a tower the moment he stopped, intrigued all of a sudden by the strings of his pull-up pants. He had a set of brand-new foam building blocks in many shapes and colors. Analyzing this episode later, Greta had to admit she was itching to put those untouched blocks to good use, her mind craving some meaningful activity; she just did not have a moment of respite to fulfill her wish.

The tower grew ever taller. Greta got so caught up in her pursuit, she did not realize that all the movement and noises from the fuzzy navy form that Greta knew was her Jimmy, had stopped. Then, with her side view, she perceived a bright spot on the peaceful navy background of Jimmy's outfit. Reluctantly, she paused and looked straight at Jimmy. A small hand was stretched in her direction. It held a big red building block. Too scared to breathe, not to push away the newly found partner, Greta took the block from Jimmy's hands and put it at the very top of her masterpiece. Two little hands started to clap.

Later, she took him outside for his nap, since he absolutely refused to nap in his crib. Maybe ideal children in the ideal world did, but not Jimmy, and certainly not with Greta. Even getting him dressed for a walk and putting him in his stroller was not a task for the faint of heart. Sometimes, giving him a snack while pulling on his winter garb worked to distract his attention. She would blabber whatever came to her mind with as much conviction as she could muster, and the child would finally condescend to be dressed and strapped into his outing device, apparently fascinated by the ability of adults to produce so many nonsensical sounds at such a speed.

Greta would usually stroll along a wide avenue near the Greens' building until Jimmy's eyelids started to droop, his eyes lose focus, and he would fall asleep. That was a glorious moment, the highlight of Greta's day. She then could find a quiet nook, take off her gloves, and consume her lunch tubes, holding them intermittently with one hand and putting the free one into her pocket to warm it up. It was a particularly bitter winter.

Such lunches were rather sad affairs, but that was the best Greta could come up with. She could not duck into any food joint for that would wake Jimmy up immediately. After lunch, she would pace the avenue for two and a half hours, the time Jimmy needed to nap. The only disturbance that could throw the perfect plan out the window was the unbearably loud sound of the fire engines and ambulances' sirens. These vehicles had a special altitude designated for them exclusively, but they still used their sirens as an extra precaution; their speed was two or three times greater than the speed limit for planocars.

It usually took Greta quite some time to quiet down the awakened child and sometimes he would not go back to sleep. It was especially annoying if one of those vehicles happened to pass when Jimmy was about to fall asleep, for it usually put the happy moment off for an unpredictable amount of time, or could even prevent him from napping altogether. No wonder Greta dreaded them. She was constantly on the lookout for the approaching sounds and would try to hide in a side street until the vehicle flew by.

That day was no exception. Jimmy was carefully cocooned in several wool blankets so that only his nose and eyes were showing. Empowered by her modest morning success, Greta felt much more in control. She was proudly pushing the stroller along several blocks up and down the avenue, smiling encouragingly at Jimmy. Suddenly she felt much more comfortable operating the clumsy contraption. She could now pay less attention to the road, avoiding passersby and other navigational hazards. A fire truck appeared out of thin air, its siren growing louder by the second, filling the space of the entire block with deafening sounds. Surrendering to the inevitable, people covered their ears or dodged into the first door that came their way. Greta looked at Jimmy. He was not yet asleep and his eyes, like two dark gems, were glaring at her from the woolly softness of the covers, apprehensive and inquiring at the same time. Greta nodded to him, smiling, as if to say not to worry about a thing. She saw the little face relax, and in a moment or two when she glanced at him again, he was already peacefully asleep.

That day, the Greens were shocked to witness a very unusual sight. Greta was sitting on the carpet in the middle of the room, her legs comfortably stretched. Their precious son who could not sit still for a moment, was leaning against Greta's legs and trying to stack his new building blocks one on top of the other. He looked at Greta for support and acknowledgement of his success from time to time and she would just smile at him encouragingly.

• • • • •

The sides presented conflicting reports. An investigation followed. The well-being of a child was at stake. The Greens were shocked and annoyed at suddenly being in the limelight. They resented getting in the middle, especially considering a dispute between the two allegedly best friends smelled fishy to begin with.

The last thing they needed as independent parents was additional attention. Their knee-jerk reaction was to play the situation down. They said they remembered the episode, but vaguely. They lied.

"I told you it was going to blow up one day!" fumed Allen, Jimmy's father.

"I know, I know, you were right. We should have sent a report that our child was not happy with Susan, but they don't say that in hindsight everybody's vision is 20/20 for nothing." Meagan tried to keep a level head and figure out what line of defense to pursue.

"We could lose our rights now because of this nitwit Greta, who didn't even bother to find a decent replacement for herself. What a formidable prospect!"

They remembered that night very well. They were at a concert, a recital by a pianist they were looking forward to attending for a long time. The evening, however, was off to a bad start. Allen, a doctor, was unexpectedly summoned to the hospital, and they had to leave shortly after the intermission. They had side seats, as always, to be prepared for such eventualities, but their departure still caused a lot of displeasure among fellow audiophiles sitting in their proximity, some of them friends. When Meagan came home, she found Jimmy in tears. By the looks of him, he had been crying for quite some time. She quickly dismissed Susan, who was filling in for Greta, thankfully, for the last time, and quieted down her little boy.

The good thing was, they were not themselves in the crosshairs; Greta and Susan, as prospective mothers, were. So, as long as she and Allen stuck together and provided a coherent and believable version of the incident casting blame at one of the two and leaving the Greens in the shadow, they would most likely be fine. Greta was allowed by the terms of the contract to find a replacement in case of emergency, so the Greens did nothing illegal by accepting Susan.

They should have, however, as diligent citizens, filed a complaint against Susan, to put on record her lax approach. Meagan noticed her switching her PAT from video to standby mode. She was obviously watching something instead of taking care of Jimmy. Meagan just got lazy. On the other hand, who could have thought it would come to an investigation? That was their only weak link. They could have denied any crying on Jimmy's part, but unfortunately neighbors heard him, too, and on more than one occasion. One of them mentioned the next day that Jimmy had been crying a lot lately. Those pesky concerned citizens! Meagan was in a hurry, and not disposed to go into any details, so she said Jimmy was teething, just to get the neighbor off her back. Bingo! Of course, they had to make it look like Jimmy was a little sick during that time.

They said at the last hearing that they did not remember any trouble with either of the girls. Greta did have a bit of a rough time in the beginning, but she seemed to have found the right approach to their little Jimmy later on. And as a matter of fact, Greta still sent him occasional gifts and dropped by once in a while to say hello to him and have a cup of coffee with Meagan.

They did not see Susan but one time. She had substituted for Greta two times, and the first time Greta came back before the Greens. Once Meagan came home earlier than planned, so she met Susan personally. She did not pay much attention to her. Their son was safe, that was all that mattered, and they knew that was the last day of Greta's unexpected unavailability anyway. Their son was teething at that time; she did remember Jimmy crying when she came home, but it was not a meltdown, he was just fussing. There was nothing Susan could have done in addition to what she had already done, to ease his pain. She seemed very level-headed and dependable.

CHAPTER THIRTY-ONE

After the quarreling friends had left the bar, the remaining two couples remained silent for a while, assessing the information and its potential ramifications. Then they all started talking at once.

It was a shock on many levels. No one had ever seen the two best friends quarrel. Everyone agreed that Susan bossed Greta around, but also that she helped Greta in their social circle and protected her.

"Whom do you believe?" Lisa, a small, blond, mousy-looking woman finally grabbed the bull by the horns. Her small face was transpiring the impatient eagerness of a great lover of rumors and gossip.

"Greta and Susan are both so nice, it's just a misunderstanding, I'm sure," countered Nelly, a big, dewy-eyed brunette. "Susan must be scared."

John, her husband, a narrow-shouldered, frail-looking man with a thin face, delicate features, meticulously parted black hair and a thin mustache, cut in, "Greta just tried to score points at Susan's expense. Conniving woman. She put Susan on the spot. I would not be surprised if it was her who provoked the child in the first place. We should look at personalities, not just facts. Greta is an icicle, whereas Susan is so warm and caring."

"I can't agree with you more, John," Lisa intervened. "Remember the birthday party Greta threw for Susan? Such a self-promoting, calculating woman. Put out all this expensive rosé Susan didn't care for, just to show off. So arrogant, too! She acted like she owned the place."

"You are not being fair," broke in Nelly. "Those emulsified oysters with fake caviar, for example. They go so well with rosé. Besides, Greta did have beer for Susan in the fridge. Everybody else prefers wine to beer, including you, Lisa. Isn't rosé champagne your drink of choice? Look, you're sipping it now. Remember how you were raving about that Veuve Clicquot champagne?"

"The party was not about the guests, Nelly, it was about Susan. And she was very disappointed, I remember her saying so after the party. I bet she felt slighted. I wouldn't even put it past Greta that she wanted to humiliate Susan by exposing her tastes as inappropriate for such an upscale venue as the Old World."

"That requires such a devious mind. But I agree with you, Lisa, that would be very much in Greta's character," chimed in John.

"I'm pretty sure Greta just wanted to throw a great party for her friend, and honestly, I think she succeeded. She spent a lot of her own money on it, and she certainly invested a lot of time and effort. Everybody loved it."

"Believe what you will, Nelly, but frankly, I think you're being too gullible and falling right into her trap. I'm pretty sure the only thing on Greta's mind was to show off. She is such a hypocrite. Look, she just sent me a birthday card, just general niceties, and a small bouquet of lilies-of-the-valley." Nelly and Tim gasped, for they had forgotten about Lisa's birthday. "Susan, on the other hand, sent me a bottle of Veuve Clicquot, exactly the kind we drank at her party and that, I don't deny, is my favorite. So, now that no one is watching to sing her praises, when there is no fanfare, who is more thoughtful and generous?" said Lisa triumphantly.

No one saw the need to draw attention to the fact that fresh lilies-of-the-valley must have cost Greta an arm and a leg this time of year.

Tim, a big blond brawny guy had pointed out that Greta provided reasonable proof, and there was nothing to discuss here. If anything, it was Greta who was a bit of a pushover, and if one of them were to deceive, it would be Susan, not Greta.

"Indeed, no good deed goes unpunished. Just listen to you."

At that point, he left the table and went to play darts with a group of rowdy men at the other end of the bar.

"Just like you, Tim," said Lisa. "Passive people like you put our society in danger. You refuse to take sides and try to get to the bottom of it!" Tim just waved his hand dismissively.

The table remained abuzz late into the night. In a few days all four of them submitted their independent accounts of Greta's and Susan's child-caring experiences and their thoughts about their readiness to become mothers. Lisa and John took their duty very responsibly and spent hours on meticulously documenting their thoughts. Nelly, having forgotten half the facts by the next day, tried very conscientiously but was not able to present anything but a lamentable hogwash of contradicting shreds of information. Tim's report was very succinct and contained just a few sentences stating, more or less, that he believed Greta did nothing wrong.

Their reports, together with those of the Volunteer Service and the Greens, were to be examined by the Parenthood Commission, to determine whether the couples qualified. The Commission's decision was considered final and could not be appealed. The couples could, however, restart the process in two years.

CHAPTER THIRTY-TWO

The Commission convened on December 10, 2120, to come up with their final list of independent parents approved for 2121. The city's slots were subject to a particularly harsh competition that year. Arianna, head of the Commission, started the meeting and outlined the situation.

The percentage of women and men for whom raising children was all they desired for personal fulfillment had been rather stable for the past decades. The present scheme, established three years ago, took this fact into consideration. The number of independent slots matched those figures and slightly surpassed them, making sure no individual willing and deserving was left behind. Most importantly, these numbers were not high enough to jeopardize the needs of the economy, should the independents fail. Already, so early in its implementation, the number of contestants was by far exceeding the theoretical calculations and continuing to grow at an alarming pace. It was too early to draw any long-term conclusions. Was it just a statistical bump of no significance or was it an early sign that the general strategy was faulty? Why this change of heart? A hot discussion ensued.

"Ungrateful, as always! I don't understand modern women. So much is being done for them. They are given a unique chance to fulfill their professional dreams without dealing with the downside of motherhood. No sleepless nights, no worries over bruises, broken bones, illnesses, bad grades, college preparation process, you name it! Now they are truly on equal footing with men. And they can still see their kids often enough.

"Shush! Don't even try to tell me that men and women were equal in that respect for more than a century. Baloney. It was still considered by many a woman's job." The tirade was purely rhetorical, for no one tried to object in the first place.

"This is mind-boggling! What else could they possibly want? The numbers are too high to write off as bad career placements, which seems to be the case as far as male contestants are concerned. Oh, I'm sure many of them just don't know what they want and are ready to blame anyone but themselves for their troubles," ranted Betsy.

Betsy was Arianna's deputy of many years and her self-proclaimed devout supporter, not that the latter needed any, or was allowed to have one by the voting rules and regulations of the Commission. She was a middle-aged woman who carried her body, presently clad in a gray business suit, with dignity and poise. She was known for her common sense and an uncanny ability to redirect information flow from every source straight to her, and as a result, being always in the know about everything. Betsy transferred to join Arianna, whom she knew from her college years, from the HR department of a big firm; they attended the same psychology classes.

"Maybe people don't want to be helped?"

Everybody looked at the man who dared to question Betsy's words, waiting for the continuation. Other members of the Commission preferred not to mess with her. He was not young, but his bright blue eyes had kept their boyish vivacity. His name was Mark. He wore a simple navy crewneck sweater and navy slacks; his gray hair and short beard were impeccably groomed. Although the smell recognition was not added to business VR applications for money-saving reasons, one could bet he was wearing a barely perceptible but exquisite cologne. He was well into his seventies, and an emeritus psychology professor of a prestigious university.

"It looks to me to be part of a broader issue. Maybe people just want to live their lives the way they choose, make their own mistakes, find their own ways to fix them, be able to claim their victories as well deserved? What if they want to earn that right and fight for it rather than have something handed down to them on a golden platter? Maybe they prefer to be free to being perfect and happy and want the same for their children. Perhaps, deep inside people are moral, after all, in a twisted sort of way, in that they have a natural desire to earn what they have and not just enjoy the spoils." Mark threw in this controversial firecracker of a statement quite intentionally. He loved debates. He lived alone and had time on his hands to indulge in his passion. Betsy would have none of it, however.

"Don't patronize me, Mark! Children don't have to suffer from their parents' lack of educational talent and experience. Let's not condone making a child's soul a playground, even worse, a battlefield, for a clumsy parent."

"Most parents are not monsters; they want what is best for their children."

"Listen, we've been there before. The truth of the matter is that most parents are not equipped nowadays to raise labor for the modern economy. Full stop. For many centuries, parents complained about the hardships of the process and how it prevented them from doing what they had dreamed of all their lives. Now that they're allowed to do just that, they want their previous lives back. As I said, ungrateful."

"We are drifting away from the task at hand, Betsy, Mark, please," interfered Arianna. "Let's not waste time on pointless discussions. We have to deal with the issue one case at a time. We already have enough strong contestants to fill the independents quota for 2121. This is pretty unusual in itself, since we're normally not full until the end of December. We are down to just two families this year who may qualify and be offered the final secret test. The males in both families are highly satisfactory. Both Michael and

Gregory would be terrific fathers, we all agree. Now, we have to decide whether Susan and Greta are fit to be good mothers.

"We have to keep our eyes on the ball. Our goal is to determine whether the contestants would be able to raise the child in accordance with modern requirements, that is, whether they have what it takes to raise a happy member of our society who could realize his or her potential. We are not trying to find out whether they're good people. We need to determine who's able to be a good *mother*. Keep in mind our secret motto, the judgment of King Solomon on the character of a true mother. So, what do you think about Susan and Greta?"

"Greta seems to love children and have a good rapport with them. So, the child will probably be happy growing up," volunteered Emma.

Emma was a young graduate with a philosophy major, working on her PhD. Her face was dominated by big eyes that looked scared and nearsighted, even though she must have had the corrective operation by now. Her thin nose, a shade pinker than the rest of her face, was constantly dripping so that she always had a tissue at the ready, clenched in a small fist crowning a wrist so narrow, one might think it would break from a most quotidian task. Her shapeless sweater was a bad choice for her small frame. It was hard for the other members of the Commission to take her seriously.

"Unless it's all hypocritical manipulation, and no real love from her is involved." Betsy disliked Greta's kind that "put on airs" and lacked simplicity.

"What makes you say that? Why would she seek to raise a child?"

"Maybe emptiness, or laziness. No real achievement in professional life. She lives in a world of her own, that's for sure. She has no interests. She is imaginative, which is a requirement of her profession, of course, but clueless. I'm alluding to her explanation of why she wants to raise a baby herself. It is poetic and a strong image, sure, but lacks substance. There's also this incident with the toy. It seems she is jealous of her friend Susan, who is a very brilliant young lady, well-read, interested in the cultural life of the city, good at sports, attentive to her friends, articulate, and smart. Susan graduated from Armard! Guillard is also a great school, but Armard! One must be exceptional to get into Armard."

"But you contradict yourself. A clueless dreamer would not have the smarts to connive against her friend. Wouldn't it be more in Susan's character, as one of the inspectors who had reported the incident had suggested?"

Leaving Mark's remark without answer, Betsy changed her line of attack. "Greta doesn't even seem to have good friends. Nelly and Tim did not bother to invest a decent amount of time and effort to write adequate reports in her support, just short, inconsequential and unconvincing notes; no solid proof, no profound analysis. To judge by their writings, one would think Greta's great moral character goes without saying. Lisa and John seem to really like Susan. They presented meticulous, logical, and well-formatted reports; they must have spent hours on them. What a touching detail about a bottle of Lisa's favorite champagne for her birthday! There's no proof, but off the record, it looks like Greta tried to hide behind her friend in the Greens incident. The Greens deny any wrongdoing on Susan's part, and the neighbors might have confused the dates; the incident took place more than two years ago."

"Let's not bring in unproven and at this point already unprovable statements," cut in Arianna. "Our decision has to be based on hard facts. We don't want it to be influenced by incorrect or biased information. I would say the Friends and Family part shows that Greta, undeniably, is good with children. She likes them and they like her; the fact was corroborated by parents and neighbors alike. Susan, on the other hand, is good with adults. She is respected and well-liked. Greta's child is more likely than not to grow up happy, but will she be able to steer her baby in the right direction? I have no doubt that her strong-willed and down-to-earth friend Susan will.

"As to your assumptions...Greta is aloof, inattentive, has no real bonds with anybody. In her only true relationship, outside her marriage, of course—the one with Susan—she is clearly the sidekick, a fact that this contest made all too apparent. Greta may have lost her imperturbable congeniality that she seems to be known for and did try to usurp the toy idea. After all, it is Susan who has the story of a favorite toy from early childhood, not Greta, who just mentioned having one, without further details. She pretended she didn't even want to show it, but it looks more like a clumsy ruse. Who would hide something in a room that was supposed to be thoroughly inspected? For the same reason, she might have tried to blame Susan in the Greens' case, as a desperate attempt to make herself look good by pinning the disasters of her first days, when Jimmy was crying a lot, on Susan. We don't have enough information to substantiate Greta's claim that Susan did not pay enough attention to Jimmy. But as I said, let's not allow our speculations to influence our decision.

"So, let's recapitulate. Sticking to the facts, we may safely assume the following: Susan has a full, successful life. If she contemplates such a drastic change, it means she seriously wants to dedicate her expertise, knowledge, and talents to raising her child; Greta doesn't seem to have much going for her. She could just consider raising a child out of boredom. She is an average journalist, but other than that, has no footprint, if you know what I mean."

"Of course, being aloof as she is, she must rarely touch Mother Earth," Mark uttered softly. Everyone laughed readily, relieved from the stress of the seriousness and difficulty of their task. "Susan approached this challenge as a job assignment. And it was a job well done. Strictly speaking, it is a no-holds-barred assignment. I'm not talking about clearly illegal activities, of course, but a certain amount of cleverness, to spice things up a little, is not unwelcome. We do not want it to become too stuffy an affair, do we?"

Mark stopped, hoping for a response that would allow him to defend his highly uncommon point of view, but everybody was too tired by that time to react to his new provocation.

"Susan, by the same token, has a great chance to succeed at child-raising, with her businesslike approach and iron grip. Greta is lacking pretense to a frightening degree. One is wondering how it is even possible to live into your thirties and remain so, I would say, unpolluted and polarized. As we age, the black-and-white contours of our early perceptions become fuzzy and blurred, gray areas take up more and more space as we make allowances. For some of us, the initial colors switch altogether, blacks become whites, and whites become blacks. That is outside the scope of this discussion, however. People like Greta are quite unpredictable, and things could go either way, but we have to admit that integrity is extremely important in the child-raising process. Her approach could be compared to creating a piece of art. Inspiration can do wonders, but then again, the undertaking can fall flat. So, Susan's kid will probably know all the ropes, but will he or she be happy, ecstatic? I wonder.

"Child-raising is hard work, but it is not a job. Parents should not go into it expecting compensation; their child's happiness should be their only reward. It could not be considered an investment either, for the same reason, not even a long-term and risky one. You have to toil long years and be prepared that your children may not live up to your expectations, and still, you must have it in you to love them just the way they are and not consider them failures. We need patience and humility. This is counterintuitive from the business approach point of view."

"This is nonsense." Arianna was visibly shocked. "There are no unknown quantities here; parents understand well in advance what they are expected to achieve. We cannot make allowances for going back and forth, searching for the right answer. We need stability, predictability, and elimination of waste. If the business approach to child-raising is what gives us those, the business approach it must be."

"Mark, you talk just like a man defending a beautiful woman," intervened Betsy immediately, now that the boss's position was finally unequivocally stated.

"I can say the same about you, Betsy. You are just a catty woman, attacking one of your own. Why, you think a beautiful woman can't be worthy?"

"It is so clear that Greta just doesn't qualify, and you are trying to make a case on pure speculation. Greta has been known for being happy and well-wishing, I'll give her that, but that's exactly because she doesn't want or care about anything deeply enough to fight for it! Look at her PAT charts. There are no spikes lately. Susan, on the other hand, has more and more of them as the competition tightens."

"But it was not supposed to be a competition!"

"Let's not fool ourselves. We think we have slots for every woman that needs this kind of activity and that our job is to identify them. But there are obviously scores of women who apply for this right without sufficient gifts for it, and very often for reasons of their own. And I don't think they will readily accept defeat. They will fight, and they may fool us and win spots reserved for potentially better parents who are not as good at fighting. This is one of the major difficulties of our task—to avoid awarding the wrong ones. If only people were happy with what they deserve. No, they will always bargain for more. And that tends to get ugly sometimes."

"I think this is an excessive precaution. The concern is moot. Come on, our tests are so straightforward, it's practically impossible to use any unhealthy methods of competition, if you are determined to call it that," insisted Arianna. "Besides, we can afford to make a few mistakes. We have all the reins."

"You wouldn't know—" started Mark, but he was interrupted by Emma. She was more attuned to her thoughts than to the pronouncements of others and always started talking whether it was timely or not, and as a result, was very often cutting people off in mid-sentence.

"We should remember that we're looking for just potential here, a gift that has not yet materialized. So, great achievements in other fields have no bearing here. We should be looking, in my understanding, for a capacity to love. Such people are easily overlooked, for they are not very interested in getting things, but rather in looking for opportunities to give. Sometimes they don't even realize it themselves."

"Emma, please stop your philosophical nonsense! This is too deep for me, and for everybody else, I'm sure." Nobody commented. "Anyway, this is too far from real life and the issue at hand." Stanley, dubbed the "metro male" behind his back, decided it was time to put in his two cents. Stanley was an oddball with no graduate degree, but he was a very successful fashion entrepreneur. "Greta, in my opinion, is just a self-absorbed, arrogant woman who thinks she is above everyone and always right."

"She's just out of your league, Stanley, and you know it!" Everybody knew Emma had a crush on Stanley, so no one usually paid much attention to her bickering with him. This time, however, Mark agreed with her.

"I don't think Greta feels superior to anybody, or inferior, for that matter. It doesn't occur to her to compare herself to anyone. She is peacefully secure, happy at how the dice fell, so to say. She is enchanted by her particular uniqueness and finds every little detail of it endearing and clever. I think she is rather childishly satisfied with herself and gladly accepts others for that very reason."

"Stanley, Mark, please. May I remind all of you again that we are not here to pass judgment on Susan or Greta's character. It's getting late. I think everyone made their position clear enough and had a chance to share their views. Let's cast our ballots." She was the first to put the virtual balls into the bag. A white one for Susan, no doubts here. A black one for Greta. At the last moment, she remembered their interview and saw two autumn leaves dancing in the air, trying to stay together, but blown further and further apart by the merciless wind. She let go of the black ball and threw in a white one.

Susan got one black and four white ones. She was granted the right. Greta got three white and two black ones. This meant conditional granting with a one-year probation period.

The meeting was over. Arianna lingered in the virtual conference room, as was her custom. She sat there for a few minutes, in the empty room. Then, with a sigh, she disconnected.

CHAPTER THIRTY-THREE

Susan received the Commission's decision exactly one week after its final meeting. Susan printed out the letter and put it in front of her on the dining table, facedown, and just stared at it. The contents of this letter had the ability to shape her life and determine its course for many years to come. The sun disappeared behind the clouds, and it made the letter look even more portentous. She invested so much energy in this fight, she now felt drained to the last drop, lifeless. Doomed either way. The mere thought that all this work may have been in vain, that she may have lost, made her sweat. No, anything but that. She stubbornly tossed her head. She had to forge ahead. She had to win. She rose and quickly and resolutely flipped the paper. Her eyes immediately singled out the word "GRANTED" in bold letters at the end of the page.

Susan sat again. So that was it. She did win. Curiously, she remained totally calm, if not apathetic. Her VS device was peacefully pulsating in green. She reached for the report again and read it carefully this time. The report noted her high level of maturity and impressive level of social awareness, as well as warm and understanding nature. A great rapport between the spouses was particularly stressed. It was also noted that she had a propensity for overkill, for trying almost too hard, which sometimes would only obfuscate her positive core. She did rather poorly on her Friends & Family section. But, taking into consideration the fact that she was voluntarily helping out her friend who thus put her in a difficult situation, as well as the favorable reports from the interviewers and inspectors, the Commission was granting her, Susan Baldwin, and her husband, Michael Baldwin, the right to raise their child in their own home, as long as they remained married and complied with obligatory monthly inspections.

Carefully, as if it were made out of glass, Susan put the sheet back on the table. She was satisfied. One could say she was happy. She could legitimately relax and do nothing, and think of nothing, for the rest of the day. Mike was working in his room. She did not feel like telling him just yet. She stood up from the couch and went to the window. The Christmas season was in full swing. The elaborate projections of red and green lights all along the river and its lean elegant bridges were interspersed by jolly snowmen and Santas in their sleighs, shooting for the stars, bags full of presents, and Christmas trees behind their backs.

She thought about the tree in their home, invariably very small, when she was growing up. It was usually put in the bucket her mother used to wash the floors and for all kinds of household chores. It was then hidden from view by her mother's only winter scarf, bright red in color. Both items were temporarily removed from daily usage. This must have caused considerable inconvenience for her mom, Susan suddenly realized, but neither her nor the other members of the family were aware of it. The ornaments were usually fruit and candy. They also would pierce eggs at both ends, blow the contents out. and then use the emptied shells to make clowns, or just paint them and cut chains and lanterns out of pieces of colored paper. They were all engaged in the process, and all loved the results.

It felt like her mother was reaching out to her across the years, smiling at her and taking off her only warm scarf once again and putting it around Susan's shoulders this time. Susan smiled. It would be nice to have a little girl with dark eyes and dark hair just like herself, to take care of. They would decorate a huge Christmas tree with hand-blown toys in wonderful bright colors and open presents all morning long, snuggled on the huge living room couch, with Mike smiling at them from across the room. *Who said opportunity knocks but once?* whispered Susan and went into Mike's study to tell him the good news.

•   •   •   •   •

Mike had been acting strangely lately, always hiding behind his computer. Something was definitely going on, but with the intensity and drama of the final stage of the child-raising battle, she had no time to look into it. Oh well, she knew she didn't have to worry about Mike, she could always rein him in, if need be. Let him sulk and miss her really badly.

Contrary to Susan's expectations, Mike took the news without enthusiasm. He slowly stood up from behind his desk, then, without looking at Susan, unhurriedly turned off all the pieces of his equipment, one by one. Then, looking straight into her eyes, he asked, "What about Greta?" His question was said in a quiet neutral tone that alarmed Susan more than a possible outburst of rage or anger.

She shot back, without carefully thinking over her answer, which was not a frequent occurrence. "What about her?"

This is really ironic, thought Susan. She had secured them a victory, and he looked at her as though she were a bug to be squashed. Oh, those scrupulous ones! She suddenly thought about Greg. Greg, too, so positive, so dependable, always knowing the right thing to do and having the solution to any problem. Susan wished Greta knew how his arm unmistakably trembled when she put her fingers on it after their last tennis outing. *If he weren't so engrossed in his obnoxious viruses, I would have given him two days before he ate out of my hand and forgot all about his precious little Greta! I really wish I could see how she handles the mess she's in now.*

"Look at you! You feel so proud of yourself! You are thinking now, no doubt, that you selflessly toiled for our mutual good, have won, and I, the useless, ungrateful one, don't appreciate your travails. Isn't that exactly what you were going to say? Well, you betrayed your best friend to get there, Susan. You coldheartedly threw her under the bus! No, don't deny it. It's clear you have planned the whole charade, thinking over every word of your diatribes. You're a monster, Susan! I'm not sure I still want to have a child with you. I'm not sure of anything anymore."

Susan's VS device was choking. In helpless fury, she smashed her wrist against the sharp edge of Mike's desk. The LED screen shut off with a soft popping sound; thin white cracks formed an intricate web on its suddenly black face. Susan's wrist started to swell, but she did not seem to feel any pain. Mike's calm rebellion did not bode well. She liked to think that people could be put in motion with just a pull of a switch, that her pawns wouldn't dare make moves of their own, messing up her game. He was supposed to be the father of her child, support her endeavors and stand behind her. Mike was not supposed to think; that was her job. Least of all, to judge her. Who did he think he was? Susan was in rage.

Mike grabbed his coat off the hook and left in such a hurry he forgot his hat and gloves on an antique console by the entrance door. They were both very proud of that console. They had snatched it for a fraction of its original price at a second-hand auction site less than a month after their wedding. Back then, whenever an individual decided to replace a piece of furniture, he or she had, under the Responsible Use Act, the precursor of the Anti-Clutter Law, to sell it first to another consumer through an online auction. The person was allowed then to replace the piece. Susan loved the site and soon she and Mike made it their first stop when shopping for their home.

• • • • •

Mike was slowly moving along the avenue. Despite his distraught state, he could not help being surprised by the beauty of it. He rarely walked, and had forgotten how enticing the tall shiny windows of the restaurants and lobbies of the buildings looked, especially when it was getting dark, and lights of various shapes and sizes lit the big city. Almost every building was a work of art designed by a world-renowned architect or a landmark of centuries past.

He had not lived in the city long enough to consider himself a true New Yorker, so these buildings did not speak to him personally. They did not have the additional appeal of memories or nostalgia, like they did for most of his friends. Every such plaque chained them to the city by one more link, making the dazzling city a monument to their everyday cherished events and achievements, and slowly transforming people into voluntary hostages.

The process had, however, begun, and Mike already had a few memories of his own. Presently, he stopped, thunderstruck, in front of an impressive residential building. The irony of life or subconscious yearning brought him to the building where Mary, his erstwhile girlfriend, had lived, and where he had met Susan. How long ago it seemed. He felt almost strangled by regret and shame. *Where is she now?* Mike wondered. She was such a nice girl. She was very much in love with him, too, and made no secret about it. He thought she was becoming clingy at the time. In hindsight, she appeared refreshingly genuine. And she was pretty, too. He voiced her name into his PAD, but it didn't return any address. He went into the closest coffee shop, and with a frothy cappuccino in hand, started to call everybody he thought could give him Mary's present whereabouts. He vaguely remembered hearing she had left the city, but he wasn't sure. He felt so alive. Funny, he had forgotten this feeling.

Soon he got in touch with her closest friend. The girl sounded cold and unfriendly and was unwilling to part with any information at first. The sincere urgency in Mike's voice finally made her change her mind and she told him that Mary had moved to L.A. a couple of years ago and lost touch with her soon after. Always a devout Catholic, she was apparently running her own charity now. She gave him her phone number. Mike left Mary a voice message on her PAT.

·　·　·　·　·

More than two hours had passed. Where was Mike? *Oh, whatever. He won't go far.* He was hooked, he needed her. No woman could give him what she could. Susan was raw, vibrant, unbridled like life itself. He would be back.

The elusive winter sun had already set. Susan was sitting on the couch, sunk deep into its cushions, motionless, in total darkness. She was absolutely calm now, looking for a way out. She did not care for the light. She did not want to stand up and interrupt the train of her thoughts. That was an unforeseen turn of events, to say the least. The blow came from where she expected it the least. She spoke too soon. She had weakened her vigilance. It served her right. Unlike Mike, however, she still knew exactly what she wanted and was prepared to fight for it again—as many times as she had to.

A very peculiar thought came to her mind. If she wanted to raise a child by herself, first, she had to secure a man. Back to prehistoric times, full circle. Only now it was considered an honor, not a tedious necessity. How funny was this. Something Greta would have a kick talking about for hours. Susan's face twitched at the thought of her former best friend. Then, suddenly, it lit up in a eureka moment. She sprang to her feet and turned all the lights on.

Susan went into the bedroom and took the theatrical makeup kit from her nightstand drawer. It was good thinking she did not throw it out after Greta's birthday. Now it was coming in handy again. She carefully applied it in very thin layers, so that the results looked natural at close range. Pale, with dark circles under her eyes. Yet she made sure the makeup did not make her look repulsive. She examined her face carefully in bright light, then in their dimly lit hallway. She was pleased with the results. Played up by the expertly applied makeup, her eyes looked bigger and brighter, and the paleness, with just a hint of pink, allowed her face to retain its freshness, and not look sickly greenish. She also applied some of the white stuff to her fingers. Mike loved her hands. The effect was stunning. She looked startlingly beautiful in a very dramatic sort of way. At first, she was tempted to discard the remaining makeup, just to be safe. After a moment's hesitation, however, she put it back into the nightstand drawer and stashed it under her daily vitamins and old cosmetics. Why throw out a perfectly good product? Mike never went through her things.

After she was done, she sat in a chair, to ensure she didn't accidentally fall asleep—who knew when Mike would come back—and got ready to wait.

The minute she heard the elevator door open, she sprang from the chair and stood by the door, grabbing Mike's hat, twisting it nervously with her white-as-chalk fingers. The navy blue of the hat accentuated their whiteness marvelously. Mike's eyes tried purposefully to avoid looking at Susan's face. Her hands were the first thing they encountered. Involuntarily, he looked up and met Susan's eyes. They were full of grief and remorse. Their burning stare was a silent plea.

"Please, Mike, hear me out, I beg you! I know I did an awful thing and there's no forgiveness for me, but please, let me explain!"

Mike, unable to look away, started to slowly take off his coat, which Susan interpreted correctly as an invitation to proceed. Susan noted with satisfaction that she could still override his moral scruples. Making sure she had him hooked, she continued.

"I got carried away, I lost sight of right and wrong, Mike, I was so focused on winning. Anything is worthless to me without you. I do not want to lose you, Mike. I can't imagine my life without you. I'll do anything you say. Please, don't leave me, Mikey!"

Her blazing eyes were drilling holes into his, setting him on fire. He could not resist this woman. He hated himself for it, and yet he slowly, like a zombie, walked straight into her arms. At this moment he heard his PAT ring. He looked at the screen. Mary was returning his call. Like two white graceful birds, Susan's arms flung to his shoulders and clasped around his neck in a steel embrace.

CHAPTER THIRTY-FOUR

The peace was precarious. Mike still hadn't forgotten that Susan had wronged Greta big time. Susan did not push her luck and tried to lay low. She was moving about the house as a fleshless ghost, self-effacing and unobtrusive, as humble as humanly possible. She tried foreseeing and tending to the flimsiest of his desires, preferring to stay out of Mike's sight, especially when he was not working.

One such afternoon Susan was sitting on her building's roof, in the winter garden, to give Mike some space and avoid provoking him inadvertently. After updating her own, she was lazily checking her friends' online diaries. She did not enjoy them as much as usual. She just needed something to occupy herself, not to ignite unwelcome curiosity on the part of their neighbors.

The Anti-Clutter law had put a lid on one of the favorite pastimes: how to accumulate the most things one usually had no room for and no time to use, for the smallest amount of money one often did not have—also known as shopping, for short. The released mental energy gushed to conquer the vastness of the virtual space with redoubled determination. Those who wanted to *be*, mostly read. Those who wanted to *seem*, mostly wrote. Only the very lazy ones (and the consumed introverts) did not write at least a few lines a day into space. Informational chaos was looming. The digital clutter, thankfully, was proving to be less damaging to the Earth's ecosystem, so far.

The screen lit up as a new email came in. It was from the Parenthood Commission. Smiling at the thought of her success, Susan opened the message. Her VS device data in the few days since the Commission had notified her about its decision, were disastrous. They were not in conformity with the norms established for prospective mothers. In view of the growing number of fraudulent cases in connection with VS devices, in order to contest the data, Susan had to undergo a blood test. Susan had no choice but to comply.

She was supposed to appear for additional tests on Wednesday at nine a.m., which meant less than forty-eight hours. She wouldn't have time to get rid of the alcohol in her blood. Would they be able to see that she was smoking? And her diet was not particularly healthy lately. The way things were, there was no way she could pass that test. She indulged way too much upon hearing the good news and after the stress Mike's behavior had caused her. *Snakes! Perfidious snakes!* Susan was choking with anger. Almost immediately, realizing that her viral signs were diligently recorded and processed, she ordered herself to calm down.

She certainly could not ask Mike for help now. She could not, obviously, ask Greta. Or could she? She learned from Lisa that Greta was granted permission, too, but apparently there were some strings attached. It came as a big disappointment to Susan, who considered it a huge injustice. She thought that Greta did not deserve such an honor, and Lisa fully agreed.

Susan grabbed her PAT. *I'll teach you how to mess with me, Greta, dear.* She chose a gorgeous bouquet of flamboyant red roses, Greta's favorite. She spent an obscene amount of money on them, but she thought they were worth every penny, under the circumstances. Her eyes shone wantonly, the contours of her face became sharper. Susan was in a rush, every minute counted. The card that accompanied the flowers read as follows:

Dear Greta,

I know there is no forgiveness for what I did. I became so focused on the victory, I stopped paying attention to the bigger picture and lost sight of the most important thing in our lives—the people we love. I also know that you are not like other people. If there is one person that would be able to put the despicable things I did behind us and start anew, it is you. Please, Greta, forgive me! I love you. I can't go on without you.

Your Susan

Susan reread the card and clicked "Submit." Only then did she relax a little and sat back in her chair. In a few minutes she went back to their apartment. She was alone in the house now. Only the house robot was toiling and going noiselessly about its business.

"I hope the sucker falls for it," said Susan out loud with feeling. "Oh, I do need her, indeed."

. . . . . .

Greta had not spoken to Susan after their altercation at the bar.

It was true, now Greta knew it for a fact. She was not familiar with the ways of the world, as Greg had put it, and she had learned the hard way. It was not about forgiving, it was about reassessing, redrawing the whole world around her, its magical pristine picture tarnished overnight. She was hurting, as if some of her bones were broken, as if not only old constructs in her mind had to be readjusted, but her skeleton itself had to reshape to accommodate new realities, with her previous views shattered to pieces.

Greg was worried; he had not anticipated a reaction that deep. But then it was the problem of reckoning with the real world so late in life. It was the same with children's diseases, like measles, when adults tend to have more severe symptoms and serious complications.

After a while, Greta did not feel sick anymore every time she thought about Susan. It was like a storm that had brewed for a long time and finally made a landfall. Along with damage came purification, catharsis. She felt ashamed. Greg had warned her so many times, and she was foolish not to believe him. Who was the real Susan? Was there a real Susan at all, behind those mirrors she surrounded herself with that had distorted her image beyond recognition? She saw now that Susan was using and patronizing her, but in her own way, Greta was using Susan, too, and that was probably why she so tenaciously held onto her beliefs and refused to see the obvious. When she said as much to Greg, he became unbelievably angry.

"No need to castigate you, Greta. You are being unreasonable, if not downright masochistic! You always find a way to blame yourself for other people's faults. You have done nothing wrong. You took care of Jimmy so well he didn't want to let you go, have you forgotten? You did marvelously at the bar. You stated the facts precisely. You did not crumble. It does not mean anyone else will be on your side. Tim seems to be a good chap, but I think he's so fed up with his wife's predisposition to intrigue he would try to avoid getting involved. Nelly seems to have good instincts, but she is so insecure and unsure of herself I wouldn't be surprised if she changed her mind several times a day. But I don't look at you through their eyes, Greta, I have my own. I'm proud of you. This is your right of passage. Let's celebrate you."

Greta wished she felt the same way. She was not sure there was anything to celebrate. At least Greg was fantastic. Not a single "I told you so." He acted as if nothing happened. As if Susan had never existed. She had probably never really existed for him anyway. Greta did get a sense that he missed Mike, but he never said anything to that effect.

In due time, Greta received their report. It stated that although some members of the Commission found Greta to be a kind, nice person, being a nice person was not enough to be a good mother. However, the Commission saw potential for improvement and growth in the right direction, and granted her, Greta Baker, and her husband, Gregory Baker, the right to raise their child in their home with the understanding that they would agree to a one-year probation. It meant more frequent assessments and a higher likelihood of having to give up privileges.

When she broke the news to Greg, his face became white under his year-round tan, giving it a ghoulish effect.

"Oh, darling, don't take it so close to heart! We still made it, which is a miracle, under the circumstances, don't you think?"

Greg said, "I had no doubts we would make it."

"I'm sure we will satisfy all the conditions," Greta went on happily.

Greg realized with dismay that all this time after John's offer he did not, for a minute, believe they could actually win, and was unprepared for the outcome. He just stared at Greta.

Greta hurried to the kitchen to bring him a glass of water. *I had no idea he took it so close to heart,* she thought. *So stupid and callous of me. I'm an awful human being!*

CHAPTER THIRTY-FIVE

Greta was not surprised to hear from Susan. She heard from their mutual friends, Lisa and Nelly, that Susan and Mike were granted the right to raise their baby at home. Greta was not angry, just sad. She had always thought that saints had such sad expressions because they knew people were incorrigible in their sins, and there was nothing that could be done about it.

Greta could almost feel some unhealthy vapors rising from the note, and even from those gorgeous flowers. Perfect velvety petals were so intensely red, they seemed to be pulsating. Their regal magnificence was so unsettling, so out of place, so fake. Greta threw out the flowers without unwrapping the paper. She had immediately calmed down. She had an important test in a day. Apparently, the Commission had to make sure her VS data was not faked. She'd better rest.

* * * * *

Susan had waited in vain. She did not hear from Greta that evening or the next day.

Susan was up earlier than usual the day of the test. She spent a sleepless night trying to come up with a solution, but still saw no way to pass the test. She decided to skip coffee and her beloved muffins and had been nibbling on an apple for more than thirty minutes now, thinking feverishly. Nothing came to mind. The house robot started to vacuum instead of doing laundry. Susan registered the change in the usual sequence of house chores, but she was too absorbed in her thoughts to analyze the sudden quirkiness of her house helper's routine. She just waited morosely for it to finish its work around the table. All of a sudden, the robot lost control and almost rolled over, jerking its metallic arms in a purely human movement to keep its equilibrium. It looked quite funny, and Susan probably would have laughed at another time, but now she was not in the laughing mood. Besides, one of the robot's arms painfully poked Susan in the chest. She hit the robot so hard, it almost fell for the second time.

"Ouch, you clumsy idiot. Stay away from me! Now I'll have a bruise on my hand, thanks to you," she added, cooling off a little and inspecting her hand that had hit the robot.

The robot blinked pitifully for a few seconds, then uttered, "Sorry, Susan!" in a barely audible voice. The smart device wheeled away. *I must be losing my mind. I have a feeling this thing hates me,* thought Susan. *It's just so flawed. And I have no patience for imperfect personnel.*

Susan was known for keeping her team on a short leash. To begin with, she did not encourage free thinking. All the thinking had to be done by her, and her only. Second, Susan had to reap the results of every achievement. Those were the unwritten rules. She had myriads of ways in her arsenal to appropriate the results of their labor and make them feel useless at the same time. Those who agreed to follow her meticulous instructions and be servilely loyal, were adequately compensated. Those who failed to understand or accept the rules of the game were subjected to Susan's unrestrained fury until the insane person who dared seek independence was annihilated or forced to resign.

•   •   •   •   •

At 8:45 a.m., Susan was at the testing facility. There were a few women ahead of her. None of them talked, visibly on edge. The unexpected summons made everyone nervous. At nine o'clock sharp she was taken into a small office and asked to wait a few moments for her technician. Susan's eyes were examining every inch of the counter, every piece of equipment, slowly crawling from one item to the next in search of the solution. Greta had let her down. Susan was counting on her. She was hoping she could swap their vials at some point; Greta never paid enough attention to anything. Now Susan had to find another way.

The test technology was kept rather archaic for fear of substitutions. She looked at a stash of label sheets with her name on them. She approached the counter and had a closer look. There were five narrow strips of labels, four labels on each strip. Surely, they would not require twenty vials of blood. There must be extras. Anyway, whatever they were for, that was her only chance. She took one strip and put it into her pocket, making sure to make the incident appear as if she had just lost her balance and tripped while wandering around the office. In all likelihood, the room was equipped with a camera. Not a moment too soon. A young girl—the lab was staffed almost entirely with medical students—came into the room and greeted her cheerfully.

"Good morning, Susan, my name is Susan, too. Isn't that nice?"

Susan felt that not everything was lost. She could work with this type. "Good morning, Susan, what a coincidence, indeed. I mean, what are the odds. Isn't that a great name? A great name for a beautiful girl like you, in any case."

"Oh, thank you, Susan. You are a gorgeous lady. I'm pretty average. Please roll up your sleeve." Susan complied immediately.

"Susan, let me tell you something. You are very beautiful, and never let anybody make you believe otherwise. Also, and this is very important, never react to praise or compliments in such a manner. Just say thank you with a gracious smile, as if you hear it all the time."

While still talking, Susan let the girl draw her blood. She needed to keep the girl's undivided attention for just a few more minutes. She went into detailed praises of her hair, skin, eyes. When Susan had exhausted all her body parts that could be complimented without sounding foolish, the girl, having affixed the label to the last vial, mesmerized by the words she had obviously never heard before, put the extra ones in the shredder without looking at them.

Susan left the office and lingered in the corridors until one of the technicians told her to leave. Susan was ready for this and pretended she was looking for a bathroom. She was scornfully reminded that the bathrooms for patients were in the waiting room area. Just as Susan turned to leave, she saw her Susan at the end of the hall. She was carrying vials with blood. Susan saw her enter an unmarked room and reappear in the hallway in a matter of seconds empty-handed. Having seen what she wanted to see, Susan exited the restricted area with profuse apologies.

Susan left the premises of the hospital and started to pace the street. She stopped in front of a beautiful facade, all gleaming metal and multicolored glass, unsure what to do next. Suddenly, her eye caught a familiar silhouette reflected in the wide molding. Greta! Susan looked at her PAT. 9:45. Greta seemed to be in a hurry. Susan almost choked with joy. It looked like Greta would help her, after all.

She waited patiently, hidden from view from the hospital's entrance. Her eyes glued to the entrance door, she was waiting for Greta to leave the building. At about 10:20, just as Susan had anticipated, Greta reappeared. Susan waited a few more minutes. Then, taking off one of her earrings and putting it in her coat pocket, she headed back to the hospital.

Susan's plan, though daring and not foolproof, worked like magic. It was her lucky day, sure enough. She stormed into the lab waiting room in tears, claiming she had lost one of her earrings, a gift from her mother. Without waiting for the registering nurse's approval, she went back into the hallway and quickly ducked into the room where all the vials were stored, awaiting their turn. She saw Greta's vials right away. She was apparently the last patient. It took Susan a few seconds to remove Greta's labels and stick on her own instead. Then she found hers; they were not hard to locate. She did not look up and was trying to hunch over the vials so that cameras would not be able to register her face or alert security of any wrongdoing. She left, and clenching her second earring triumphantly, she reappeared in the waiting room, smiling so radiantly, the personnel didn't have the heart to reprimand her for her inappropriate behavior. The story was touching, and it had happened so quickly.

Susan did not switch her labels with Greta's. She put hers on Greta's blood samples and removed her own altogether. This way, Greta's tests would be declared lost and no one would suspect foul play. At least, that was how Susan's reasoning went. None of the vials had her fingerprints on them. She had used a handkerchief to handle them. So, should any doubt arise, it would be her word against the hospital personnel's. Deep in her heart, however, Susan knew it was not likely to come to that. Susan was positive that her Susan would use only superlative terms to describe her. No one saw her entering the room where the vials were stored, and she doubted there were any cameras in the hallways. She thought she had a good chance of pulling it off.

•　•　•　•　•

Linda arrived at her office fifteen minutes earlier than her official business day was to start. She had bought herself two donuts and was looking forward to eating them peacefully before everyone else showed up. She had a separate office just outside the maternity test laboratory with scores of security monitors. Cameras were placed in strategic locations throughout the facility. Strictly speaking, she was supposed to keep the door shut at all times, but privacy was not something she missed. Still, the buzzing busy noise from the reception area was quite distracting. Staring at the monitors at all times was not part of Linda's job description. Security software was very good at automatically picking up on unusual activity and signaling potential problems right away. She was supposed to deal with such problems, should they arise. They seldom did. The recorded information was kept for twenty-four hours.

Linda loved her quiet little routine. She poured herself a generous amount of latte from the office machine and took a disposable plate. Linda liked her job at this hospital. One could immediately tell it was a major institution. The coffee machine and biodegradable plates and utensils were top-notch. Linda closed her eyes and gave a few moments of undivided attention to the stimulating aroma of her coffee. Then, she started her computer and perused the new messages. Nothing major. A fire drill was planned for the afternoon. It was always a huge pain in the neck, but at least the weather wasn't too bad.

She waited a little before biting into the guilty deliciousness of one of her donuts. These donuts – jelly and Bavarian cream were her favorite – had been around since time immemorial, and she knew why. She developed a craving for them during her second pregnancy. Granted, they were not a paragon of healthy food, but they were the only blatantly unhealthy item in her diet, and she managed to stay within her recommended norms.

She was on her second donut when she saw an unusual message. It came from an unfamiliar address and the subject line was empty. It seemed to be a video. The system did not detect anything suspicious, so Linda clicked on the file. The quality was poor. The camera was not aiming straight and was always at an awkward angle. The image was fuzzy, the camera focused on random objects, but some of the filming was unmistakably done in her hospital. A woman walked back and forth through the corridors of the test facility, putting vials with test blood in storage, fussing over some of them. It was not clear what the problem was. It reminded Linda of those long accidental recordings on PATs. But why send it to the hospital's security unit? Linda was seriously annoyed. The incident ruined what was usually the highlight of her workday. She put the donut away and looked through the video one more time. It was probably a prank by one of the lab technicians. Too bad it wasn't possible to see who it was.

Linda's coffee was getting cold since she never used the tops on disposable cups—they hurt her upper lip. Resolutely, she hit the "delete" button. At that moment, she realized it might have been possible to make out the names on the vials, and figure out who tampered with them. It was too late. She'd better not mention the incident to anybody. She sighed and went back to her donut, but the pleasure was irreparably ruined. Before leaving for her lunch break, still a little shaken, she checked the recorded data from the storage room camera. Just due diligence. She did not expect to see anything unusual. Indeed, she saw nothing but lab technicians entering, bringing new vials in and taking some out. They rarely stayed for more than a few seconds. Linda put the incident to rest, her conscience at peace.

●　　●　　●　　●　　●

In the evening, after her successful test operation, Susan was in for a pleasant surprise that almost brought her to tears. She was unwinding on the couch with a bottle of Beck's in hand. She stared mindlessly at the display screen—she opted for a show she had seen many times not to be too distracted—and replayed the day down to the smallest detail in her mind. The robot approached her noiselessly and hugged her, without saying a word. Susan's great mood had made her feel suddenly magnanimous; mostly, however, it was the complete unexpectedness of the move that made her hug the robot back without any utterances. The robot's strong metallic body had an almost imperceptible jolt and seemed to have shrunk. It seemed surprised. *Poor thing! Maybe it does have feelings, after all. I should be more careful, just in case.*

The robot, once out of Susan's view, readjusted the fourth navigational camera it had planted in Susan's blouse that morning and proceeded with the self-cleaning cycle two hours before schedule.

CHAPTER THIRTY-SIX

Mike felt tired. His thoughts were in disarray, and he needed to finish his paper by next day. He needed the boost pill. Health insurance companies allowed one per week, with a mandatory twenty-four-hour rest after use. He had no history of using them, but Susan popped them rather regularly, hers and Mike's share, too. He knew she kept them in her nightstand somewhere amid her cosmetics. Hesitantly, Mike entered their bedroom and approached Susan's nightstand. He felt awkward, letting himself in on a secret without her consent, and it bothered him. Moreover, he was not simply invading Susan's privacy, he was uncovering the sacred mystery of a woman's beauty.

But he needed the pill, and Susan wouldn't pick up. The drawer was a mess. Mike fumbled through boxes of pills, cosmetics, scraps of paper; presently, he saw a rather big unmarked black box. He opened it. It was theatrical makeup. The whites and blacks were almost gone, but the other colors were barely touched. Mike felt queasy. The memory of Susan's white hands on his hat and dark circles around her eyes shot through his mind, painful, sharp as a razor blade. He put the box on the stand and ran into the bathroom. He washed his face with cold water and waited. He felt better in a few moments and slowly went into the kitchen to have a glass of water.

He waited for some time, the empty glass in his hand. Then, almost smashing his glass against the counter, he dashed into the hall, to the console where his hat was kept. He did not see it right away and worried it was gone. But it was there, under his gloves. He grabbed it and went slowly to the window in the living room. He stalled a little before looking at the hat in the bright afternoon light. The navy wool had barely perceptible white marks all over it that he had not noticed before. He went into his study, sat in front of his computer, and remained there for some time without turning it on. Then he stood up, took his bag, threw in his computer, and left the house.

·   ·   ·   ·   ·

Susan felt something was wrong the minute she opened the front door. The house stood dark and silent. Mike was always home at this hour. She slowly wandered through the apartment in the direction of the bedroom. She felt as if she were on a roller-coaster approaching the high point, listening to the cringing sounds of the carriage and awaiting the unavoidable dip into emptiness.

She entered the bedroom to check if Mike's clothes were still there. Before she approached his closet, her gaze fell on the black box on her nightstand. She stood there, breathless, suddenly weak and helpless, wishing she could yell and scream and bang her fists against the wall. *All this work for nothing?* She opened the closet. All of Mike's clothes were there, untouched. All of a sudden, she felt in control again. *I won't lose him. I can't lose him*, she thought, tossing her head. *I always get what I want. I always win.*

·   ·   ·   ·   ·

Upon leaving the building, Mike stopped. He hesitated for a minute, and then firmly walked in the direction of the monorail. *Why Mary? Why now?* Mike was thinking sitting in a comfortable seat on his way to the airport, alone in the empty carriage. He hadn't thought about her for five years. Was he running away from his troubles to somebody he was sure would accept him even five years later, no questions asked? *No*, he thought. His conscience was clear. He was going back in good faith. He felt like he had just woken up from a bad dream. He was going to reclaim the lost years, to make it up to Mary. How could he forget how alive she had made him feel? When he exited the monorail already in L.A., near Mary's house, he noticed a fresh-flower stand. They had almost disappeared now that prices for cut flowers had reached astronomical heights. The few stands that remained required preorders. Mike noticed a bouquet of delicate pale pink roses in the window. It looked like somebody had cancelled last minute. A stood-up lover? A cheated-on husband? Mike interpreted it as a good sign.

The huge bouquet in his hands, Mike walked faster. He was almost running when he entered Mary's building. His heart racing, he pressed the bell. Mary opened the door. Mike was taken aback by how happy and radiant she looked. Not happy to see him. Just happy.

"Mike! You? I can't believe you remembered my birthday! After all these years! How long has it been? Five years?"

"Who is it, honey?" A tall thin man with a beard and long hair pulled in a tight ponytail appeared in the doorway. Hugging Mary, he looked at Mike with friendly interest.

"Steve, this is Mike. Remember I told you about Mike?"

"Mike, this is Steve, my husband. But do come in, please, we have company for dinner and were just about to go to the table."

Mike mumbled something about being in the vicinity for business and hastily shoved the flowers at Mary, the wrapping paper brushing her face. He left taking the stairs, without waiting for the elevator, before either Mary or Steve, too astounded to speak, could say a word.

CHAPTER THIRTY-SEVEN

Susan's prognostications proved to be correct. In three days, she received notification that she had passed the final test and she and Mike were granted the right to raise their child in their own home.

Greta received the notification the same day. Hers stated that, unfortunately, her vials were nowhere to be found and she had to come back in two days to repeat the test.

"Greg, my test results got lost! I will have to retake the test in two days." At the sound of his name, Greg's body jolted, as if he suddenly awakened from deep sleep.

"I'm sure it's just a stupid little setback. You will be fine, Greta." He quickly corrected himself. "*We* will be fine."

There was not much conviction in his voice, but Greta did not pursue the issue. After a few tender words and a kiss, she left him to his lonely sulkiness.

He had been preoccupied and withdrawn since after the inspection, more or less, but the last few days were simply unbearable. He would stay sitting on the terrace for hours on end, indifferent and listless. All of Greta's attempts to find out what had happened were unsuccessful. He kept repeating he had a lot of work, but no problem of any kind, so she had nothing to worry about. *He must have had a setback or a colleague got promoted ahead of him and he was too proud to tell me,* thought Greta. She did not insist, just left him alone and became invisible. She reasoned that the best way to be supportive would be to be unobtrusive.

Two days later at seven a.m., the city authorities issued a shelter-in-place order. An outbreak of a novel viral disease was recorded in the city. The epicenter and the only hotspot so far was the Carnivore. Poachers were providing real wild game to the restaurant, and a spillover occurred. More than a hundred people had tested positive and there were already a few deaths. All New York dwellers had to shelter at home except for first responders until the tracing results were examined and the potential infected patrons rounded up. The pandemic protocol was strict. There were no exceptions and no way around it.

Greta realized that everything was over. She would not be allowed to retake the test before the end of the fifteen-day quarantine period. This would bring her to January 2121, and so her hopes of getting permission to raise their child at home would not materialize in the coming year. The painful truth was slowly sinking in. She did not know how long she stayed still, staring blankly at the message on her PAT.

At last, she stood up and went to share the news with Greg. She found him on the terrace, his usual spot lately, nursing a glass of wine. Greta was taken aback by how much older his face looked. Tanned all year round, a touch of brownish ruddiness on his cheekbones, as if they had been rubbed with sandpaper, it was now ashen in color, lifeless, cheeks sunken in, as if all his boisterous ambition and spirit were syphoned from his body. He reminded Greta of a deflated balloon forgotten on the back of a chair after a hastily cleaned-up party.

Greta's heart filled with tenderness and love. The man must be going through so much pain. She wished she could help him, and instead she had another blow to deliver.

"Greg, my test has been postponed until further notice because of the outbreak. We did not make the cut this year," she started. She saw no pain, no devastation; rather, some sort of cautious disbelief.

"What did you say, Greta?"

Greta repeated her words, unable to take her eyes off of him. She could almost see life being pumped back into the lifeless body that was slowly reclaiming its familiar shape, straightening proudly, screaming with relief, deliverance, ecstasy while he spoke in a low voice, as if from far away. He lifted his eyes on Greta.

"I can't believe this, Greta. I don't know what to say. I'm so sorry!" He stepped forward and hugged Greta. Without letting her go, he added, "We'd better get ready to go underground. They'll start in fifteen minutes." The preemptive cleaning by radiation was set for eight a.m. The city population had to descend into special bunkers constructed below the underground system.

Shocked by the fantastic transformation, Greta was unable to move or say anything. She must have missed some of Greg's words, for she heard him again at mid-sentence.

"...but we will not be deterred," he was saying forcefully. "We will raise our child ourselves! I love you, Greta," said Greg with so much passion and sincerity, it seemed to have mopped all the misery of the last few weeks out of Greta's memory in one stroke.

"What are you saying?" asked Greta.

"I do not think we should accept the present state of affairs. If this is as important to you as it is for me, and I know it is, I propose we join our colony on the Moon. You know the rules are much laxer there. We will be able to have as many kids as we want there and raise all of them ourselves. We will still have inspections and assessments, of course, but I'm sure you will be up to par. You will be a terrific mother, Greta!"

"You would do that for me, Greg? What will you do there?"

"They have a branch of the Institute for Viral Research there. I am ready to work my way up; with God's help and my perseverance, I'm sure I will get ahead in no time."

"I'm not sure I can accept such a sacrifice from you, Greg. After all, it's my fault we didn't win here. Just as you have always said, I was a poor judge of character."

"I'll be alright," exclaimed Greg. "Life gives us a second chance, Greta, let's not miss it," he went on vehemently. "You will be happy, that's all that matters. We both will."

"This is all so drastic, Greg…"

"Think about it! Why should we accept defeat? Besides, you know it and I know it, the decision was not fair. The judges failed to see the truth. How can we entrust such people with the life and happiness of our child? Why should we depend on them?"

"You have a point there, Greg. But life on the Moon is so different. There is certainly more freedom, but the consequences of our choices could be more dire. And we will have to think about so many things we are not used to thinking about here."

"Well, Greta. We will have access to the same technology and data, only we will not have to pay the price we have to pay here on Earth. We won't be nudged in any direction by fines and outright limitations. The choice will be ours. Maybe we will not be our healthiest and most successful selves, but we will be the way we want to be. We will be able to decide for ourselves, unconditionally. Think about it, Greta! This is mind-boggling! This is not like the Mars colony, where you have ready-made clothes only and you have to shop for food and cook your meals unless you're loaded and can afford to dine in restaurants every night. And the real estate is free."

"Oh, Greg, don't overemphasize the logistical aspects. The crux of the matter is that we're both happy with the way things are here. We don't suffer from the pressure of being steered to using our physical and intellectual potential in the most efficient way possible. We want it ourselves. We do it of our own accord. Besides, what about the ecological problems? We know very well that the Moon will face the same problems Earth did in the last century unless the present laissez-faire policies change. And they will, when there are enough colonists."

"No, Greta. The crux of the matter is that we can raise our children ourselves there." *I will tell her,* thought Greg. *Someday, I will definitely tell her.* But he knew he never would.

• • • • •

It was early morning when they boarded the space shuttle. The cabin was full. Greta noticed only one empty seat, just across the aisle from them. She looked through the window. It was still dark. Despite the early hour, the flying field was bustling with activity. In the uncertain glow of the sparse lights Greta saw a legion of square-faced robots, with their uniform swift and precise movements and bright yellow torsos undistinguishable from one another, swarming around the shuttles. Their human supervisors, clad in black as usual, scurried about the field performing last-minute checks.

At the end of the twenty-first century, when robots all but replaced humans in the service industries, old-fashioned attire for them was in vogue. Doormen donning long coats and white gloves and house help in white aprons became ubiquitous. It did not last, however. Two quarreling women on a sidewalk were mistaken for robots with conflicting programs, and a robots' supervisor was called. A multimillion-dollar lawsuit ensued. After a few other similarly awkward situations, a strict protocol regarding robots' uniforms was put in place.

The area was teeming with trucks of every conceivable shape and size delivering various supplies and the passengers' luggage. On the far end of the field, the air traffic control tower stood proud and tall. Its powerful searchlights were zipping through the air in every direction, their bright clutching fingers grabbing an impassive metal face here, a delivery dolly there. Thick double windows prevented any outside sound from entering the cabin, so it seemed that men and machines worked in complete silence, which contributed to the eeriness of the scene. Greta felt suddenly uneasy. *It's just a flying field at dawn. There's nothing creepy about it. I had to get up in the middle of the night, and now everything is giving me goose bumps.*

After a short crackling noise, an announcement followed. "Robert White is kindly requested to report to the registration desk immediately." *Robert White! That must be our Bob! So, he did decide to leave, after all. Why isn't he here yet?*

She got up from her seat and went to the bar stand at the far end of the cabin. Greg, in all appearance, firmly back to his normal self, was engrossed in one of his colleagues' articles. The fact that he may not see his planet for many years did not seem to have any effect on him.

Greta began perusing the impressive wine list. The crew members were chatting in the back behind a curtain. The robot at the bar was patiently waiting. When Greta reached number 68 on the list, she heard the familiar name, Robert White, pop up again. She stopped reading and listened closely. She heard the words "quarantine" and "Carnivore," but then the bartending robot, having registered that Greta had lifted her eyes from the wine list, enquired what would be the lady's poison. When Greta listened again, the crew had already gone about their business. Suddenly losing interest in a drink, she went back to her seat. She hoped nothing bad had happened to Bob. Back at her seat, she took out a magazine, *The Moon Monthly*, wrapped herself in the provided cashmere blanket, and closed her eyes.

CHAPTER THIRTY-EIGHT

Greta felt suddenly cold. She shivered and her eyes flew open. She was sitting in her favorite armchair in the living room, a champagne flute in her hand, miraculously not broken in her sleep. A bowl of big, almost translucent grapes was standing on the side table near her chair.

Greta stood up and adjusted the room temperature on the wall panel manually, instead of from her PAT. Her body felt sore and numb from sleeping in an uncomfortable position and she wanted to move a little to warm up her body and her muscles.

What a weird dream! Greta shivered, still not fully recovered from its grip. What a preposterous idea, children taken from their parents to be raised by the State. And Susan! Her dear friend Susan! What on Earth made her dream up such a monstrous human being? Greg, too! Such nonsense. *We don't even have a colony on the Moon. Just a few research stations and a hub for tourist shuttles.* She was wandering mindlessly around her apartment, reliving her dream, part by part, incredulous and immensely relieved at the same time that it *was* just a dream.

Greta went to the windows and looked out. HAPPY NEW YEAR 2120! she read. The sign, in huge red letters, was taking up the whole expanse of the dark sky, although its eastern edge was beginning to lighten up. It was the only embellishment at this hour, except for the mysteriously twinkling stars. All the holiday decorations were already gone. Only streetlights and signs were shimmering in the frosty air.

Greta stood there a long time. The eastern walls of the tall glass-paneled buildings with incongruous rotating solar batteries on their roofs began to shine with all the hues of orange and pink, as if they were squeezing the color from the sign that still adorned the sky. The big city was waking up to a new day, a new year.

She went to take the pregnancy test. It was positive. Slowly, full of wonder at her own body, she joined Greg and spooned comfortably with him in her usual manner, careful not to wake him, and trying to catch the first signs of new life inside her. Her body became numb after a while. Greg suddenly jerked and grunted, and just as his heavy arm was about to lock her securely into place, Greta rolled away, her limbs free and full of joy and excitement in her new comfortable nook.

She impatiently reached for her PAT to call her best friend Susie to share her big news. Her hand stopped in midair. All of a sudden, she changed her mind. She really had to become more responsible; there was somebody who needed her now. She'd better wait.

THE END

ABOUT THE AUTHOR

Daughter of a Russian diplomat, Helen Trepelkov graduated *summa cum laude* with a master's degree in International Economic Relations from the Moscow State Institute for International Relations, dubbed the "Harvard of Russia" by Henry Kissinger. Shortly after, she followed her husband to New York City and, quite unexpectedly, became a stay-at-home mother to their two daughters. Forty years later, now a grandmother, Helen still lives in New York City with her husband. Her first book, *Postgraduate Studies in Motherhood,* a memoir, was published by Black Rose Writing in August 2018 and won the 2018 Maxy Award runner-up in the nonfiction category.

NOTE FROM THE AUTHOR

Word-of-mouth is crucial for any author to succeed. If you enjoyed *The New Year's Resolution of Greta Baker*, please leave a review online—anywhere you are able. Even if it's just a sentence or two. It would make all the difference and would be very much appreciated.

Thanks!
Helen Trepelkov

We hope you enjoyed reading this title from:

www.blackrosewriting.com

Subscribe to our mailing list – *The Rosevine* – and receive **FREE** books, daily deals, and stay current with news about upcoming releases and our hottest authors.
Scan the QR code below to sign up.

Already a subscriber? Please accept a sincere thank you for being a fan of Black Rose Writing authors.

View other Black Rose Writing titles at www.blackrosewriting.com/books and use promo code **PRINT** to receive a **20% discount** when purchasing.